Kyra, Just for Today

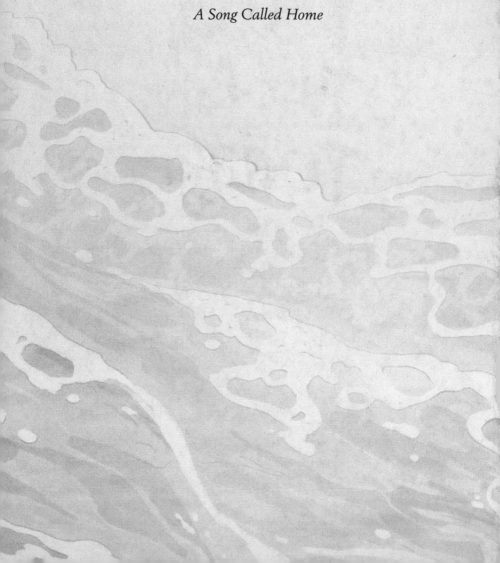

ALSO BY SARA ZARR

A Song Called Home

Kyra, Just for Today

SARA ZARR

BALZER + BRAY

An Imprint of HarperCollins*Publishers*

Balzer + Bray is an imprint of HarperCollins Publishers.

Library of Congress Control Number: 2023937488
ISBN 978-0-06-304513-2

Typography by Andrea Vandergrift
23 24 25 26 27 LBC 5 4 3 2 1
First Edition

Kyra,
Just for
Today

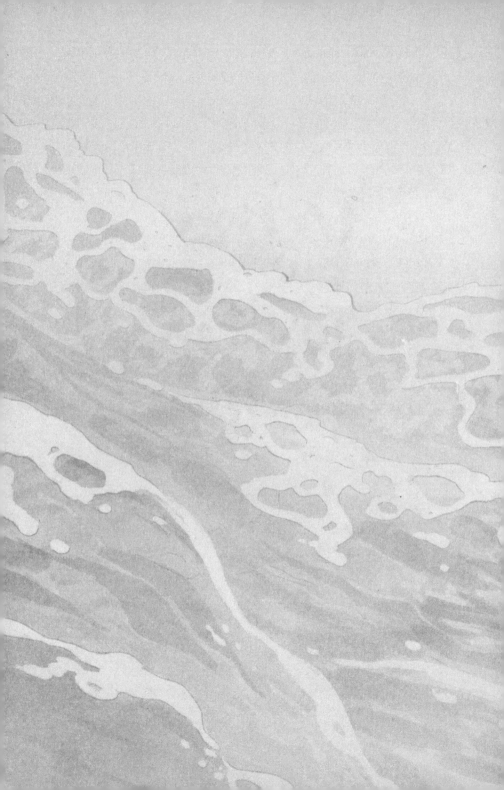

PART I: NOVEMBER

An Attitude of Gratitude

I

It's the Saturday before Thanksgiving and we have houses to clean.

A lot of Mom's clients are either having guests in, or hosting big family celebrations, or renting out their houses while they go somewhere else for the holiday. Some of her clients are managers of full-time vacation rentals, and those have a lot of turnover right now, too.

All the houses are too much for just Mom, but we need the extra money and can't turn down work. It'll slow down in January. Since we live on the coast near San Francisco, where everyone wants to visit, January is about the *only* time it slows down. Last summer, Mom decided I was old enough to help if I wanted, and it gave me something to do during the days. I like cleaning the way I like to watch my teachers erase the whiteboards, or the way I like to check off a shopping list. It's satisfying. I hope next summer I can work with her more and maybe start getting paid for it, too. For now, all the money goes to bills.

Mom keeps the due-this-week bills under the California Republic magnet on our fridge. The next one up is PG&E; $158.23 for electricity and gas from last month plus the $25 we pay every month on last winter's bill. We'll make all that today, easy. Underneath that is the car insurance: $166.75. We should be able to cover that or most of it with today's work, too.

"Caught you looking," Mom says as she comes into the kitchen.

"Oops."

She doesn't want me to worry about bills. But they're right there in front of my face, so it's hard not to think about them, and thinking almost always leads to worrying.

She comes up behind me and moves the *Count Your Blessings* magnet on top of the PG&E bill so I can't see the numbers. "I'd rather count blessings than pennies." She gives my shoulder a pat and asks, "What smells so good?"

I'm making us breakfast sandwiches: English muffins with an egg and a slice of smoked cheddar cheese and some grilled onions. It's easy to make grilled onions along with the eggs, and it makes them taste so much better.

"Onions," I say, smiling. "And butter."

"Yum."

I learned to cook a long time ago. I had to, because Mom

wasn't reliable when she first got sober, or before that. Mom's friend Steve—who also happens to be my best friend's stepdad—taught me. Now I'm better at it than Mom. I cook and make our grocery lists, and a lot of times I clean our house, and of course go to school. She works and goes to AA meetings and does most of our laundry and also cleans here when she can.

It's only the two of us. And that's mostly okay.

I assemble the sandwiches and wrap them in paper towels so we can eat in the car, and put some bananas and trail mix in a bag.

"Do you want to wear one of my shirts?" Mom asks.

She means the T-shirts for her cleaning business. They're pale orange with a simple white logo of a bucket and Meg the Maid in block print underneath. I like them better than the first T-shirt she had made when she started her business. That one had a cartoon of her (she's Meg) holding a bucket in one hand and a mop and broom and feather duster in the other, with a vacuum hose hanging around her neck.

That one was a little embarrassing. This one isn't, and it makes me feel official.

"Yeah," I say. While I fill our water bottles, she gets me a shirt from the pile by the dryer.

"Did you check supplies?" I ask. She told me last night to remind her to check if we need to buy anything on our way to the first house.

"Gonna go do that now."

Clients are supposed to provide their preferred cleaning

supplies, but they can forget, and you never want to be caught without something you need—surface cleaner, garbage bags, extra rags.

The trunk of Mom's car is full of plastic bins and baskets with everything we might need. There's a set of mops and dusters in there, and we also throw our own vacuum into the car just in case.

I go to my room to strip off my sweatshirt and put Mom's T-shirt on. We're the same size now—the logo stretches a little across my chest just like it does on hers, and I don't like that. I put my sweatshirt back on over it.

"I think we're set," she says when I go outside with our breakfast and snacks.

"Charger?"

She points to the phone-charging cord plugged into the car dash. "Yep."

"Hair ties?"

She pats her pocket. "Got 'em."

Satisfied we've thought of everything, we start on our way, eating our sandwiches. I like this feeling—a new day, and no school next week. It's just after seven now, and even though the part where I actually have to get out of bed feels impossible, once I'm up I like being out on a weekend morning. The streets are quiet, and the sun is only now starting to light up the sky. Being up at this time of day when I know the next thing I have to do is school isn't as fun.

Last year, I didn't mind. But seventh grade is a whole other thing.

We drive two blocks and then Mom swears, swerves the

4

car to the curb, and gives me a look. "I remembered the charger, but I left my phone in the bathroom."

I laugh. It's always something. "Nobody's perfect."

"Especially me," she says.

We zoom back home, and I run in and get the phone from where she left it on the sink while she was drying her hair, and pull up the schedule and addresses so we know where we're going.

First up are two vacation rentals near Rockaway, right next to each other. Someone owns these two whole houses with views of the Pacific Ocean *plus* whatever house they live in. It doesn't really seem fair.

We can hear but not see the ocean from our house, but we don't have to walk far to get to it. That's good because it's special to us. It's kind of our church.

The first rental isn't too dirty, but it still takes time to get the bedding washed and dried, do the tidying and dusting and vacuuming, sanitize the bathroom. At the second one, there's a big mess in the kitchen, like the renters didn't even attempt to clean up after themselves at all.

"I bet they left food in the fridge," Mom says, wheeling the vacuum through to the living room. "It's ours now if you see anything in there you want. Do you want to tackle this disaster, or do floors?"

"This disaster," I say. The worse something is when you start, the more satisfying it is to see it when it's done. And floors are boring.

She grins. "I knew you'd say that."

I pull on the gloves with the long cuffs from our bucket of supplies, and scrape and rinse dirty dishes. The trick is to not look very close or breathe very deep. Just scrape and rinse and run the garbage disposal and don't think about what the food was before it turned disgusting. I put the scraped and rinsed dishes into the dishwasher, then run hot soapy water to hand-wash the nice wineglasses.

The sour-smelling alcohol residue at the bottom of the glasses has attracted fruit flies. I don't understand fruit flies. We get them at home sometimes around our bananas. They magically appear when there's aging fruit sitting around and then magically disappear as soon as that fruit is gone. Where did they come from? Were they just waiting around, hiding out until something rotten woke them up? Where do they go after you clean up? Back into hiding?

"Where do fruit flies go?" I call to Mom.

"What?" she calls back from the living room.

"Where do fruit flies live when everything is clean?"

"Good question," she says, then turns the vacuum on.

I dry the wineglasses and find where to put them away. It's weird to me that a lot of people have entire sets of glasses that are made just for drinking alcohol. Different-sized wine-glasses, small tumblers, medium tumblers. And I know not all these people are alcoholics. *Some* people can have *some* alcohol *some* of the time and not want to keep drinking and drinking until they pass out, day after day, no matter who they hurt and what they lose.

Mom isn't some people. Mom's an alcoholic.

6

She says it can be something in a person's biology. Last month we did a genetics unit in Ms. Scheiner's class. Like where eye color and hair color come from. While other kids were filling out a worksheet on recessive and dominant traits in dogs, I was wondering if I might inherit alcoholism.

When I asked Mom, she said, "Maybe. It tends to run in families, but they don't know if that's biology or environment. You know, nature or nurture."

We talked about that in class, too. Nature is like . . . what you were born with. Nurture is how you were raised, and when, and where.

"With a lot of traits that aren't strictly genetic, it's harder to prove cause and effect than correlation," Ms. Scheiner said. "And there's so much we don't know."

It's easier to figure out what color eyes your baby will probably have than if they might be an alcoholic, in other words.

"I won't drink, then," I told Mom. "Just in case."

"Given that you just turned thirteen, I think that's a good idea." Mom said that with a laugh, so I guess she's not worried and thinks I shouldn't be, either.

Now, while she finishes floors, I clean the kitchen counters. First with a dry towel, sweeping crumbs right into the trash. Then with the cleaning supplies and wet towels to get up all the sticky spots and grease splatters and wine spills, and one last time with disinfectant and paper towels.

I enjoy this feeling. Making order out of chaos. The thing I like about doing the rentals is that while they can be dirty, there's hardly ever any clutter. Like, books and toys shoved under a bed, or piles of clothes all over the closet floors. These houses have only what a guest might need and not much else. So when they're clean, they're neat and tidy, too.

Then I remember I still need to clean out the fridge. I find a bunch of takeout containers, which I stack up to take to the compost bin in the driveway. There's also almost a full pound of the good Irish butter we usually can't afford. I put that in a paper grocery bag that got left behind, along with a bottle of ginger-lime salad dressing they didn't even open.

In the fridge door there's a bottle of beer. It's the brand Mom used to drink.

The color and design of the label triggers a sudden and intense buzzing that starts in my brain and shoots out to my fingers and down to my toes. I clench the handle of the fridge.

Mom comes back through with the vacuum; I shut the fridge door and stand in front of it.

"Wow," she says, admiring my work. She squeezes my elbow gently. "You want to skip high school and go into business with me?"

I know she's only teasing, but I say, "Yes!"

"Find anything good in the fridge?"

"Fancy butter. And . . ." I step aside and open the door. It's clean and empty except for the one bottle of beer. "What should I do with that?"

Mom hasn't had a drink in over five years, but it still feels a little awkward, staring at her old favorite beer. Like it's a bomb that might go off if we don't handle it right.

"Oh," she says. "We can leave it here, or pour it out and recycle the bottle—"

"Pour it out," I say.

She reaches past me to grab it, and finds a bottle opener in a drawer. After she pops off the cap, she turns the bottle upside down over the sink and says, "Down the hatch."

The smell makes me dizzy. I remember being little, smelling the smell. Of this beer, or wine or liquor, whatever alcohol she could get. Mom likes to joke she wasn't picky.

She looks away from the bottle in her hand now. "Gross, huh?"

I nod. Except I know that her life used to revolve around it, no matter how gross she might say it is.

Used to. Her drinking days are in the past. Even if the smell or the sight of certain things can sometimes remind me of the time before she was sober, now she is, and that's what matters.

She hands me the bottle to take out to the recycling as she runs water in the sink to wash the smell away. I drop it into the bin and watch it crash against the other bottles and break apart. I close the lid and decide not to think about it anymore.

When I come back in, she says, "Let's see how fast we can make the beds. Three bedrooms, four beds. Who will be queen of the derby?"

She's talking about roller derby. Mom was on a team when she first got sober. She said that knocking into all those other women and letting herself fall and get hurt only to get up again helped her find a strong part of herself she didn't know was there. Then she fractured her wrist and decided she didn't need to be *that* strong.

Now it's a game we play to make cleaning more fun, and we only pretend to knock each other over.

I get down into the roller derby starting position, crouched low with knees and elbows bent like I'm already running.

"Kiki Krash in position," I snarl.

She crouches, too. "Marauding Meg ready."

In roller derby, you get a special name that tells your opponents how tough you are, how scared they should be.

Mom looks at me. "Aaaaand *go*."

She races past me and pushes me out of the way, cackling.

"That's not fair," I scream, also laughing. "I don't even know where the rooms are!"

"No one said derby is fair, babe!" she yells back, and thunders up the stairs at the end of the hall.

2

Saturday nights are for my group meetings.

My group is kind of like Mom's. They're both based on the Twelve Steps of Alcoholics Anonymous, which go from step one—recognizing there's a problem you can't handle on your own—and go all the way to step twelve, which is about practicing all the steps as much as you can to help you live sober, which is more than just not drinking.

Our group doesn't use the steps the same way Mom's does, and sometimes we don't talk about them at all, because our group isn't for alcoholics. It's for kids who live with them or have them in their—our—lives. Also, our group is only once a week, while Mom can go to hers every day if she wants. But usually she goes once a week, depending on her schedule, because her recovery is in a good place.

I never miss group, and even though I'm tired from cleaning all day and hungry because we didn't have time to make dinner between finishing the last house and group, I'm not going to miss it tonight. It's where I get to see my best friend, Lu, outside of school, and we can talk about real things instead of school things.

We've been friends since the middle of fifth grade, when she transferred from San Francisco to Pacifica, our little suburb by the ocean. Lu moved because her mom married Steve, my mom's friend. Steve is a few years older than Mom, but they became friends in high school and stayed friends off and on all the years after. He was especially around when Mom was first getting sober. Then Mom made some recovery friends and focused on her business, and we didn't see Steve much for a couple of years and didn't go to his wedding. But when I realized that my new friend Lu was also Steve's new stepdaughter, it seemed like fate that we had to be *best* friends and that Mom and Steve should get back in touch. It's different now, because Steve is married, but I'm glad we're all friends again.

In a lot of ways, Lu's the opposite of me: petite and dark-haired with a tiny nose, like a cute little elf. Personality-wise, we're kind of different, too. She's quiet, more shy and careful. She cares more about fitting in. I've never fit in, so I don't care. Well, I care, but I don't think there's anything I can do about it, so I try not to. The fact that she's more popular than me makes me worry, sometimes, especially since we got to middle school. But like I said, there's nothing I can do about it. And no matter what happens, I know there's one thing we'll always have:

Group. And why we're in it.

Lu comes with her sister, Casey, who's in high school. Casey's cool and pretty and nice enough to me even though I'm only her little sister's friend.

There's another high schooler who comes, named Owen. He's kind of new. I think he'll stay, though. It's his fourth meeting in a row, which means something. A lot of people come to one or two and then we never see them again.

We've all kept our coats on because the church basement heat only works half the time. Since it's the last meeting before Thanksgiving, we're talking about gratitude.

"It's a little different from thankfulness, I think," Gene says. "What I've learned is that gratitude is an action, not a feeling. It's a practice. Which means we *do* it, we don't just feel it."

Gene has bushy white hair on the sides of his head and no hair on top. His eyebrows are less white than his head hair, more gray, and his mustache still shows some blond and always looks like it's curling into his mouth.

This group is for ages twelve to eighteen, and he's our sponsor. That means he shows up every week no matter what. He mostly kicks off our conversation, and also brings books and pamphlets about living with alcoholics, in case anyone needs them. He makes sure we have the freezing-cold room in this church basement reserved, and he has the key.

Gene's an alcoholic, like my mom and like Lu and Casey's

bio-dad and like Owen's dad and aunt and grandma. Gene and my mom have long sobrieties—years—but they still think of themselves as "in recovery," not recovered, because they don't think there's a cure or ever a time you can just decide you're not an alcoholic anymore. Owen's dad has zero sobriety. Lu and Casey's dad has zero right now. He's been off and on.

Everyone who comes into this room for this group has been affected by someone else's alcohol or drug abuse. Like Gene sometimes says, it's a club no one wants to be in. But we are, and so we're here in the freezing basement, our folding chairs in a circle.

"How can gratitude be an action?" Owen asks.

"You don't wait for it to come to you," Casey says. "Like, you can choose it." She glances at Gene. "Right?"

"Well, what do you guys think?" Gene looks around at us, raising those thick eyebrows. He's not here to give us answers or tell us if we're right or wrong.

"Hi. I'm Kyra," I say. That's how we do it when we want to share, even though everyone here knows each other's names.

"Hi, Kyra," everyone answers. That's another tradition.

"You can write down three things you're grateful for every day," I say. "That's an action. Also, you can tell people when you're grateful for them." In the middle of talking, I remember we're supposed to use "I" language. "*I* can tell people when I'm grateful for them."

Owen tilts his head down and looks at me like what I said was dumb. But he doesn't know this stuff the way I do yet. My mom has been in recovery for over five years. It's easy to remember because she quit on my eighth birthday and we recently celebrated her fifth sober anniversary on October 9, the same day as my thirteenth birthday. She goes to her meetings and talks about it and reads me things from her journal sometimes or from her books. So I'm a little bit of an expert, even if I'm younger than Owen.

"I can say I hate school, or I can say I'm grateful for education," I continue, trying to make my point to Owen even though we're not supposed to be fixing or arguing or trying to convince each other of things in this group. "That's a choice."

"Why can't you say both?" Owen asks.

Casey laughs, and Lu looks at me with a smile.

I raise my voice a little. It's still my sharing time. "Okay, so I had a pretty good week and I'm grateful to be here, and for my mom's sobriety, and that school's on break now." Because even though I am grateful for education, I *do* kind of hate school. Not the learning part but other stuff. Like, there are these eighth-grade boys, Juan and Gabe, who are always together and have started to notice me. I'm taller and bigger than most of the other seventh-grade girls and am easy to notice. Juan and Gabe have decided they don't like what they see. And I don't like talking about it or thinking about it, so I choose to focus on being grateful that there's no school next week.

"Today I was helping my mom with work," I continue, "and there was this beer. The kind she used to drink when I was little. It was just weird when I saw the bottle and had all these, like . . . memories that weren't really memories. Feelings, I

15

guess, about being small and scared and not knowing what was happening. But I do remember how sometimes I'd see a six-pack of those exact bottles if I got a snack before bed, then they'd all be gone in the morning when I opened the fridge at breakfast. I guess she always cleaned up after herself and took her empties and the cardboard out to the recycling bin, and I'd wonder if I'd even really seen it the night before."

Everyone's listening. Owen nods like he knows what I'm talking about.

"I'm grateful I don't have to think about that anymore," I say. "That's all."

"Thank you, Kyra," Gene says. "You were heard."

Lu goes next. "Hi, I'm Lu."

"Hi, Lu."

"I'm also glad we're on break, I guess. Except we're leaving tomorrow to spend most of it in Ohio at my grandma's, and I hardly know that part of the family, and they're meeting Steve for the first time. And I feel like I only started to feel relaxed at holidays in the last couple of years, since my mom married Steve, and I want it to be like that, not all . . . different."

I know what she means. A certain kind of predictability in life is comforting, where you know you'll be doing *mostly* the same things and seeing *mostly* the same people in some regular way. With enough variety now and then to keep you from getting bored.

"Yeah, it's going to be kind of like spending the holiday with strangers," Casey adds. "Um, I'm Casey, as you know."

"Hi, Casey."

"I'd rather stay here with the problems I already know I have," she says, "not in an unfamiliar place worrying about new ones that might come up."

"Maybe nothing bad will happen," Gene says with a smile. "It's always possible."

We all laugh a little. That's a big reason I love group. For that laugh that means we understand each other.

After everyone has had a chance to share, Gene reminds us that even though next weekend is a holiday for a lot of people, he'll be here with the key, setting up chairs like any other Saturday.

We stand in a circle and hold hands and say, "Keep coming back."

As if I ever wouldn't.

3

In the parking lot, I give Lu a hug goodbye. She has to get on her tiptoes to put her arms around my neck.

"Have a great trip," I say. "Text me."

"I will."

I walk her to Steve's truck, where Casey is waiting behind the wheel. A lot of times they give me a ride, but tonight Mom dropped me off on our way back from the last house we cleaned and she'll pick me up. Eventually. She's good at recovery but not the best at being on time.

"Bye, Casey," I say as Lu climbs into the truck.

"See ya, Keek. Wish us luck."

"You don't need luck. Just keep it simple!" I tell her. "Keep It Simple" is a recovery slogan we use in group sometimes to remind ourselves to try to stay grounded in what's happening in reality, not what we imagine *might* happen.

Casey smirks and rolls her eyes while Lu laughs.

We know that like a lot of the slogans, it's easy to say and hard to do.

Gene waits with me in the lot. We both put our hands deep in our jacket pockets and hunch our shoulders against the damp chill.

"You say you like this weather, huh?" he asks.

"It's better than being hot." I *hate* being hot. Being too hot makes me want to scream, break things, and shave my head. Bright lights, too. I taped cardboard on the inside of my bedroom window because it faces the sun all afternoon and would turn my room into an oven if I didn't do something.

"Let's see if you still think that when you're my age and your bones turn into ice cubes." Mom's car zooms up the driveway. "There she is," Gene says.

While I get in, Mom rolls down her window and calls, "Thanks, Gene! Have a good Thanksgiving!"

"You too, Meg," he says back with a wave while walking to his car.

"Hey, Gene!" Mom shouts as he unlocks his door. "Do you have somewhere to go on turkey day? Plenty of room at our table!" She glances at me. "It's okay to invite Gene, right?"

I can't exactly say no at this point, so I nod. But Gene calls back thanks and he's got plans but he appreciates the invite, and I'm relieved. It's like what Lu said about holidays. I like Gene, but I also like it when it's only me and Mom on the days she doesn't have to work, which don't come all that often at this time of year.

"How was group?" As usual, she forgets how steep the exit driveway is and takes it too fast. The front bumper scrapes the pavement with a jolt.

"Mom!" Someday she's going to break the car. Then what would we do?

She laughs. "Sorry!"

"Group was good." I turn up the heat in the car to try to defrost my hands. I may not like being hot, but I also don't like frozen fingertips. "The church still hasn't fixed the heat."

"I think twelve people go to that church and they're all about eighty years old."

"Gene says old people hate the cold, though."

"Yes, but my point is I don't think they have any money to fix it. Churches count on donations from members, and if the members don't have money, then neither does their church."

"Oh." Money is stupid and annoying. I hate that we don't have it. I hate not being able to buy the things I want to buy—like this new set of pans I saw on a cooking video the other day. I hate worrying about money and knowing Mom is worrying. Sometimes I hate people who have money and don't *have* to worry.

I try to steer my thoughts away from my list of hates and back to gratitude. I'm grateful we have the house, which Mom inherited from her grandmother when she died the year I was born. Otherwise I don't even know where we'd live. There's still the property taxes and utilities and insurance and all that to pay for; Meg the Maid barely makes enough to cover everything.

"Where'd you go, Keek?" Mom asks.

"Nowhere." I don't need to worry her with my worry. We're almost home already. "Can we stop at the beach for a minute?"

"I thought you were cold."

"Now I'm too warm." I turn off the car heater to prove it.

"Aren't you starving for dinner?"

I am, but I deny it. So instead of turning on our street, she stays on the main road and crosses the highway at the light to get to the beach side and pulls into the parking lot near the discount grocery store. We ignore the No Beach Parking signs. Mom grew up here and her mom grew up here and her grandma moved here when the town was first incorporated. We kind of feel like it's ours even though it's turning into a place only rich people can live unless they've had their house in their family a long time, like us and like Steve.

We walk down the sandy footpath in the dark, and perch on one of the pieces of driftwood that's been here forever.

In group and in Mom's recovery, we talk about having a higher power. For some people, it's God. Mom grew up in religion and her mom forced her to go to church every week and she always felt judged and guilty, and she says it ruined the idea of God for her. So she's worked out a higher power that isn't called God and isn't like what she learned in church. Only that it's something bigger than her, than us, than what we can always see or understand.

21

"I've always felt that way about the ocean," she told me when she was figuring this stuff out. "It's bigger and wider and deeper than I can comprehend. From here, it looks eternal. It's always there, even when I can't see it. It's full of hidden life. And it doesn't trigger all my religious baggage."

I don't know if religion is all bad. Lu goes to church in the city almost every week with Steve and her mom. Casey goes sometimes. Lu likes the singing and candles and going somewhere every week where people know you. "Like group," I said when we were talking about it once. She thought about that and answered, "Sort of. And sort of not. You can come with us some Sunday if you want."

Group is enough for me. I've been to church with my grandma and didn't like it. And I wouldn't want Mom to get triggered.

Religion is part of why Grandma doesn't really talk to us, except sometimes on holidays. Or why we don't talk to her. There are other reasons, too. I haven't seen her since I spent some of my summer with her when I was ten. Mom was working through her ninth step and making amends to people she'd hurt, and tried to repair her relationship with Grandma. So we drove down to the central coast, where she lives now, and visited awhile, then Mom left me there a couple of weeks.

What I liked: the neighborhood where her apartment is because I could hear and smell the ocean like at home; watching *Jeopardy!* and *Wheel of Fortune* together every single night; looking at photo albums of my mom plus a whole part of the family I don't even know. What I didn't like: Grandma criticizing the way I did everything, like how I hung my towel, how I set the table, how I cut my meat; having to go to church and wear a dress.

Worst of all, though, was this one day we were going to take a picnic to the beach. I was folding up the pullout couch and ready to pick out my clothes. Grandma came over to me and said, "Last night I set out granola bars to take to the beach. Now they're gone. Did you take them?"

"No?" I don't even like most granola bars.

She pursed her lips together and tilted her chin down. "Kyra, don't lie."

That had never happened to me. Mom had never accused me of lying. "I'm not," I said.

Grandma turned away from me and said, "Just like your mother."

Then she didn't talk to me other than to say things like, "We're leaving in five minutes," and "Don't forget your sandals," and at the beach we sat there not talking. I saw a whale spout way off the coast and wanted to say, *Look!* but I was scared to say anything.

She unpacked our lunch onto the blanket, taking out our cheese sandwiches, cut fruit, and sodas. Then she froze with her hand in the tote bag. A few seconds later, she pulled out the granola bars and put them on the blanket. "What do you have to say about that?" she asked.

I wasn't sure what she meant. I said, "You must have already packed them and forgot."

23

"Well, I don't think so."

She didn't apologize for accusing me. I told Mom about it on our drive home, and *she* got way madder than I even was and called Grandma when we got home and cursed her out on the phone. She handed me the phone, and Grandma finally apologized, but Mom could never fix what needed fixing with her. Part of that was about our house, the one we still live in now, and the fact Mom's grandma left it to her and not to Mom's mom. I don't understand why that could make you never want to talk to your daughter, but then I don't understand most of what adults think matters. It's also about all the years my mom wasn't sober and how it affected her mom. Grandma seems like she doesn't trust Mom's recovery, like she's just waiting for it to all fall apart, the way my grandpa's apparently did.

Mom says religion is no good if it doesn't change you for the better, and she doesn't see Grandma changing for the better. Anyway, when it comes to a higher power, the ocean works for us.

Tonight, the air is extra salty, and the fog is thick in the dark. We can hear and smell the ocean more than see it. I take deep breaths, like I could inhale it all into me and take it home.

"Smells good, huh?" Mom says.

I used to like it when Mom would say aloud what I was thinking in my head. It was like she was in my thoughts with me. Lately I don't like that so much. I want to have my thoughts and feel like they're all mine instead of as though we're always sharing them.

But right now, it doesn't bother me quite as much. "Mm-hmm."

She puts her arm around me. "I'm grateful for you, Keek."

I lean into her. "Why?"

"Why am I grateful for you?" she asks with a laugh.

"Yeah." I like to hear it specifically.

"You're my baby girl. You're my light. You help keep me grounded." She squeezes me. "You're a heck of a good cook. And I'm hungry." She lets go of me and stands, then extends a hand to help me up. "Shall we?"

I visualize what's in the fridge at home. "There's leftover lasagna."

"Oh, I know. I've been thinking about it all day."

We walk back up the path, still holding hands, the sound of the ocean following us all the way to the car.

4

After we finish off the lasagna and the pan is soaking in the sink, and we've shared the last few bites of ice cream that were left in the carton, Mom asks, "Should we do journals?"

In October, when it was my birthday and her sobriety birthday—the anniversary of the day she decided to quit drinking—she got us each a journal. One for her, one for me. They're special journals with writing prompts for people in recovery, and she thought it would be nice to each be writing in them and then share what we wrote.

It seems like the point of a journal is having a private place to keep your private thoughts. Not to share what you write. And besides, I wanted a new set of measuring cups for my birthday, with the scoops for dry ingredients nesting right into the cups for liquid ingredients. The markings on our old plastic measuring cup that I use for everything are almost all scratched off now.

But the journals and the sharing seem like a big deal to her, so I try. I forget and miss a lot of days and have to catch up with her like it's forgotten homework. When I do remember, I imagine reading it aloud to her, and that changes what I write.

"I haven't written in it since Tuesday," I say.

"That's okay! Go get it. I'll boil water for tea."

I go to my room. It looks so inviting, cool and clean, and I have a blue kitchen towel draped over my bedside lamp so that it's not totally dark but not too bright, either. After starting early and cleaning all day and then going to group and having a late dinner, all I want to do is sit on my bed with my back against the pillows and watch some cooking videos and text Lu before her family leaves for Ohio tomorrow.

I find the journal on my desk under some homework and go back to the kitchen. She smiles at me while getting out the boxes of tea.

The prompt for Tuesday was "What Is Serenity to Me?"

I wrote:

Serenity is being at home.
Serenity is being free to be myself.
Serenity is being alone, sometimes. Or sometimes it's being with Mom when she's not thinking about work and I have her all to myself.
Serenity is looking at the ocean.

27

Serenity is a clean house and a full refrigerator.
Serenity is cooking good food for me and Mom.

I read her everything except the one about being alone and her thinking about work.

"I love those," she says. "Mine is more like a few paragraphs than a list. A list is a good idea."

"Lists are faster."

"Good point. Let's see . . ." She flips through some pages with one hand, holding her hair back with the other—it's a yellower blond than mine but the same sort of messy.

I dunk my tea bag a few times. It's peppermint, the only one I like. Mom likes the fruit and flower ones. To me those smell like hand lotion, which I wouldn't want to drink.

She glances up at me. "I wrote one for today while you were at group. The prompt was the usual Saturday one, about reflecting on the week."

That sounds long. She starts reading.

"Today was the best day of the week, because Kyra was my buddy for client work. She's so helpful and I enjoy her company. I never got along with my mom when I was her age or any age, and I'm grateful she still likes me. Or seems to." She steals another glance at me, and I say, "I do," and then she keeps reading. "Today a client left a beer in the fridge. I think it stressed Kyra out. She acted like she wanted to hide it from me at first. She probably has no idea how many clients' houses I'm in every day that are full of alcohol. When she watched me pour the beer out, I felt like I wanted to make it funny,

28

make her laugh. But I know it's serious, too."

She closes her journal and looks at me. "It did stress you out, didn't it."

I almost say no, because I don't like her thinking that *I* don't trust her sobriety the way her mom doesn't. But I also want to be honest. "It was your brand. I had, like, a physical reaction to it."

"You remember my brand?"

"Yeah, I used to always check when it was and wasn't in the fridge."

She groans and puts her hand against her cheek. "Of course you did. At six or seven you must have been old enough already to have an emotional association with the beer bottles and wine bottles and liquor bottles you saw around here."

"Yeah." I put my nose close to the peppermint steam floating up out of my mug and close my eyes. I wonder if Lu is packing right now or if she's already packed.

"Do you not want to talk about it right now? It's okay if you don't."

I open my eyes. "I'm just really tired." In group, we've read about HALT, where you try to avoid getting into emotional topics when you're Hungry, Angry, Lonely, or Tired.

She picks up her phone, which she's had face down on the table. "Holy smokes, it's almost ten-thirty."

"Am I coming with you again tomorrow?" I ask.

"I don't think so. I arranged it so most of my clients tomorrow are in the city, and I'm going to hit a meeting there, and I don't want to drag you that far from home all day. Especially

29

after you worked so hard today. Is that all right?"

I hesitate for a moment, then nod. "That means I get the house to myself tomorrow," I say, choosing the upside: I can stay in my pj's and watch the Food Network and start planning our Thanksgiving dinner.

"I thought you probably wouldn't mind." She stands up and leans over to kiss me on the head. "Sorry I kept you up so late. I'll be getting an early start again in the morning, but you just sleep in, okay?"

I know that I'm going to get up and make her breakfast and help her make sure she hasn't forgotten anything, and I think she knows it, too. "We'll see."

She laughs. "I love you, baby."

5

I texted Lu last night but she never answered, so I text her again before I get up to make Mom a breakfast burrito.

Did you leave yet?? I'll miss you. Have a good trip! :)

There's only one egg left, so Mom's burrito is mostly pinto beans and a slice of Swiss cheese. Swiss is not the best cheese to go with beans and eggs—that would be Monterey Jack or cheddar. But it's the only cheese we have left right now, and a burrito definitely needs cheese.

Mom comes into the kitchen with her hair wet and dripping on the shoulders of her Meg the Maid tee. "You're supposed to be sleeping in!"

"I woke up anyway." I scrape the eggs and beans from the pan onto the tortilla (with cheese). I already warmed it up in

31

the microwave so it's easier to roll.

"Do we have any green chili sauce left?" Mom asks.

"Check the fridge door."

She finds the hot sauce and hands it to me with a smile; I add a few dashes before I fold up the burrito and then wrap it in foil.

"Thanks, Keek." She fills her travel mug from the pot of coffee I made. "Any fun plans for today?"

"Everyone's out of town."

"You mean Lu's out of town."

I want to say, *I don't have any other friends!* But she knows that, and also it's embarrassing to say. "I'll probably read and watch TV and stuff. And make a grocery list."

"Text it to me and I can stop on my way home."

"I want to go with you, though." Sometimes she doesn't get exactly what I put on the list, and she almost always forgets at least one thing or says she can't find it because she gives up too easily if she doesn't already know where it is in the store.

"Maybe we can go tonight after dinner?"

"Okay," I say. "Try not to be too late, though."

"I will try." She's checking her pockets for something when she says it, and I'm not sure she listened.

I pack her a few snacks and fill a water bottle from the tap, and we make sure she has her phone and everything else she needs for the day.

"If you decide to go down to the beach or anything, just shoot me a text to let me know where you are," she says. She pulls me into a hug goodbye. "Thanks again for your help yesterday. And this morning. Have a good Kyra day, okay? Do whatever you want. I know you'll miss Lu, but sometimes it's nice to do your own thing, right?"

I do my own thing almost all the time. She's in a rush, though, and there's nothing she can do about it anyway, so I agree with her that it is nice, and I tell her I love her, then she's out to the car and on her way.

After she's gone, I make my own breakfast. Since Mom got the last egg, I have a burrito with just beans, cheese, and salsa. It's still good. I take the little bit of coffee that's left in the pot and set it aside in a cup to maybe use in a recipe later.

I do like having the house to myself, except it's not clean right now, the way I said I like it on my serenity list. And the fridge is not full. I can do something about the house even if I can't fill the fridge until Mom takes me shopping, and there's enough there for me to put together dinner for us later.

Steve taught me to cook a long time before he even met Lu's mom. The first year of Mom's sobriety, when she was going to meetings almost every day and also starting to build her business, she'd call Steve to come over and hang out with me, or she'd drop me at his house. All Mom's other friends were still drinking and partying; there was a gap between when she stopped hanging out with them and when she found new sober friends. During that gap, Steve was pretty much the only adult she could rely on.

He taught me how to use recipes and also how you don't really need recipes, except maybe for baking. He taught me the safe way to use a knife, and how to not make a mess, and how, when I'm planning a dinner, to think ahead to leftovers and lunches.

When I'd go to his house, his mother was there, too, before she died. She looked about a hundred years old—Mom said she only looked that old because she was sick—and was always in her nightgown. She walked in a wobbly shuffle as if she was about to fall. I was scared of her, or maybe scared of her falling. One time she came into the kitchen while we were making corn bread and stared at me and asked, "Are you my granddaughter?"

"This is Kyra, Ma," Steve said. "You remember my friend Meg? From high school? This is her daughter."

"I know, but is she my granddaughter?"

"No, Ma."

I don't think she understood why he was suddenly spending all this time with me.

I'm not as good a cook as him yet, but I'm pretty good. Like I said, better than Mom. Mom's better at cleaning than me, but I'm the one who's here, so I'll do it today.

I go around the house and pick up shoes and clothes and school stuff and dirty dishes. I sort the mail and put the junk in the recycling. I can't vacuum because Mom has our vacuum for work, but I sweep and unload the dishwasher, then load it with dirty dishes. Then I go through everything we have in the fridge and pantry.

Less than half a head of broccoli that's starting to shrivel.

A lot of condiments.

A pack of vegetarian hot dogs.

A little bit of onion, a little bit of spinach, a little bit of chicken, half a lemon. A few more slices of Swiss cheese.

I check the cupboard. There's one last can of tuna. Spaghetti. And a partial head of garlic in the bowl on the counter.

When I see the tuna, I know exactly what I'll make for dinner: spaghetti tonnato with broccoli and garlic. The lemon will help give it a nice bright flavor. I learned from Steve that you can call anything "tonnato" that has tuna in it because "tonno" is the Italian word for tuna. It sounds fancier that way.

My phone buzzes on the counter; I lunge for it.

We're at the airport!

It's Lu. There's another text right after it:

There's a girl from school here who's on the same flight as us. We're going to try to sit together so it won't be so boring. We're getting on different flights after Chicago though.

Who? I ask.

Till Melloy? She's in 8th. She's in chorus with me.

I try to picture who she means, and can't. Then Lu sends a selfie of her with Till Melloy. I've seen her at school. She has big brown eyes and clear braces.

Oh yeah, I write. **What's the airport like?**

I've never been. And there's nowhere I need or want to go, but I'm curious. I wait for Lu's reply, staring at the screen, until I lose patience and write, **Well have a great trip!**

With the house picked up and my plan for dinner in place, I wander around from room to room. I open windows a crack

35

to get fresh air, even though it's chilly out. I close the curtains where the sun is going to be too bright later this afternoon. I take a bubble bath.

I look up where fruit flies come from and where they go, and I wish I didn't. They squeeze in through cracks and window screens or their eggs are already on the fruit. They only live a month, but they can lay five hundred eggs before they die. They can breed in the plumbing or even on an old sponge.

It's gross.

One article says you can make a vinegar trap to try to get rid of them, so I watch a video on that and then put apple cider vinegar at the top of my shopping list. Meanwhile, I make a hot bleach bath in the sink and put the kitchen sponge in and also our cutting board. By the time I do all that, I'm hungry for lunch, and so I make a salad with the chicken and spinach and wrap it up in the last tortilla.

I guess Lu is in the sky now, sitting next to Till and getting to know her. I wonder if I ever saw someone from school in an unexpected place if I would talk to them, if they would talk to me. If they would even know who I am! I've never had more than one or two friends at a time. And Mom. Like I wrote in my journal, I do like being alone. But not *all* the time. And especially during school breaks, it would be good to have a few more friends. Or a sister. Or a brother. Or a father.

That's the kind of stuff I don't like to think about too much. It's almost as bad as thinking about fruit flies.

I turn on the Food Network, but they're showing a marathon of shows I've seen before, so I go to YouTube instead for

Thanksgiving ideas. I've never made acorn squash. That could be good. I want to make cheesy potatoes. I want to make corn casserole. I want to make pull-apart herb bread. There's only so much the two of us can eat, so some of these things I'll have to do when it's not Thanksgiving.

I make the grocery list and divide it up into regular stuff we need and then holiday stuff.

I text Mom.

What time should I have dinner ready?

Not sure. Will let u know later. Busy busy busy!!! xo

I send her a kissy face even though I would have rather had an estimate of a specific time.

So that I'm prepared to cook as soon as she says she's on her way, I wash and cut up the broccoli and garlic and leave it on the cutting board with a kitchen towel over it. I fill a pot of water for the spaghetti and set it on the stove. I put the can of tuna next to the cutting board.

There's no homework to do, no more cleaning, no more lists to make, no more texts to send. It could still be a couple of hours before Mom is done. I don't want to walk to the beach. Not by myself.

If Lu weren't on a plane, she might text right now and say, *Let's walk to the beach*. Then I'd want to. Or we'd ride bikes to the park or to the shopping center, like we do sometimes, or I'd go to her house and make videos of her playing her guitar, or we'd learn a dance to do and post. We're not that good at learning dances, but it's fun to try.

Last Thanksgiving break, her mom took us to Stonestown—

a big mall on the south end of the city—and we got Christmas presents for our families and for each other. I got her a small box of See's chocolate and she got me a Shake Shack gift card that we went back and used during winter break.

We haven't done anything like that in a while. I count back and realize we haven't *really* done anything special together since my birthday in October, when we went to Round Table with both our families. We see each other at school and go to group, but lately that's been basically it. She hasn't suggested anything else lately, but neither have I.

Why?

Like fruit flies and fathers, I don't like thinking about this too much.

Since there's nothing else to do, I write in my journal, knowing that Mom will probably want to share later. The prompt is "Things I Worry About," which is the last thing I want to think about right now. I sigh and write them down anyway while watching more cooking videos and waiting for Mom.

6

She forgets to text me when she's on her way home, but I figure it out by tracking her with my phone. We both have our phones set so that we can locate each other if we need to. Her dot is moving south from the city toward Pacifica, so I start to boil the pasta water. While the spaghetti cooks, I sauté the broccoli and garlic, add the can of tuna, and juice the lemon.

I check her dot again and it's stopped around Vallemar. Probably traffic. Highway 1 is the only way in and out of Pacifica, and it can get very backed up on the weekends, with people enjoying beach days even in winter. Except it's nearly seven-thirty, and by now most of the traffic should go north toward San Francisco, not south toward us. Anyway, the spaghetti is done and I'm ready to eat, so I drain it and toss it into the broccoli, garlic, olive oil, and tuna sauce, and add the lemon juice, salt and pepper.

Her dot is still stuck, so I fix my bowl and text her that I'm going to eat. I eat as slow as I can, and stop halfway through so we can still technically eat together.

Finally, she gets home.

"I'm sorry!" she calls as she comes in the door. "I'm sorry, I'm sorry!" Her sorries get closer, then she's in the kitchen. "And I'm starving! It smells so *good*."

"It is." I get up and fill her bowl, and add a little more to mine.

"The traffic was a nightmare. I don't know why everyone and their brother was coming this direction tonight. I almost pulled off at Rockaway to have a good scream, but then cars finally started moving again."

"Do you think we'll still have time to go to the store?"

"I think so," she says, coiling a huge forkful of spaghetti tonnato against her bowl. "This is great, babe. How was your day?"

I shrug. "Kind of boring." She pauses and looks at me, and I can tell she feels bad or is going to want me to say something about my feelings, so I keep talking. "What's the airport like? I was texting Lu and asked her, but I guess she had to get on the plane before she could answer."

"Oh gosh, I haven't been in a long time. Like fifteen years, maybe? I'm sure it's all different now."

I twirl up some spaghetti. "Where did you go? Fifteen years ago?"

"Las Vegas," she says, and cringes. "With my party posse.

40

For a while we were taking trips a couple of times a year. Vegas, San Diego, Palm Springs. Anywhere we could let the desert heat cook the fog out of our bones."

"Was that when you worked at the convention center?"

"Mm-hmm. Well, for the logistics company that contracted with the convention center."

Before she was Meg the Maid, she worked doing all kinds of business and hospitality services, and before I was born she mostly worked at the South San Francisco Conference Center. That's where she met a lot of the friends she drank with. And where she met the man who was my dad for about ten minutes before he decided he didn't want to be one.

"You know," she says, "you don't have to be flying somewhere to go to the airport. We could just *go* to the airport. Most of the good stuff is past the security gates, and you wouldn't be able to see that, but you'd get an idea of what it's like."

That could be interesting. At least we'd be getting out of the house for something other than cleaning. "Maybe we could do that on Friday? The day after Thanksgiving?"

"I bet we could."

I eat my last bite of spaghetti and get lost in thoughts of Mom traveling to fun places with her pack of friends. She never talks specifically about what the party posse did, and I know that was from a time when her drinking was at its worst, but I can't help but think that parts of it were probably fun. Way more fun than being home alone all day or going to only the outside parts of the airport.

She puts her fork down and reaches out to touch my hand.

"I know I've been working way too much."

"It's the season. You'll have more time off after the holidays."

"*You* won't, though. I just wish . . . I don't know. I wish we had a few more options. I wish I could give you that. Options. Things to do, people to see . . ."

"It's okay," I say quickly. But I feel suddenly sad thinking about how when it comes down to it, it really is only the two of us. Our little life. Group and school and work and not a lot else. I should be grateful for those things, which are good to have. I swallow the sad and pull my hand out from under hers.

She reaches to take it back. "It doesn't have to be okay."

"It is, though," I insist, and get up to rinse our plates. "Can we go to the store?"

"Yes." She pushes herself up out of her chair, wincing a little when her one knee pops. "I need to check in with Antonia real quick first, okay?"

Antonia is her sponsor, the person who helps her keep her sobriety on track. They have regular check-ins, and this is an example of how sometimes, no matter what Mom says, it *does* have to be okay, even though I want to say, *Mom! You said you wouldn't be late! You said we would go to the store!* Her sobriety is more important than groceries.

She makes her call in the living room while I clean up. When I'm done, she's still talking, so I grab the car keys to go get the vacuum so I can finish cleaning our house later or first thing in the morning.

"Keek?" she says suddenly as I open the door. "Where are you going?"

"Getting the vacuum?"

She waves me back and holds the phone to her shoulder to say, "No, no, honey, I promise I'm almost done. I just need a little privacy, okay?"

She could have it if she'd let me get the vacuum!

I sigh and go to my room and pull out my journal to write down three things I'm grateful for this week so I'm not a hypocrite for what I said to Owen at group last night.

That I know how to cook
No homework

I tap my pen on the journal and look all around my room for ideas for a third thing. There's the side table I got at a garage sale last summer for seven dollars; I like it, but it feels depressing as a thing to be grateful for.

I think about Lu on a plane and feel a twinge of envy. I want to go somewhere.

I need a third thing. A gratitude list of two feels worse than no list at all.

In the other room, I can hear Mom's voice, talking to Antonia in low tones, but I can't make out the words.

The ocean

It feels like cheating because I always put that, but at least it's done.

7

On the drive to the store, Mom seems tense.

"Seems" is the word I try to hold on to. I know from group that people who live with addicts and alcoholics have a habit of reading too much into how other people are acting, or guessing at how they might be feeling or what they may be thinking. It makes us feel safer to know or to pretend we know, so that we're not caught off guard.

So when Mom seems tense, I want to know exactly why.

Is she tired? I know I am. That's one-fourth of the Hungry-Angry-Lonely-Tired of HALT. I'm lonely, too. And I even might be a little angry at having to wait for her. Is she mad at me for something? Does she wish she could have gone to the store without me instead of having to double back after dinner?

I should know it's not a good time to try to guess at what it means when she whacks the turn signal harder than she needs to or whips into the parking spot too fast. My brain wants to guess anyway.

"Got your list?" she asks.

"On my phone," I answer, holding it up.

"Let's rock and roll!" she says happily, but it seems forced. *Seems.*

In the store, I round up prices and add as I go and only get about half the things I want to. Since our Thanksgiving is just us, I don't need to make enough food for ten people.

In the cheese section, I pick up a wedge of smoked Gouda and stare at the price and get stuck.

This happens to me once in a while when making decisions. I freeze the way my phone screen sometimes freezes. The cheese is expensive, but I know it would make the *best* cheesy potatoes. I could get this and not get pecans for the acorn squash, or I could get a cheaper cheese and do both.

Mom is leaning on the cart, watching me. "What's the holdup, babe? You've been staring at that cheese for like three minutes."

"I'm just thinking."

"Can you think faster?" she says. I look at her, and in the split second between when she sees me looking and when she thinks I'm not, her face is blank and her eyes are unfocused, faraway. Then she winks and smiles. "Get the expensive cheese. It's okay."

When I still don't move, she reaches to grab it out of my

45

hand and puts it in the cart. It's an agitated, impatient movement. But she laughs, so maybe she was only pretending to be impatient. I finish the shopping as fast as I can anyway.

Out in the parking lot, she says, "Hold on a sec," as she pops the trunk of the car to move some things around and make room for the bags. I go over to help, but she waves me away and gestures to the cart. "I got it, Keek. Want to return that?"

She keeps loading the car, and I push the cart to the cart return, running with it and jumping on to glide a few feet at a time. I push it into the back of another cart with a satisfying clatter.

In the car, Mom asks, "Radio?" and I say sure.

All the way home, she blasts her favorite station with music from when she was in high school.

We talk through our plans right before bed, like always. I'm going to help her with a job tomorrow morning down the coast, then we'll come home for lunch, and she'll do her afternoon jobs on her own and I'll take care of dinner.

She sits in my room, and we read from our journals. I go first, flipping back from my sad gratitude list to my "Things I Worry About" list. I don't want to read all these to her because there are a lot, and I feel like Mom was already worried enough about whatever was bothering her all evening, and I don't want her to think about that anymore. So I leave out certain things while I read.

"I worry about climate change. I know I'm supposed to

'accept the things I cannot change' and I'm just one person, but I don't accept it and think everyone should do better."

That's a general worry that everyone has, so it won't feel personal to Mom. I skip over what I wrote about how I worry Mom will never have time to be here more, especially when I get to high school and homework will be harder and I won't have so much time to help. That's still almost two years off.

"I worry . . ." This next part is about Lu. And Mom is friends with Steve, and Steve is Lu's stepdad. Should I say it? I glance up, and Mom is looking down at her own journal, so maybe she's only half listening. "I worry that Lu doesn't like me as much as she used to. She has more friends at school than I do this year. Eighth graders think she's cool. They would never think that about me."

I stop there, even though there's some stuff about bills and war after that.

"Oh, babe," Mom says. "Lu loves you."

So she was listening. "That's not the same as *liking.*"

She pauses, then says, "Middle school is hard."

She says that like it's supposed to be comforting. It isn't.

"I'm gonna close my eyes while you read yours, okay?" I say. I'm so tired. I settle down under the covers.

It's our normal routine, but it doesn't feel normal. I keep picturing how she grabbed the cheese, how she waved me away when I tried to help unload the groceries. She's not usually like that. There was also how low her voice got at the end of her call with Antonia. That's not *that* unusual by itself.

47

Maybe it's just the little things all together that are getting me tangled up.

I concentrate on listening:

"'Sometimes I wonder if starting my own business was the right thing for me,'" Mom reads now from her journal. "'It's just so much work for one person. I'm the boss and the front-line employee and the accountant and the human resources department. And my own resources as a human feel a little low right now.'"

She pauses, and I can tell she's watching me to see if I'm asleep yet. I pretend I am, careful not to move or let my eyes open. It's funny how closing your eyes is so easy, but then the second you really *try* to not open them, they want to open. Mine flutter from the effort, and she keeps reading, her voice getting softer.

"'I have plenty of clients and get good reviews and tips. I manage to take care of us without any help, even though it's a struggle so much of the time and property tax is overdue and I try to do everything right with recovery. I don't know why, with all that, I still feel like a failure.'"

She pauses again, and then I hear her close the journal.

So maybe that's it. That's what's been bothering her all night. Maybe I should open my eyes all the way and tell her she isn't a failure. She isn't! Maybe I should assure her I'm all right. That it's okay if we don't have enough money to get all the ingredients I want. And that I can stand being bored for the rest of break. It's not forever. *This Too Shall Pass*, as it says on one of our fridge magnets.

Maybe letting it pass is better than saying something right now. I make myself into a rock, willing my eyeballs to freeze and my eyelids to stay closed while she kisses my cheek and smooths my hair.

"I love you, Keek," she whispers. "I'm sorry. Sweet dreams."

8

One thing I remember about Mom before she stopped drinking was how she was always saying, "I'm sorry."

I remember waiting to be picked up from day care and my teachers whispering to each other because Mom was always late. "Sorry I'm late, Keek," she'd say, pulling me along too fast on the walk home.

I remember being small and how she liked to sit on the floor of the bathroom with a drink while I took my bath. She would talk and talk and I'd watch her take sips and gulps from a tall glass of ice with clear liquid that wasn't water. I'd have to show her how pruney my fingertips were getting and tell her I was cold to get her to stop talking and wrap me up in a towel. "Sorry, sorry," she'd say, rubbing my hair dry too hard. "I'm sorry."

I remember babysitters who needed to be home by ten

still waiting for her until midnight or one. I'd be awake in my room, listening to them on their cell phones, calling their parents or friends, calling my mom and leaving her messages. "I'm *so* sorry," I'd hear her tell them when she finally got home. "So sorry!"

Other times she'd climb into bed with me at night, crying and apologizing. Or laughing and apologizing. Smelling like what I'd learn was alcohol, and sometimes smoke. Those times, I didn't know what she was sorry for, specifically.

The way she said "I'm sorry" last night when I didn't know what she was sorry for didn't sound exactly like those apologies. But it didn't sound *not*-like them, either, and a new little pocket of unidentified worry opened up somewhere in me.

When Mom left my room last night and I could stop pretending to be asleep, I typed out a text to Lu.

I hope you're having a good trip. I wish we had group again already. I think my mom is stressed out.

My thumb hovered over the send button. I wanted something to assure me that Lu remembered I still exist here while she's on vacation, but then I thought, *What if it's too late in Ohio and I wake her up?* And if she couldn't or didn't reply right away, I might get stuck all night checking my phone and feel worse than if I sent it. So I didn't send it.

This morning, I do all our getting-ready stuff: make coffee, make breakfast, pack snacks, fill water bottles, go through the departure checklist. I try to close the pocket of worry and hope it goes away. I decide to be grateful instead.

51

I'm grateful that the place we're cleaning today is this cool house in Moss Beach that has a gray-and-wood exterior and a roof that tilts in only one direction. When we use the key code to go in, Mom stops and puts her hands on her hips, surveying the big living room with its leather couch and love seat, grand piano, and huge picture window facing the ocean. There's hardly anything on the shelves or coffee table.

I go the window and soak up the view, looking for whale spouts or dolphin fins.

Mom says, "Every time I come to this place, I have to stop in my tracks and think about how freaking rich some people are."

I turn and look at the room again. It does look like something from HGTV, when they reveal the makeover and everything is new. Like it's never been dirty and they want to keep it that way.

"At least it's not a mess," I say.

"Yeah. Only the rich can afford to be this minimalist. I think they have another house in Tahoe they live at half the time. She's some fancy pianist. Ooh la la." She lets out a big sigh and turns away from the ocean. "I need an attitude adjustment."

On impulse, I grab her hand. "Attitude adjustment. Starting now."

"Okay. Fake it 'til we make it."

She squeezes my hand, and we work out who will start where—me in the kitchen and her in the bedrooms. For the rest of the morning, whenever we pass each other we paste on big clown smiles to make each other laugh.

"How's your attitude, Kiki?"

"Amazing. How's yours?"

"Couldn't be better!"

By the time we go home for lunch and she leaves again, she's in a better mood.

Whatever was going on with her last night, maybe I fixed it.

The next few days go kind of like that. Mom works, sometimes I help, and I also hold down the house. It's boring and I'm lonely, but I don't say so.

I text Lu to see how her trip is and she replies, Fun! and then doesn't text again or ask me how *my* vacation is going. The day before Thanksgiving, I text her, **Remember when we went to Stonestown and got all our Christmas presents?**

She replies, Yeah I remember! It was just last year!

I write, **I miss you.**

She leaves a heart sticker. That's not the same as saying "I miss you" back.

Finally, it's Thanksgiving. Mom takes that day and the day after off.

Thursday she sleeps until almost eleven while I get our Thanksgiving meal together. It's canned ham, because it's hard to find a turkey sized for just two people. Plus we have the baked acorn squash and the cheesy potatoes with the expensive smoked Gouda. I wanted to make pecan pie, but canned pumpkin was on sale and pecans are expensive, so I did pumpkin instead. With vanilla ice cream and chocolate sauce.

Once she's up and showered, we eat.

She compliments me a lot on the food. "I wasn't sure about acorn squash, but this is great." And, "Are these the best potatoes you've ever made?" And, "I'm excited about ham sandwiches tomorrow."

But something about it feels forced. Or maybe I only think that because I'm looking for problems after what she read from her journal the other night.

When we're finishing up, she says, "I'm sorry I slept so long and didn't help. I'm just so exhausted from all this work. . . . I'm going to do all the cleanup, okay?"

"We can do it together—"

"Just let me do it, Kyra." It almost sounds like she's snapping at me, but then she takes a breath and says gently, "I want to do my part."

"Okay."

After she cleans up, we watch the two Star Wars movies we haven't seen yet and then have some leftovers and sit on the couch and write in our journals.

The prompt for today is about gratitude, of course, which I'm getting a little bit sick of, but I manage to list a few things that I read out to her:

Cheesy potatoes
Luke Skywalker

Our house
No school

She's on the other end of the couch, leaning on the arm of it with a blanket over her legs. She says, "I also had Luke Skywalker. And our house." She glances at me, then down at her journal. "You, of course. Um . . . that's all."

"Did you really put Luke Skywalker?" I ask.

"Of course! Who wouldn't?"

"Lemme see." I crawl over her to try to get to the journal. She holds it over her head to keep it away from me. I'm laughing and she's laughing, too, twisting her body to avoid me getting hold of the journal. "Give it!" I shriek, and I can't stop laughing. We're Kiki Krash and Meg the Marauder.

Then in an instant, we're not.

"Kyra, stop it!" She pushes me off her onto the floor, hard.

I'm still laughing, sort of, and trying to catch my breath. When I look at her, her face is red and she's not smiling anymore. The journal is pressed against her chest.

"Sorry." My voice is small. I get up on my knees and shuffle over to the coffee table to start clearing our pie plates. Saliva collects in my mouth, and my eyeballs feel hot.

"Keek, wait."

I stand up as I if I didn't hear her, and carry our plates to the kitchen to rinse and load. Even though I want to clatter dishes and slam the door of the dishwasher, I do everything extra quiet and take a lot of breaths.

Journals are private, and I wouldn't have wanted her to try to take mine.

But I thought we were playing. And she's the one who always wants to share.

"Babe."

Her voice comes from behind me in the kitchen. I turn around and see her holding her journal, then quickly look away.

"I shouldn't have pushed you," she says.

"I know."

"Can I show you my journal?"

I shrug. She comes over to me and opens to the Thanksgiving page and holds it in front of my face. It's just doodles. No list of what she's thankful for. No Luke Skywalker, no me.

"I'm tired," she says. "It's my first day off in a long time, and I just . . . didn't feel like writing anything. I figured I'd come up with something on the spot. That was all true. And I am thankful for the house. And you. Maybe not Luke Skywalker."

I don't care what she writes in the journal, or if she even does at all. I don't even like the journal. I do it for her. That all comes out as "I don't care."

"It's okay if you do care."

She doesn't understand what I'm trying to say. I don't know if I understand it. "I was only playing around," I say. And then I got pushed. And then I got yelled at because *she* lied. But I also shouldn't have been trying to read her journal. Were we both wrong? I don't know. "You're the one who said we should do our journal prompt."

She squeezes her eyes shut, then opens them again. "I

know. I know. I'm sorry. You made such a wonderful Thanksgiving meal. Everything was perfect. I should have just said that." She holds her hair back against her forehead with one hand and looks over my shoulder at the wall. "I think I'm going a little crazy right now. You know I always think about my mom and everything at the holidays. . . ."

Here's something we can talk about that's not me, not her, not whatever is going on between us. My breath relaxes. "Do you miss her?" I ask.

"Yes. Also no. But . . . she's my mom. And I guess I've been dreading our annual holiday call. Antonia says I don't have to do it, but I think it's a good ritual." She lets her hair fall and focuses on me again. "Should we call her? We could do it tomorrow, and then it's done, and I won't be stressing about it between now and Christmas."

Suddenly, it's my decision. "If you want."

"Well, we'll sleep on it." She steps closer. "Hug?"

I let her hug me. I hug her back. We're the same height— we only noticed that recently. My eyes land on the refrigerator and the recovery slogan magnets.

Live and Let Live.

One Day at a Time.

Easy Does It.

Keep It Simple.

Together We Can Make It.

9

In the morning, we make the call.

Mom puts her phone on the kitchen table and turns on the speaker and we listen to it ring. Once, twice, three times.

Mom glances at me. "Maybe she's at work."

Ring.

"Don't teachers have today off?"

Ring.

"Yeah, but—"

"Hello?" Grandma's voice sounds curious and a little worried.

"Mom? Hi!"

"Is everything okay? Is Kyra all right?"

Mom rubs her forehead. "Yeah, Mom. She's right here. Everything is fine. We just wanted to say Happy Thanksgiving."

"Hi, Grandma! Happy Thanksgiving!"

"Well, Happy Thanksgiving to you, too!" She sounds like she's trying as hard as I am to sound cheerful and normal. As if we talk on the phone all the time and there's nothing awkward at all about our relationship. "What did you two do yesterday?"

"Kyra made us a feast and we just hung around, enjoyed being lazy." Mom pauses. "How about you?"

I can hear the strain in her voice in that simple question.

"I baked half a dozen pies this week for church, for our Thanksgiving potluck. Two each of pear, pecan, and apple. We have a new associate pastor, and he requested the pecan pie especially. His name is Jim—I think you'd like him, Meg. If you ever wanted to bring Kyra down on a weekend and join me. Anyway, there were nearly fifty people at the potluck, and we had to use most of our tables and chairs. Lots of folks brought family members who were visiting."

She lets that hang there for a few seconds. Mom's head is in her hands as she stares down at the phone.

"I made pie, too," I say. "And acorn squash. Have you ever made that? Like, I cut it into rings and glazed it with butter and brown sugar. It was really good with ham."

"I haven't made any kind of winter squash in years. It's hard for me to cut because of the pain in my hands. Sometimes I buy butternut squash already cut up, but that's a bit pricey."

"How's work?" Mom asks.

Grandma laughs in a way that doesn't sound happy. "Worse every day. Just counting the months to retirement. Seven more to go. We'll see if I make it."

There's a long silence where Mom stares and stares at the phone, as if waiting for something, and I can't think of what else to talk about. Then Mom says, "My work is going pretty well. Lots of clients. A little tiring, but that means I'm busy. Work, meetings, spending time with Kyra. That's it in a nutshell."

"Oh? Still going to all those meetings?"

"Yeah, Mom. That's how it works."

"Well, it didn't work for your father. Do they still tell you that God can be anything you want him to be? That you can call a pumpkin God and that's your higher power?"

Mom shakes her head and looks at me with a half smile. "That's right. That's exactly right. Kyra and I worship pumpkins."

I half smile back even though there's a knot in my stomach now. I don't know why they can't even talk for five minutes without this happening. Grandma's church is her whole life, and technically it's the same Christian religion as Lu's family, but the way she talks about her version of it is way different from how Lu talks about hers.

"No need to be sarcastic, Meg," Grandma says.

"You know that's not what a higher power is about."

"Do I? I know what God is about. That's what I know."

"I'm glad you're so certain," Mom snaps.

"Mom," I whisper.

She grabs the phone and takes it off speaker before getting up and walking out of the kitchen. I hear her say that she and I are happy with our beliefs and would appreciate a little of the respect that we show hers. She's quiet a minute, then says a little more that I don't hear, then comes back into the kitchen holding out the phone. "Say goodbye to Grandma."

I press the warm phone to my cheek. "Bye, Grandma."

"Will I talk to you again at Christmas?" she asks. "I hope so. I love you, honey."

She does? How? She doesn't know me. The last time I saw her she accused me of stealing. "Thanks" is all I can say.

When we're done, Mom says, "I'm going to take a quick walk around the block." After a second she adds, "Want to come?"

I jump up from my chair and shove my feet into flip-flops.

It's cool and cloudy out, the way I like it. Mom takes some big gulps of air, blows them out slowly through tight lips.

"I just wanted her to ask about my work."

That must have been what she was waiting for during that big awkward pause. "I don't think she thought of that," I say.

"Why not, though, is the question. It's human interaction 101. She says what *she* did for the holiday, we say what *we* did. I ask about *her* work, she asks about *mine*. Anyone can do it. Except her."

We walk a little more, and I think through the conversation. "Maybe because she hates her job she doesn't enjoy work, like, as a topic."

Mom stops. "That's not the point!" Her face is flushed, her eyes intense. "It shouldn't be about her all the time! She doesn't ask me anything about my life, ever. It feels like she doesn't give a crap!"

I flinch, and the knot in my stomach pulls tighter. "Sorry."

"It's . . ." She takes another deep breath and puts her hand on my shoulder. "I'm not mad at you. Don't be sorry. I'm mad at her, only I can't do anything about it or express what I want to express, and I feel like I'm never going to not be mad at her, and I don't even know why I still want her to care."

"Like you said, she's your mom."

She sighs and drops her arm. "Yeah."

We keep walking. I want to ask if we're still going to go to the airport and people-watch, like we planned, but I also don't.

Yesterday when she shoved me and just now when she yelled at me, that's not normal for her. I think it's stress, and I think if I keep doing my jobs around the house and do what I need to do at school and go to group, and she does her work and goes to her meetings, we'll get through this busy, stressful season and then life will return to how it's supposed to be. We can go to the airport some other time.

A breeze from the ocean blows up the street and brings with it the distant sound of the waves crashing onto the beach. There's something bigger than us. Not Grandma's God, but not a pumpkin, either. Something wild and big and powerful, and always there.

10

Lu and Casey and their parents get back from their trip late Friday night, and Saturday morning Steve calls Mom to invite us to come over for dinner before group.

"Yay!" I say when Mom tells me. Later, I text Steve to ask what I can bring, and he replies:

Just yourself unless you've got something you're trying to get rid of. I'm doing a turkey since we couldn't bring leftovers back from Ohio!

I *do* have the ingredients for the green bean casserole with fried onions that we usually have at Thanksgiving. I didn't make it on Thursday because we already had enough food. So I make it in the afternoon and pull it out of the oven just in time for us to get over to Lu's.

She never replied more than a sticker to my *I miss you* text, and I'm a little nervous about seeing her, but as soon as we walk in, she gives me a big hug. The house is warm and smells like the holidays, like family. Not that our Thanksgiving didn't smell good, but it wasn't like this.

Lu's mom takes the casserole from me, and Steve gives me a hug, too, then Lu drags me to her room to tell me all about being with her Ohio family. "They were really nice, I guess, but also it was weird and boring. My grandma and grandpa left the TV on all the time, like *all* the time. They loved Steve. I got to see a lot of pictures of my mom from when she was little and pictures of all these people in the family who are dead now."

She's lying on her bed, holding a pillow, and I'm sitting on the floor.

"What was the plane like?" I ask.

She sits up. "I hardly noticed. I was talking to Till, like, the whole time."

"Oh yeah." I'd forgotten about how she made a new friend.

"Casey changed seats with her and slept through most of it."

There's a knock on her door. It's Mom. "You girls want to come out and help?"

"Sure." I pop right up, but Lu grabs her phone and stays on the bed.

Mom goes back to the living room, where she's been chatting with Lu's mom. I don't know where Casey is.

In the kitchen, Steve is checking the temperature on the turkey with a meat thermometer. He glances over at me and smiles. "Just about perfect, I think." I go over and look. It has a few more degrees to climb before it's officially safe, but usually it will go up a little while it sits.

"You want to shape the rolls?" Steve asks. "I settled for frozen bread dough since I haven't even had a day to prepare, but I figured we could make some garlic butter and we'll never know the difference."

"Yummy."

I wash my hands and dive into the dough. I could do regular round rolls, or I could do cloverleafs, where you put three little pieces together into muffin tins, or I could make triangles and roll them up like crescents. Regular round ones will be quickest, so I do that.

Steve presses some cloves of garlic into a bowl and mashes in butter he's been softening on the counter.

He's tall with gray curly hair. He and Mom are around the same age, but he's always seemed older to me. Older and wiser and like a real grown-up, whereas with Mom I'm not always sure she knows what she's doing.

"How was your Thanksgiving?" Steve asks.

"It was okay."

"What did you guys cook?" That's what he always wants to know. It's okay, because it's what I always want to talk about.

"I made ham and glazed acorn squash and cheesy potatoes. And pumpkin pie."

"And what did your mom make?"

I set a roll on the baking sheet. "Dirty dishes?"

He laughs. "She's been pretty busy, I bet."

"Mm-hmm."

"Well, I missed being home. I would always rather be here than anywhere else."

"Me too."

We fill up the sheet with rolls—me shaping them and him smearing the garlic butter on. Before we put them in the oven, he sprinkles just a little bit of salt over the tops.

After dinner, me and Lu and Casey pile into Steve's truck to go to group, with Casey driving. Mom's going to go to her own meeting, and then I'll see her back at home.

"I'm *stuffed*," Casey says.

Lu agrees and says she hopes she can stay awake through group.

I'm just happy. Stuffed and happy. It's been a whole week since I was with anyone but Mom. "I missed you a lot," I say to Lu, still hoping she'll say it back.

Casey scoffs. "Weren't you guys texting, like, nonstop?"

"Hardly at all," I say.

"Who were you texting the whole week?" Casey asks Lu.

"Oh," Lu says. "It was Till."

"That girl from the plane?" Casey says.

"Yeah. I told you." Lu says it in a quiet but intense way to Casey. The way you talk to someone who you're trying to remind to keep a secret.

We don't talk again until we turn onto Highway 1 and Casey asks what I did during the break because most of our dinner conversation was about their trip.

"Literally nothing," I reply.

"You did *some*thing," Lu says.

"I mean, I helped my mom some with work. I cooked Thanksgiving dinner and we watched movies. I organized the towel closet."

"That sounds nice," Casey says. "Better than being among a dozen awkward relatives you barely know and trying to sleep in a room filled with creepy dolls and bird figurines."

Lu's pocket buzzes; she pulls out her phone and answers a text.

"Is that Till?" I ask.

"Yeah." She doesn't look up.

11

We start group with a moment of silence.

Gene brought a little space heater that makes a lot of noise, so it's not *that* silent right now, but the point is we try to get still and remember that we're *here* now—in the church basement, in the safety and routine of our meeting—not out *there*, where anything can happen.

My mind is still out there, though.

Lu was talking to Till through her whole trip, and even in the car on the way to group? After not seeing me for a whole week? Why didn't she text *me* while she was away? I'm the one who was stuck at home doing nothing while everyone else was going on trips.

Someone hands me the binder, and I realize it's my turn to read aloud from some of our materials. Today it's the description of what an alcoholic is.

I know all this stuff. I can almost do it from memory. It's about how all kinds of people are alcoholics and it doesn't always look like it does in movies, where they're stumbling around and obvious. It's about how most alcoholics could even seem fine, but their drinking is affecting other people or their work or themselves. I speed through it and pass the binder to Owen on my right.

Instead of reading, he says he wants to share. No one objects.

"My Thanksgiving sucked," he says. "Everyone in my family got drunk. Like, every adult except my uncle. Even one of my cousins, who's my age, and nobody said anything about that. From the minute we got to my grandma's house, it started, and when my mom had her second drink at ten a.m. I was like, yo, Mom, what are you doing, and she goes, '*I'm* not the alcoholic, Dad is, and this is a holiday, so chill out.' I hate her."

Those words snap me out of my fixation on Lu and Till. I don't know how anyone can say aloud they hate their mom, especially when she's not even the one he's here for. It's his dad he always talks about, his dad who drinks every day and loses his temper, his dad who is the problem.

"Um, that's it," Owen says. "I'm done." He folds his arms and stares at the box of tissues in the center of the circle, and then at the space heater a couple of feet from that.

Casey says, "Thanks for sharing; you were heard."

Then Lu has a comment about the reading I did, how

alcoholics hardly ever look like the "drunks" you see on TV and stuff.

"My dad does look like that," she says. "Or he did. Everyone could tell by looking. If you saw him on the street, you'd cross over. He fell down the bus stairs once when it was just me and him and we were getting off and he hit his head and it was gushing blood, but he said, 'I'm fine,' and kept walking me home. He took off his jacket and held it to his head. Everyone we passed stared. I don't know why someone didn't stop and ask if he was okay, or if I was okay. It was weird. I don't know if it's worse to have an alcoholic parent who acts like a drunk or one who hides it so well that you don't even know."

I think about the clips from my memory, of Mom apologizing all the time. How she'd crawl into bed with me at night and apologize until she fell asleep, and how she smelled like that wine in the bottom of the glass at the Rockaway rental. I guess she was kind of an obvious alcoholic, too, but also she kept going to work and making me lunches and paying bills. So maybe not.

While Lu finishes sharing, I plan in my head what I'll say. I'll talk about calling Grandma yesterday and how I wish Mom and Grandma could get along, and how the week was really lonely, and maybe even Mom lying about her journal and pushing me off her.

Then I think: *I bet Till doesn't have all these complicated problems and is a lot more fun to text and talk to.*

Maybe Lu needed a break from me. Maybe I'm too much.

"I had a good Thanksgiving," I say. "I cooked and got to help my mom. We called my grandma and went for a walk. I'm grateful for my mom's job and our house, and that there was no school for a week. That's all."

I feel Owen looking at me like he knows I'm lying. Or at least not telling the whole truth. He says, "Thanks for sharing," but it sounds kind of sarcastic. I feel that knot in my stomach again.

Casey does a long share about what it was like to be with so much family that she doesn't feel close to, and being angry at her mom, and angry at her dad, and angry at Steve, and just generally angry. Between her finding a million ways to be angry and Owen hating his mom, the mood is a lot more negative than usual.

Gene does some closing readings and reminds us that everything we say here stays confidential. We don't talk about who we see and what we hear. "Take what you liked and leave the rest," Gene says.

By the time we come up out of the church basement, Lu is already looking at her phone again.

12

On the first day back to school after break, Mom drives me. Starting tomorrow, though, I'm going to have to walk or take the bus for at least the next two weeks because her schedule is so packed.

I can tell she's stressed from the way she drives. Too fast and doing rolling stops instead of complete ones and forgetting to signal.

"Don't get a ticket, Mom."

She makes a scoffing sound and waves the idea away. "I went to high school with half the cops around here. I know all their secrets." In the drop-off circle, she almost rear-ends the car in front of us. Kids turn to see where the screeching tire noise came from and Mom says, "Oops."

"Do you have your snacks and water?" I ask.

"Got 'em." The phone charger is plugged into the dashboard now, charging her phone, so I don't have to ask her that. I open the door to get out, and she says, "Bye, babe. I'll probably be late tonight."

"Are you going to a meeting?"

She freezes for a tiny second, then reaches for a piece of gum from the pack she keeps in one of the cupholders. "No, I have a client. It's just nonstop work right now. You have your bus pass?"

"Yeah."

"Love you."

"Me too."

I close the door and scan in front of the school for Lu, worried in this moment that she's not going to be there in our usual meetup place. She is, though, and waves and smiles, and I feel a hundred times better than I did all day yesterday. I don't even pay attention to the sound that I know is Mom peeling out onto the street too fast while other cars honk at her.

I bounce a little on the balls of my feet as I hurry toward the rock where Lu waits. As I get closer, I realize the person standing near her is Till. Are they going to start meeting every day at *our* rock?

"Hi," Till says to me, right after Lu does.

"Hi." I wave. "I'm Kyra."

She's short like Lu, but curvy. Her hair is dark brown and wavy. Mostly what I notice are her eyes.

"Was that your mom?" she asks. "With the Meg the Maid sign on the car?"

I look over my shoulder as if the car is still there. "Yeah."

"I think she cleans our house."

It's not the first time someone at school has said that to me when they notice the car. I don't mind, as long as people don't say it in a way that makes me think I'm supposed to be embarrassed. I don't *think* Till means it that way, but I don't know her.

"She cleans a lot of people's houses," I say. "That's what she does. It's her company."

"I know. My mom likes her."

Lu smiles at me as if I'm supposed to love Till simply for saying that.

A couple of other girls walk over. I'm guessing they know Till, because they're eighth graders, too. The one with streaky hair who's almost as tall as me is named Jaymison, which I know because *everyone* knows who Jaymison is, and the other one I've seen but don't know her name. She runs track and I think does other sports, too.

"Hey," Jaymison says to Till and Lu. Her eyes scroll over me like I'm a picture she just swiped past on her phone without hearting, then turns back to Till and Lu. "Did I leave my sweater in your mom's car?"

I assume she's talking to Till, but it's Lu who answers. "I don't think so."

She won't meet my eyes no matter how hard I stare at her, then the morning sun comes out from behind a cloud over her shoulder and glares right at me. Burns. That knot in my stomach that's been there off and on since calling Grandma is now a double knot.

"I have to get something out my locker before homeroom," I blurt before dashing inside. It's darker and cooler and I can think.

What was Jaymison doing in Lu's mom's car? When? Why?

In homeroom, Mrs. Novotny has everyone go around and say what they did over break. It's one of those time-fillers I think she does when she's not ready for school to start and needs to drink her second cup of coffee while we do the talking. Maybe when it's Lu's turn I'll get the answer about whatever she didn't invite me to.

No one else went as far away as Lu and Till, but lots of people went other places. It seems like half the class went to Lake Tahoe to ski and snowboard. Mom calls Tahoe a rich-people place. I've never been. Never even seen the snow. Lu tells about visiting family in Ohio, and someone says, "Ohio," like it's a stupid place to go.

I glare at them. Not everyone can go to Tahoe!

When I'm the only one left who hasn't talked, I say, "It's the busy season for my mom's business, so I helped her with that."

Mrs. Novotny, who I do like even though she's only half-awake, looks interested. Before she can ask what my mom's business is, I add, "I also cooked Thanksgiving dinner. The whole thing."

"So did I," Mrs. Novotny says, setting her mug down. "You sound more excited about it than I was." She looks at her computer. "Okay, let me get through attendance and these announcements. . . ."

* * *

After homeroom, Lu waits for me in the hall, outside the door.

"You went somewhere with Jaymison and them?" I ask.

She bites her upper lip with her lower teeth, then says, "Yesterday we went to a movie. I think they only invited me because no one else's parents would drive."

"Oh." I was so bored yesterday, so lonely all week. Going to a movie would have helped. But I know I can't say all that without sounding sorry for myself, and I don't want to sound that way. Even if it's what I feel.

"It was really fun when you came over for dinner on Saturday," she says. "I missed you."

I've been waiting to hear that, but now it doesn't mean anything; it feels like she only wants to change the subject. "So if you hadn't seen me Saturday, you would have invited me to the movie yesterday?"

"Yeah. I mean, probably, you know?"

I don't know! That's why I'm asking!

"Move it, Whitney," a voice says behind me.

It's Gabe, who's shorter than me and muscular. Juan, who's even shorter and small, is laughing next to him, as always. They've been calling me Whitney for a couple of weeks, and I don't know why.

I step aside and say, "It's Kyra."

"Okay, Whitney," Juan replies. They're like a relay team, passing the bully baton between them.

After they walk away, Lu scrunches up her nose. "Whitney?"

"They're just weird."

"Yeah," she agrees. Before we separate—me to math and her to chorus—she says, "See you at lunch?"

That at least gives me something to look forward to. "See you!"

At lunch we eat at our usual table on the side. I've got Thanksgiving leftovers—a ham sandwich and some cheesy potatoes, and the last little sliver of pumpkin pie. Lu has two of the rolls from Saturday night, stuffed with turkey and cranberry sauce. And some of the green bean casserole I made.

After we use the cafeteria microwave to heat up the things that need heating up, Lu keeps sneaking glances at the table closer to the middle, where Jaymison and Till and a couple of other girls are.

"So, your Thanksgiving was kind of hard, too?" I say, trying to get her attention.

"It wasn't that bad."

"Casey made it sound bad at group."

"You know how Casey is. She's always looking for reasons not to get along with people."

Laughter comes from the other table; Lu turns to watch. Jaymison is half-standing, dangling something in front of Till, who's acting grossed out. The lunch monitor strolls over to tell them to settle down.

"What's that one girl's name?" I ask, since obviously that's where her focus is. "The one on the track team?"

Lu looks around and tightens her hand around her can of bubbly water. "You don't have to be so *loud*."

I shrink back. I didn't know I was being loud. "Sorry."

"Her name is Abbie."

"Did she go to the movie, too?"

Lu lets the hand holding one of her rolls drop and tilts her head at me.

"I'm just asking!" I say. I really am. I want to know so I'm not surprised by anything later. It comes out loud again, so I repeat it, quieter. "I'm just asking."

"No." She leans forward, speaking in almost a whisper. "It was me and Jaymison and Till. We went to the movie while my mom shopped at Target and did other errands, then she picked us up."

I put a spoonful of cheesy potatoes in my mouth to keep from saying that I know they had a full car but I would've volunteered to sit on the hump between the two back seats, even though I'm the tallest.

Usually, when Mom says she's going to be late, she means getting home right around dinnertime or a little after. Seven or so at the latest. But at seven-fifteen she texts to say she's got an hour left to go.

The towels are taking forever to dry and it's holding me up.

Go ahead and eat without me! xo

I sigh. There's nothing to say to that, so I leave her a thumbs-up and get up off the couch, where I've been doing homework with the TV on. Well, watching TV with my homework nearby.

All I was going to do for dinner was heat up the last of the potatoes and chop up ham to go in them, and make a salad.

I'm sick of potatoes and ham. Salad is depressing.

We always keep some packs of ramen in the cupboard, so I'll have that. I push the dried noodles around in the boiling water with a chopstick and watch them get soft. When the starch from the noodles makes piles of foam, I blow gently on the surface so it doesn't boil over. I add in the seasoning packet and take it off the heat. Normally, I would add some chili oil and rice vinegar and maybe some green onions or something, but I don't even care.

I don't know why it should hurt so much to not go to one dumb movie. Not everyone can be invited to every single thing. While my soup cools a little, I tidy up the kitchen. Mom's recovery journal appears under some mail I clear away. For a second, I consider reading it, and my heart speeds up. It would be so wrong.

But I also feel like there's something I need to know, even if I have no idea what it is.

That's why I need to know, though!

It's none of my business.

Unless it's something I could help with?

Instead of *reading* it, I could just flip through to see if she's been making entries. I let the pages flutter past while I look with only one eye. There's her neat writing at the beginning, then it gets more scribbly, then there are whole pages where she's scratched out what she wrote, then some doodles, the ones from Thanksgiving.

I could read maybe one entry . . .

Then I picture how I'd feel if she were reading my journal, and I press the journal closed, hard, as if it's a lid that needs snapping shut. I pile the mail back on top of it.

I carry my steaming bowl of noodles and a kitchen towel to catch drips to the living room, and settle on the floor so I can use the coffee table as my dining table. There's a kids' baking competition on. I put my whole attention into it, until the thoughts about what might be under the scratched-out parts of Mom's journal are also scratched out.

PART II: DECEMBER

Feelings Aren't Facts

13

For the two weeks after Thanksgiving, Mom stays super busy. We get back into a regular routine where I make her breakfast and we talk in the mornings, but she's late a lot for dinner from picking up extra houses, or she texts me that she's going to grab fast food and not to make her anything, not to wait up.

I often fix her a plate anyway. Sometimes she eats it; sometimes it's still there in the fridge in the morning, and so I pack it for my lunch.

In the evenings, I spread my homework out on the coffee table and turn on the TV. I know it's not a good way to focus, but it's so quiet if I turn the TV off, and it's getting dark earlier and earlier, which only makes the quiet seem bigger. Sometimes my homework doesn't get all the way done.

Also for the two weeks after Thanksgiving, I watch Lu

and Till. Till isn't at the rock every single morning, but she's there most of them. And whenever I find Lu in the hallway, Till's there, too. She's always nice to me, but she's pretty quiet. Like Lu.

They dress similar, too, in a lot of colors and stripes and patterns. Things I avoid because I don't like to be noticed at school.

Lu keeps sitting with me at our usual table at lunch, and that's when we talk the most because she hasn't invited me over since Thanksgiving and when I invite her to my house, she says she can't because my mom isn't home and her mom, who mostly works at home, doesn't want her to come over if there isn't an adult there.

I keep almost saying, *I could come to your house*, or I think about texting Steve to try to get him to invite me to dinner, but I can't bring myself to do it. I think I'm scared that Lu wouldn't want me to.

Then there's this one day when I know—or I *think* that I know—that she wants to eat lunch with Till and Jaymison. It's been building up during our lunches, when she keeps looking over there and Till sometimes comes by to sit for a minute before going to her own table. So on that day, I tell her I have to do homework in the library during lunch.

The next day, we eat together again, but I'm not sure she wants to.

One morning, I ask Mom if she has a client named Melloy and she says no, and I say how about anyone with a daughter named Till, because I felt like finding something out about her life that Lu might not know, like maybe it would help me feel better. But Mom says, "I don't know, I mean kids' names don't come up so much in my line of work. It's possible? I think there are a few families from your school on my roster. It's a small town, you know."

Yeah, I know.

It's just a bad feeling, watching your best friend become best friends with someone else, and being too scared of pushing them away even more to say anything about it. Lu starts being extra nice to me at lunch, trying so hard to act like we're the same as always that it's extra obvious we aren't.

It feels like a secret we both know but won't say.

14

According to the calendar, it's Mom's turn to drive us to group.

She texts me at the last minute to say she isn't going to be finished with her Saturday jobs in time—even though this morning she said she didn't need my help—so Casey drives us in Steve's truck. We sit three across, with Lu in the middle. I feel like a giant next to her and squeeze toward the door to buckle my seat belt. It's hard to see the buckle past my chest. Lu doesn't have that problem.

"Hey, Keek," Casey says. "Where have you been? I never see you at the house anymore."

The same place I always am. "Just busy."

Lu pulls her elbows in.

In group, Owen talks about how his dad is teaching him to drive.

"He yells and swears at me like I'm supposed to know what I'm doing," he's saying, "even though the whole point is that I'm *learning*. Yesterday, he grabbed the wheel and called me an idiot. It was like I could feel *his* anger in my own body and literally I wanted to open the car door and jump into the street."

I can picture that. My mom would never call me names like Owen's dad. But when she's as busy as she is now, always running late and forgetting something and getting mad at work and mad at the fact she can't afford to turn work down, I can sometimes feel her chaos in my own body, the way Owen feels his dad's anger in his.

When Owen started coming to group, I was suspicious of him because he sort of looks like a high school version of Juan and Gabe, with his carefully ripped jeans and hoodies that look too smooth and clean, like they were ironed. But ever since that group where I could tell he knew that I wasn't being totally honest about Thanksgiving, I almost feel like I can trust him.

"Whenever we get home from driving practice, he says, 'I need a drink,' like teaching me to drive is *making* him drink even though he'd be drinking anyway. And it sucks because I just want to get my license and never have to deal with him again. But then I feel guilty for feeling that, because . . ."

Owen's going to cry. It happens to everyone in group eventually if not often.

Gene says that our no-crosstalk rule—no interrupting, no commenting on someone else's share, no giving

86

advice—includes not even handing someone a tissue from the box in the middle of the circle. We're supposed to give each other the privilege of handling our own feelings and getting our own tissues.

Owen puts his hand on his chin to hide how it's wobbling. Too late—we all know.

". . . because I've got my two little brothers and my mom and they'd still be stuck with him." He fake-coughs and clears his throat like four times. "That's all, I guess."

I know I'm not supposed to make his share about me, but I can't help thinking about how I'm the only one here with no brothers or sisters. The *only* only child. And Lu and Casey and Owen don't know what it's like to be the *only* one living with your *only* parent, not even another adult around.

"Thank you, Owen; you were heard," Gene says.

Owen sucks up his drippy nose. The sound makes me want to gag and before I can stop myself, I stretch out my leg and kick the tissue box a few inches toward Owen. Gene looks at me with one bushy eyebrow raised.

"Sorry."

Lu, on the other side of the circle, watches me with *both* eyebrows raised, probably wondering why I'm not saying anything for once in my life.

In fact, they all seem to be waiting. Everyone has shared but me, and now there's nothing left to do but pass the basket and read the closing.

I don't want to talk. I don't want to talk about what's going on with Lu or my mom, and I don't want to talk about how lonely I am at school *and* at home. I don't want to talk about how I feel like I don't even know how to be the right kind of person right now because I'm bigger, taller, and I guess louder than the other girls at school. I don't want to talk about wishing I had a dad.

"Does anyone else have a burning desire to share?" Gene asks.

I fold my arms in my lap. That's a no.

15

On the ride home, Lu asks, "Are you okay?"

No! Can't my best friend see that I'm not okay? But if she can't, I'm not going to say it.

"Mm-hmm."

"You always share in group, though."

"No, I don't. I didn't share tonight, so I don't 'always' share."

She sighs. "You know what I mean!"

"Guys," Casey says. "What happens in the room stays in the room. Right?" She turns on the radio, a little too loud.

I lean forward to ask Casey, "Are you friends with Owen at school?"

"Sort of. I mean, we have different social circles. But we're not *not* friends."

"Is he nice?" I ask loud enough so Casey can hear me over the radio.

Lu says, "You don't have to yell." I do have to, though.

"What do you mean?" Casey asks.

"Does he pick on people? He reminds me of these guys at school who do. But I don't think he's like that. Is he?" I lean forward farther to try to read Casey's face to make sure she's honest. Lu squishes herself against the back of the seat, making some kind of point about me crowding her. I ignore it. "If I were in high school right now with Owen, do you think he'd be nice to me?"

"I don't know, Keek," Casey says with a laugh. "How could I possibly know that?"

"Can you . . ." Lu gently pushes me so I'm not leaning over her lap anymore.

I press my cheek to the passenger door window. The cool glass makes me feel a little better, even though the radio is still too loud.

Usually, after meetings, I feel light, like I've put down a heavy bag and know I don't have to pick it back up again. Tonight I only feel heavier.

We get to my house and Mom's car is out front. Relieved, I have my seat belt off and the door open before Lu can even finish saying, "See you on Monday."

I don't thank Casey for the ride or look back at Lu. I just want to see Mom.

"Kyra!" It's Casey's voice calling out.

I turn. Casey sits hunched over the steering wheel, staring in a way that leaves me feeling big and exposed and clumsy, even though Casey's eyes are full of sympathy.

"Whatever it is," she says, "it will be okay. Together we can make it, right?"

"Together We Can Make It" is a slogan from group. We have the magnet.

"I know," I call to Casey before turning to go inside.

Mom forgot to leave the porch light on for me, and when I use my key to get inside, the living room is dark, too. The house is quiet, still clean from when I attacked it yesterday afternoon with the vacuum and mop, dustrag, and scrubber. Something I could tame and control.

I turn on the kitchen light. Still clean in here, too.

"Mom?" I call.

No answer.

I made dinner before I left for group and can tell she hasn't eaten any of it. I microwave the container of rice and beans, arrange it in a bowl with a scoop of chopped salad, put salsa on top, and stand a wall of tortilla chips around part of the bowl. It's pretty enough for a picture.

I carry it all to my mom's bedroom door and knock as gently as I possibly can.

"Mom? I'm back from my meeting. Do you want some dinner?"

Group is only an hour. She must have come home *right* after she said she couldn't give us a ride if she's already asleep in there. Which means she must be exhausted and needs the rest.

Still, I want her to come out and eat at the table and tell me about her day. I want to see her.

"Can I come in? And say good night?"

She could at least look at this perfect bowl of food. My heartbeat seems to move all over my body, throbbing in my throat and then my fingers and then my knees. I try to ignore it because my body doesn't always know the difference between a real problem and just me worrying.

Then the door opens. She's got on her Meg the Maid shirt and a cardigan and leggings. Her eyes do look exhausted, small and baggy at the edges. "Hi, baby," she says.

"Hi." I hold out the dish. "Do you want to eat?"

Her eyes flick down to the bowl and back to me. "I'm sorry, Keek." It sounds so faraway. "I just gotta sleep."

"Okay. You should."

"It looks great, though. Would you pack it for me to take for lunch tomorrow?"

"Yeah." If I weren't holding a bowl of rice and beans, I'd hug her. I want her to know I care and I miss her, but words aren't always that helpful. "Do you need anything else?"

She shakes her head. "Only about thirty hours of sleep." She bends forward and kisses my forehead. "Good night, hon."

"Night."

I pack up the food for her to take in the morning and try not to think about how much I miss her. She hasn't asked to share journals since Thanksgiving, and I haven't tried to peek at hers again. We haven't played Kiki Krash and Meg the Marauder. We haven't sat by the ocean.

I set up the coffeepot for the morning so all she has to do

is turn it on. I fill a water bottle and set it on the counter. I make her a little box of cheese cubes and nuts and grapes for her snack.

Everything is tidy and clean and ready for the new day.

Before I turn off the light, I look at the fridge to check the bills. The one on top is our biggest one—health insurance. I know Mom is working hard to get that paid. Holding it down is the *This Too Shall Pass* magnet. That's something I can have faith in. The busy season will eventually be over and Mom will have time again. Till will eventually go to high school, and it will be back to just me and Lu for eighth grade.

I wish the saying were "This Too Shall Pass *Quickly*."

The smell of coffee wakes me up.

I throw back the covers and check the time. It's seven-thirty. Mom doesn't have to leave for her Sunday clients until eight-fifteen. I relax.

"Hi, gorgeous," Mom says when I walk into the kitchen. She's all clean and showered and in a fresh Meg the Maid tee.

"Hi." I go to her for the hug I wanted last night. "You smell good."

"I feel good. I think I slept twelve hours. Game changer."

She moves away from me, but I hold on to her waist while she tries to move around the kitchen. It makes her laugh. I laugh, too, except there's a part of me that wants to really never let go.

"Oh, I have a cling-on," she teases, dragging me to the fridge with her.

"I'll make breakfast," I mumble into her back.

"Let me. Do we still have pancake mix?"

I let go and hop to the cupboard to check. "Yep!"

She gets out syrup and butter. I start slicing bananas while she mixes up the batter. Everything feels good, like we didn't have a hard Thanksgiving, like the last two weeks were also fine.

"I have the Moss Beach house again this morning." She puts a pan on the stove to warm up. It's the wrong one. I get the griddle pan that has a better nonstick surface and hand it to her. "Oh. Okay." She starts to heat that one up. "Do you want to help me do the house? I know you like the view over there. I can drop you off on my way back north for my afternoon."

"Yes!" I was going to catch up on homework today, but I'd rather be with her.

"You can say no."

"I want to."

It's a windy, stormy day, and I spend more time watching clouds gather and tumble way out over the ocean than dusting.

"It's dramatic, huh?" Mom remarks when she catches me frozen at the picture window again. "I love how the ocean looks a little different every day."

"Me too."

It's so green right now, the muted but glossy green of sea glass, with foam piling up where the tide meets the beach. On a day like this, I see the "power" in "higher power," and I wish

Grandma could understand why me and Mom feel about the ocean the way we do.

"This whole neighborhood will probably slide off the cliff in about ten years," Mom says.

"Don't say that!" I turn to her in protest.

She winks. "Just wanted to get your attention." She hands me the long handle for the duster so I can do the ceiling fans, then she'll do the big piano I'm supposed to not touch.

While she's doing the piano and I'm stretching to reach the ceiling fans, I say, "Did you have a lot of friends when you were my age?"

"I think so. I mean, a normal amount."

"What's a normal amount?"

She looks up at me. "I shouldn't have said 'normal.' Everyone's normal is different."

"But how many did *you* have?"

"I was one of those people who was friendly with everyone. So I had a lot of friends at school. Older friends, too, that I probably shouldn't have had. But it was all more . . . surface-level." She swipes the polishing rag with a flourish over the glowing wood of the piano. "I didn't bring anyone *home*, because my mom was so judgy. And then around eighth grade was when I started sneaking out to parties. That was where I found my friend group."

"The party posse," I say.

She laughs. "Yep, that was my first party posse."

Since she doesn't ask why I asked, I say, "I wish I had more friends."

"You will." She puts the cap back on the special polishing liquid for the piano. "Some people take longer to grow into a social life. I think you'll be one of those."

I don't want to take longer. I want to be like Lu and do it fast.

When we're done and loading our car back up, the owner comes home. Mom's little Meg the Maid car looks small and old compared to the Volvo SUV that pulls in next to us.

"Meg!" the woman calls through the window, smiling. Her dark hair is slicked back into a ponytail that explodes into a wavy mass in the back, and she's wearing big sunglasses even though the sun is barely out. "Is this your daughter?"

Mom introduces us—her name is Lucy. "Hi," I say.

She opens her door and slides out of the car. She's taller than even me, and wearing yoga pants and sandals. "Thanks for keeping my house perfect," she says to both of us. "I don't know why, but it makes such a difference to my mental health."

"I'm the same," I blurt. "If the house is messy, I feel messy inside."

Lucy looks at Mom and points to me. "She gets it. Thanks again. Sorry I'm back early. I didn't mean to interrupt."

"Perfect timing, actually," Mom says.

The wind whips Lucy's ponytail while she watches us get into our car, then she runs around and taps on Mom's window.

"What now . . ." Mom mutters before rolling her window down.

"Hey," Lucy says, leaning in, "I was just thinking. We're not going to use the Tahoe place this Christmas. I've got some holiday concerts in New York, so we're just going to hang there. Why don't you two go up while we're gone?"

"Oh," Mom says, "I don't think . . ." She looks at me.

"Please," Lucy says. "I know you'll leave it spotless! That's more than I can say for most people I loan it to."

She wants to *loan* us a whole entire house? At Lake Tahoe? For Christmas?

Lucy looks past her and at me. "Have you ever been?"

I shake my head. "I've never even seen snow!" I can feel myself smiling like I'm a little kid, but I don't care.

"Meg, come on. The child has never seen snow. At least think about it."

Mom gives a firm nod. "I will think about it. Thank you."

"Great." Lucy straightens up. "Let me know and I can text you the directions and door code information."

I wait until we're out of the driveway, I wait until Mom has made the tricky left turn onto Highway 1, I wait for her to say something first. When I can't hold it in anymore, I burst. "We have to go!"

"We'll see," Mom says, laughing. "I wouldn't be able to get our car up the mountain if there's any snow on the ground. I don't want to deal with chains and all that. I wouldn't know where to begin."

We wind down the highway and go through the tunnel. Our stupid old car can't be the thing that stops us from getting to spend Christmas in Tahoe like the kids at school. We might never get this chance again.

When we come out the other side of the tunnel, I get a sudden idea and suck in an excited breath before blurting, "We could rent a better car!"

"Babe, honey. Can you bring down the energy a little?"

I sigh.

"Renting is expensive," she says.

I know we never have money for special things, but she's been working so hard this season, it feels like it might not be impossible. Or that we don't have to let it be impossible.

I want to see the snow.

"Let me think," Mom says. "Okay?"

17

After she drops me off, I think, too.

I think about snow, and wonder what it feels like in real life, how it feels to make a snowball and hold it in your hand.

I look up the current weather at Lake Tahoe. It's snowing there *right now*.

I make Mom's favorite broccoli-cheese soup so we can have it for dinner as soon as she's home. Sunday afternoons are often vacation rental cleanup clients, and she has one of those in Vallemar, and then that's it for today and she won't be late.

When the soup is done, I pace around and ignore my homework. I get out bowls and spoons and water glasses. I clean out the fridge and take a mushy cucumber out to the compost bin.

I write a text to Lu:

Guess what??? We might be going to Tahoe for Christmas.

Right when I'm about to send it, I think that if I send the text and then we *don't* go to Tahoe, I'll feel worse. But I want to be hopeful. I send it.

Within seconds, she writes back. Whaaaaaaaat that's amazing!

I grin at my phone.

MIGHT. Maybe. We'll see.

I'll think positive thoughts!! she writes.

While I wait for Mom, I try to think positive thoughts, too.

"This might be your best soup ever," Mom says, spooning up another mouthful.

"We had a tiny bit of smoked Gouda left, so I added that along with the cheddar."

"Brilliant."

I have another brilliant idea, but I want to suggest it at the exact right time. After all, it was only this morning that she started to seem like herself after a couple of weeks where she wasn't. Her mood has been good all day, but I don't trust it yet; it still feels fragile.

I finish my bowl of soup and get up to serve us both seconds. On the way, I drop my spoon, and she kind of jumps, and I kind of jump, and I rinse it off and clean the spot of soup off the floor.

When I sit back down, she asks, "What?"

"What what?"

"You want to say something," she says. "I can tell."

"Okay, so." I watch her face. "We should ask Steve if we can borrow his truck. For Tahoe."

She puts down her spoon. "That's a big ask, Keek. You'll understand when you have your own car someday."

"You know he'll say yes! He lets Casey drive it all the time!"

"Casey is his daughter."

"*Step*daughter." I lean forward. "You'd rather miss out on a *free* cabin at Lake Tahoe over Christmas than ask your friend—your *oldest* friend—if you can borrow his truck?"

"I don't know. I'll have to think about it."

She looks unhappy now, and I don't know why she would feel unhappy. Everything about this is good—all we have to do is ask Steve and he'll say yes, and then we can say yes to Lucy.

We eat our second bowls of soup, my mind on snow. How my soup would taste even better if we were eating it on Christmas Eve by a fireplace with snow falling outside. And how I'd be able to talk about the Tahoe cabin when I got back to school after the break. I could start sentences with, *When we were up at Tahoe . . .* , and come back with a ski hat with a pom-pom on the top that I'd wear to school on cold days.

She's had plenty of thinking time.

"Are you going to ask him?"

"Kyra!" She laughs a little and shakes her head at me. "He might need his truck for work."

"Not at Christmas."

"Well, that's not the issue."

"What's the issue?" I ask.

She sets her spoon down in her bowl. "My whole history with Steve is that *I* get desperate or into trouble, and *he* helps bail me out. Ever since the first time he drove me home from a party when I was a sophomore and he was a senior and he knew the cops were coming and that my mom would kill me for that, *that's* been the situation. Me desperate. Him saving me. I get tired of asking him for help."

"But he doesn't mind!"

"I said let me *think* about it, okay?" She stands and picks up our bowls, takes them to the sink to rinse. "What do we need to do to get ready for tomorrow?"

I know it won't be worth trying to talk about it any more tonight. We go through our checklist and make a plan for the morning that includes me making the lunches and her taking me to school.

In bed, I beg my higher power to let us go to Tahoe. It's the last thing I think about when I fall asleep, and the first thing I think about in the morning.

It's not until we're on the way to school that Mom says, "I'll ask Steve about the truck. But don't mention it to Lu, all right? Just let me handle it."

I bounce in my seat, grinning. I'm sure what I already told Lu is fine because I only said maybe. I try to hug her while she's driving.

"Careful," she says, laughing. "It's not a done deal."

I sit back and just smile.

18

I'm a little early for a change, and Lu isn't at the rock yet. Neither is Till.

While I'm waiting, Gabe and Juan walk by and Juan says, "Nice shirt."

Like a reflex and because I'm in a good mood, I say, "Thanks," but they're already laughing and going inside.

It *is* a nice shirt. It's a purple short-sleeve sweatshirt, and it's almost new. My mood is already starting to deflate.

Lu gets there a minute later. She has on a green-and-white striped T-shirt and overalls and a jean jacket. She's cute and perfect; no wonder all these eighth graders want to be her friend. "Till had a dentist appointment, so she's not coming until later; we don't have to wait."

We walk together to homeroom. If she doesn't ask about

Tahoe, I'm not going to say anything. I don't want to jinx it by wanting it too much.

"So . . ." Lu says. "I was thinking I'd eat with Till and them today and—"

"It's fine," I blurt.

"I wasn't finished! I wanted to see if you want to eat with us, too."

I stop and look at her. "Do they want me to? Or just you?"

She shrugs and smirks. "I didn't ask. They don't own the cafeteria."

Well, they kind of do. "Okay," I say. "I brought my lunch, so I'll look for you in there."

"We all brought ours, too."

They planned it ahead? Which days to bring lunch and which to eat school lunch?

Before we go into homeroom, I grab her arm. "Does my shirt look okay?"

"It looks good!" This time her smile is genuine. "I like it. That color is pretty with your hair." She takes my hand and pulls me into class and says, "Come on," and everything between us suddenly feels okay again.

When lunchtime comes, I can't find her anywhere. I walk warily around the perimeter of the cafeteria. The perimeter is always good—you can slip in and slip out if you need to without having to walk in front of a bunch of people.

Abbie is already sitting at the round table toward the middle of the room where those girls usually sit. I know two things about Abbie: one, she got her black hair cut short recently, and two, she's in track club. I've seen her running along the beach path near my house before, and up and down the street the school is on with the small pack of other kids who compete in team meets.

Would it be better to wait until Lu gets here, or to take the chance to talk to Abbie while she's alone—when I might be able to warm up to talking with the rest of them?

I walk over to the table.

Her head is down, over her phone.

"Hi," I say, and sit down across from her.

She looks unsurprised. Lu probably warned them in whatever group chat they're on. "Hi," she says, glancing up for just a moment. "Lu has PE right before lunch. It makes her late sometimes."

"I know." I grimace. It's a dumb thing to say. *I know.* But like, yeah, I *do* know Lu has PE before lunch. She was my friend first.

I open my insulated lunch bag but stop before taking out any food because Abbie has three stacking tin containers, secured by a locking hinge and lid, and it's so cool that I just have to stare. "That's a really cool lunch box."

"It's a tiffin box."

"Cool." I never heard of that.

"My dad lived in India for like a year. They use them there. He's obsessed."

"Is he Indian?"

"No, he's Korean."

"Cool."

Cool. Like it's the only word I know. It hangs there between us.

She goes back into her phone, and I pretend to look for something in my backpack and see the handle of my brush. I brought it so I'd remember to actually brush my hair before lunch, but I forgot. I can't do it *now*. I run my hands through my hair, instead. Strands catch in my fingers; I shake them off under the table and hope Abbie doesn't notice.

"You run track?" I ask.

"Yeah."

"Do you like it?"

Abbie glances up. "I wouldn't do all that running if I didn't like it."

"That makes sense." While she's listening, I say in a rush, "I really love your haircut, by the way."

She cringes and touches her neck. "It's so short! When the guy finished cutting it I was like . . . oh no, oh no, oh no. Then I decided it's good. Anyway, thanks."

I run my hand up my own neck. "It would feel nice. To have nothing touching. I used to always wear braids because I didn't like to feel hair on my neck, but then I cut my hair and—"

"There they are."

I turn to the cafeteria entrance and see Lu and Jaymison and Till coming in. They each have a pink bandanna tied around one ankle. I've never seen that before. Abbie puts her phone in her pocket and pulls the tiffin box in front of her, and I lean back to try to see her feet under the table to see if she has a bandanna, too. She must have her feet tucked under.

"Hi," I say, when they get to the table, trying not to make it sound too friendly or too unfriendly or too anything. It comes out weird and flat. They all say hi back and sit down.

Till's eyes seem even bigger and browner than usual right now. Round and wide open, and staring at me because I'm staring at her.

"Your eyes are so pretty," I blurt like I blurted about Abbie's hair. She blushes and looks down at her lunch bag, then points to her face and shakes her head.

"Her mouth is still numb from the dentist," Lu explains.

We all lay out our food.

The layers of Abbie's tiffin box have rice and chicken, broccoli and ranch, and red grapes and cookies.

"Faaaancy," Jaymison says, reaching into her bag. "I hope my mom packed me something good."

Lu has a chicken drumstick that probably Steve grilled, and some potato salad and celery with peanut butter. Till has a Lunchable and a banana but is probably only going to be able to eat the banana. Jaymison has a sandwich, an orange, a bag of cookies. Seeing everyone else's lunch gives me ideas for what I could make next week.

Jaymison glances at my food. "Is that *beans*?"

That makes them all look.

"Yeah. Beans and rice."

"I . . . don't eat beans."

"Why not?" Beans are cheap, convenient, filling, healthy, and tasty. I make beans all the time. I can sometimes get five cans of beans for less than three dollars if there's a special at Safeway.

"It's just, you know," she says with a grimace. "I don't want to make booty burps all day."

Till and Lu burst out laughing and Abbie says, "Gross," before I even figure out what she's talking about.

Oh.

Beans don't do that to me, because I've been eating them my whole life. "You build up a tolerance," I say.

"A tolerance for *what*?" Lu says, cracking herself up. This makes Jaymison laugh so hard she clutches her stomach. Till and Abbie laugh, too, but not as much. Lu can be funny. I like that about her, except usually it's not because she's laughing at *me*.

Then Jaymison starts complaining that her mom put too much mayo on her sandwich and she can't eat it like that because it's grossing her out. She zips open a pocket of her backpack and pulls out her cafeteria card. "I'm going to go get one of those hummus and pretzel packs from the snack bar."

"Hummus is beans," I say as she stands up.

Abbie looks at me. "It is?"

"No, it isn't," Jaymison says.

"It's made of chickpeas. AKA garbanzo *beans*." I look to Lu. She knows because Steve makes homemade hummus all the time.

Jaymison looks at Lu, too, who mutters, "It's . . . beans."

Till nibbles at a piece of banana she's broken off, watching the conversation with her big eyes. Till is the one Lu mostly

109

wants to be friends with, she says, so she's the one I want to try to know, but she can't even talk.

We all focus on our lunches while Jaymison goes to the snack bar. Abbie says, "She's shook," and that makes Till and Lu giggle, so I laugh, too.

When Jaymison comes back with a cheese stick and a pack of crackers, she starts talking about the winter break and how she's going to New York City with her parents. "We're going to see the Christmas tree at Rockefeller Center and everything. And see the ball drop on New Year's Eve."

I piece together what she's saying based on what I've seen on TV and in movies. Christmas in New York makes me think of Lucy, which makes me think of Tahoe, which makes me wonder if Mom has asked Steve yet about the truck.

"I'm going to Tahoe," I say without thinking. Why can't I stop blurting things I don't plan to say?

Lu's head whips around. "It's for sure?"

"I thiiiink so." Mom shouldn't mind me talking about it as long as I don't tell her the part about needing Steve's truck.

"Ugh, I'm jealous," Abbie says.

Jaymison takes little bites of her cheese and crackers and stares at me. "South Lake?"

"I don't know. I've never been there."

Her arms drop to the table. "You've *never* been?"

"Neither have I," Lu says.

"Me neither," adds Till.

Jaymison and Abbie start talking about their favorite places to eat in Tahoe and the best places to ski and the hardest snowboard pipes. While they go on, I say to Lu, quietly, "I'm not a hundred hundred percent sure yet we're really going, but one of Mom's clients has a house there she said we could use."

"Would that be boring?" Lu asks. "Just the two of you?"

Would it? "It's always just the two of us."

"Not *always*."

"Mostly." Especially when my best friend isn't inviting me over. "Anyway," I say, giving my voice a positive lift, "we'll see!"

Through our conversation, I don't realize that I'm jiggling my leg hard enough to shake the table until Jaymison says, "Can you stop?"

I stop.

Lunch period is almost over. I collect my garbage and compost and start to reach for the rest of the table's, too, until I remember that my mom cleans Till's house. I leave their trash, take mine. When I'm walking back to the table, I can finally see Abbie's foot. She's got a pink bandanna on, too.

Mom is extra late tonight.

She texted me to say not to wait up, that she had an evening client, but how can I not wait up? I'm okay being alone, to a point.

That point is now.

Every noise makes me think someone's trying to break into our house.

Every car could be hers.

Even a barking dog makes me suddenly start thinking about werewolves and nightmares where I'm getting chased by a monster and about this one book of scary stories I got from the library once, when I was about nine, and there was this one story where an evil doll comes to life, and it scared me so bad that I'd cry at night trying not to think about it. It took months of Mom reading me Penderwicks books before I finally got those scary stories out of my head, but I guess we didn't really get them *out*, because they're right there waiting for me. Like fruit flies.

I look at Mom's dot on my phone and see she's in South San Francisco and not moving toward home to me yet.

I sit on the couch and close my eyes. I picture the ocean. How it's so big. How it's so powerful. How it's always there, even when I can't see it.

Then a motorcycle roars by and my eyes fly open.

My brain checks around for something else to think about, and lands on the pink bandannas. Like, what were they doing when they decided it would be cool to all have bandannas on their ankles? Where were they? Did they talk about who could be in their Pink Bandanna Club? Did Lu suggest me, and if she did, what did Till say, what did Jaymison say? Is there more to the club than wearing the bandannas, and if so, what?

After that, I turn on the TV for a while without really watching, and write texts to Lu I don't send:

What does the pink bandanna mean?

Jaymison is like the girl version of Gabe and Juan!

When they all go to high school next year I'll still be here.

I check Mom's dot again. Finally, it is moving. I follow it on Skyline Boulevard, then winding down Sharp Park Road, then getting onto Highway 1.

I follow it all the way home.

"Oh, Keek," she says as she closes the front door quietly behind her. "You shouldn't have waited up. You're going to be so tired tomorrow."

I hold my arms out from where I am on the couch.

She hesitates, like she doesn't want to come close. I think about when she pushed me off her. I wonder if I'll ever not think about that.

But then she does come over to sit by me, put her arms around me.

I pull back. "You smell like smoke."

She scoots away. "Ugh, I know. One of my new clients is a heavy smoker. *Heav-y*. The apartment is saturated with that smell. I'm going to have to tell him I can't come back. I don't think people who smoke that much even smell it anymore." She smiles. "But hey, guess what?"

"What?"

She wiggles her eyebrows at me.

I sit up on my knees and clasp my hands together in front of my chest. "You asked Steve and he said yes?"

Her head bobs in an exaggerated nod. "And I called Lucy to tell her yes and thank you, and she already sent me all the instructions and directions."

I spring up off the couch and gallop around the room

113

shouting, "Yay! Yay! Yay!"

"It means no presents. The gas and holiday groceries and everything will be our whole Christmas budget."

I don't care about presents. I collapse back onto the couch and into her lap—forget about the smoke, forget about everything but Tahoe. "Yay," I say again.

Mom laughs. "Let me guess. You're happy about this?"

I wrap my arms around her waist and bury my head in her stomach before I look up to ask, "Are you?"

She nods and smooths my hair back. "Very."

19

Mom blocks out her calendar. Nothing can bother me, even a week of eating lunch with the eighth graders and their pink ankle bandannas with Jaymison talking over us and wrinkling her nose at anything but the plainest lunches.

At least me going to Lake Tahoe is already helping with her. She keeps telling me where Mom and I should eat out while we're there, as if I won't be cooking all our meals.

"Don't tell them about how we have to borrow Steve's truck," I tell Lu. It shouldn't be anything to be embarrassed about, but it seems like Jaymison could make me feel embarrassed about anything.

"I won't. I'm glad you get to go," Lu replies, and I can tell she means it.

I make a Tahoe grocery list so I'll have the ingredients for broccoli-cheese soup and good breakfasts like bagel sandwiches with bacon, and also the stuff for my best oatmeal dark-chocolate sea-salt cookies.

Then, finally, the day is here.

Steve drops off his truck and takes our car to drive while we we're gone.

We go shopping early that morning. Mom makes me put back the expensive cheese I want for a special holiday mac and cheese, but lets me get the peppered bacon and E-Z Logs for the fireplace just in case we need them.

"How long does it take to get there?" I ask after we're in the truck with all our stuff.

"You've asked me that about five hundred times," Mom says with a laugh.

"I know but I want to be sure."

"Check the map on your phone to see what the current ETA is."

Mom turns onto Highway 1 and takes it slow while she gets used to the size of the truck. Not too slow, I hope, because the map says it will take almost four hours to get there with current traffic, which is already too long.

Once we get off 1 and onto the big freeway, there are tons of cars headed to all the different San Francisco neighborhoods and toward the Bay Bridge, like us, and maybe even to Tahoe.

"Where should we stop for a snack and a bathroom?" I ask, looking at the map.

Mom is hunched over the big steering wheel and gripping it tight. "Babe, I can't talk until we get past the bridge and Vallejo, okay? That's usually where traffic thins out, I think."

"Okay." But when we get onto the bridge, I have to ask, "Have I ever been on the Bay Bridge before?"

"I don't think so, actually." She relaxes enough to steal a glance at me. "Congratulations. What do you think?"

"It's kind of . . . dirty." It feels exactly like the freeway except there's like a ceiling above us and I know we're over water.

"It's a lot prettier on the way back. You'll see."

I watch the cities go by. Oakland and Berkeley, Richmond, Pinole. It's all new to me. You can live in San Francisco and the Peninsula your whole life and never go to the East Bay if you don't know someone there or need to get to other side of the state, like we're doing now.

Mom was right. Once we get past Vallejo, it's not so stressful. She turns on the radio; it's on country music, which Steve likes, and we leave it there. I start to feel all the worry of the last few weeks leave my body and get replaced with the excitement I felt when Mom first confirmed we were going on this trip. I think it's what we need. And then afterward, when we're back in regular life and it's not the holidays and there's more routine and her work schedule isn't so busy, we'll feel more like we did back in the fall. She won't say she doesn't have time for meetings, and I'll go to group and school, and we'll eat dinner together every night.

Maybe Mom feels it, too, because she takes a huge breath

and blows it out and says, "Let's stop in Davis for some coffee and a snack."

She gets coffee and we buy caramel corn with nuts to eat in the car. Pretty soon the flat highway turns into a hill and we're climbing up into the mountains. When I see the first white patches on the side of the road, I jab my finger against the window and shout, "Snow! Mom! Snow!"

"I see it, Keek. Pretty neat, huh?"

"Can we stop?" I want to touch it.

"I know there's a big rest stop at Donner Pass. I remember that from coming here with friends when I was in my twenties." She drives a few more seconds and adds, "I don't remember much *after* that, because as soon as we hit Tahoe we were partying. But I do remember that."

As soon as she's parked and turns off the truck, I tumble out and run to a bunch of rocks near the restrooms. There's snow all around them. I plunge my hands into it. Or I try, but it's crusted over and icy, not soft and fluffy. I run my hands over it and dig my fingers in until they feel like they're turning to ice, too.

Then something hits me in the middle of my back. I whirl around to see Mom laughing. "That's what a snowball made of weeks-old snow feels like," she says.

There's no tension or worry in her eyes.

I start to try to make my own snowball, but my hands are getting numb and I have to pee, and I want her mood to stay right exactly where it is, so we use the bathroom and jump back into the truck so we can finally get where we're going.

* * *

The house is a cabin and is smaller than we expected, and nothing fancy—at least compared to Lucy's Moss Beach house. Everything is wood: the walls, the floors, the cupboards, the furniture. It smells piney and sweet and a little smokey.

It's perfect.

I unload the groceries into the fridge and onto the corner of the counter, leaving out what I need for the broccoli-cheese soup I plan to make for first-night dinner. Mom walks slowly around the cabin, looking into every room and taking a lot of deep breaths. Touching shelves, pillows, walls.

"It's just so nice to be somewhere different," she says. "When was the last time we were anywhere *different*?"

"Never?"

"That sounds about right."

The next morning, Mom surprises me with a trip to a place called Adventure Mountain, where we get a two-hour pass and rent inner tubes and slide down snow-packed hills as many times as we can before our pass expires. Mom is kind of wild, sometimes belly flopping onto her tube to get a fast start, other times, tying our tubes together with the strap you're only supposed to use to pull your tube when you're not in it so we can go down together.

She whoops and screams, but I only make a few squeaks and yelps. There's too much to take in and feel. The cold on my cheeks, the crunch of snow under my feet, the fear and exhilaration of losing control except not really, because the course is designed to keep you safe.

The only bad part is dragging our tubes back up after every run. We don't have the right shoes, and we slip and slide everywhere, and our clothes are getting wetter and colder, too.

Freezing and tired at the end of it, we take a selfie with my phone for me to text to Lu later and get back into the truck, blasting the heat on the drive back to the cabin until it's suddenly too hot and I turn it off.

"That's maybe the most fun I've had since I got sober," Mom says.

I know it's a joke. She's made it before. I laugh like always, but this time it sticks in my head in an uncomfortable way. Is life never fun for her now that she doesn't drink? I mean, it's not that fun for me, either, but not every day can feel like vacation.

Maybe that's how life felt for her when she was drinking. Maybe she wishes it still did.

She looks over at me while we're at a stoplight in Tahoe traffic. "You know I was only kidding," she says, as if she's been reading my mind.

"I know." I smile at her to show her I get it. "It really was the most fun ever."

"I'm glad you agree." She bends over to get something out from behind her seat, then hands me a plastic bag. "I know we said we're not doing presents, but I got you this so you can always remember today."

The light turns green and she starts driving again while I reach in the bag. I pull out a pink knit cap with a white pompom and the Adventure Mountain logo. It's exactly what I wanted when I imagined coming here.

"Mom!" That's all I can say. I put it on and flip the passenger visor down so I can see myself in the little mirror.

Mom steals a glance. "That's cute on you. Do you like it?"

"It's perfect."

That night when I'm in my room and Mom has also gone to bed, I dig to the bottom of my backpack, where I'd put my journal when I packed. I thought I *might* want to write in it. Not to read to Mom, but just for me, since I've had so much on my mind.

I sit cross-legged on the bed, still wearing my hat, and open it up.

The prompt is called "Just for Today."

The instructions say: *Sometimes it can be hard not to obsess about the mistakes of yesterday or worry about what will happen tomorrow. What are some good things that are true, just for today, without thinking about the past or present?*

I start to write.

I had fun. Mom had fun, too.
Today she didn't have to work. Today I didn't have to wait for her to come home.
We have all the food we need. It's warm in the cabin.
There's nothing I have to worry about today. But there's only like an hour left in today, so that's pretty easy, and I did worry earlier. Maybe "earlier" is the same as "yesterday" and I don't have to worry about how I was worrying.

121

I think a little bit about Lu and school and Grandma and group, but that's the past or the future.

Today I'm not alone. Today me and Mom are enough.

We're there three days and three nights. After inner-tubing, mostly we take walks, drive around to look at lake views, go out to breakfast once, and watch old DVDs on the cabin TV because there's no cable.

It's not boring, though, at least not in the way Lu said it might be. It's boring in a good way, when you're hours away from your regular life and no one can bother you. There are no bills on the fridge or homework or to-do lists.

On Christmas Eve, we sit by the fire, eating the last of the soup. It's exactly like I pictured it would be, except we haven't had any new snowfall.

Then Mom says, "Babe, look."

Huge snowflakes—some that seem as big as my hand—float past the front-room picture window. I put my soup bowl on the coffee table and jump up to see.

It really is snow. Fresh snow. Gigantic flakes.

"Can we go outside?" I ask, even though we're nice and toasty and dry.

"I think we have to."

We get jackets and gloves and shoes on. And I put on my pink knit cap, which I'll definitely be wearing on the first day back to school.

Outside, we look up. We hold our arms out and let the giant

flakes settle on our faces and shoulders and hands, where they instantly melt. The pine trees climb all the way into the stars, it seems like, and the sky is endless. This feeling, that huge sky deep with stars, the trees I imagine I can hear breathing, maybe it could all be part of my higher power along with the ocean.

"I feel so small," I say. "Not in a bad way."

Right-sized. One person in a huge world where there's room to be myself and feel everything I feel.

"I know what you mean," Mom says.

Our voices are small, too, eaten up by the trees.

"I'm glad you asked Steve about the truck," I say. "Even though it was a big ask."

"Me too. That's one of the lessons I have to learn over and over. That I can't go wrong asking for help from the right people, from trusted people. Antonia tries to remind me. I still have a hard time getting it."

I haven't heard her quote Antonia lately, and I'm relieved to hear her name.

"This is magical," she continues. "It's perfect. I'm grateful." She stops staring at the sky and turns to me. "I'm grateful to be here. To be alive and well and with you, right now." She opens her arms wide. "This moment. I could never have this moment without my sobriety and my recovery and everything else that's happened in the last five years."

We let that float up into the trees.

She adds, "Now I just need to remember that."

I put my hands in my pockets to get warm and glance at

her. Doesn't she know that? Doesn't she remember that every day, or at least every time she goes to a meeting or drops me off at group or looks at our fridge magnets? Isn't that the point of it all?

"You only have to remember it today," I tell her, thinking of the journal entry.

Just for today, then on all the other days, one day at a time.

"Sure," she says. "Easy." She's still looking up.

20

Before we can leave on the day after Christmas, we have to clean.

We get up early and spend hours on it, because Lucy said she knew we'd leave it spotless and we need to make sure we do. Mom even takes the toilet seat off and scrubs the little hinges with a toothbrush. But we put on Christmas music and play Kiki Krash and Meg the Marauder, racing to see who can pack faster when we finish cleaning.

When we're packed and the truck is loaded, we do one final walk-through to make sure we haven't forgotten anything.

"It's like we were never here," Mom says. That's how it *should* look if we've done our job, but she sounds sad.

"We were, though." I point to my Adventure Mountain hat to show her the evidence.

She smiles, opens her arms to the room, and says, "Good-bye, cabin!"

"Bye, fireplace!" I wave like a princess. "Goodbye, snow!"

Mom laughs, but I can tell the sadness is still there.

The closer we get to home, the more Mom's mood seems to go down.

"Back to reality," she says with a sigh, as we sit in bumper-to-bumper traffic a little past Sacramento. Then for a while she's quiet except for swearing at other drivers.

In group we've talked about trying not to interpret silence, that just because someone is quiet doesn't mean anything bad. "Chances are," Gene said once, "in the absence of words, you're gonna make up something real bad and work your-self into a ball of worry. I try to accept silence as silence—no more, no less. Let the other person speak when they're ready."

But I can't accept silence as silence. Not with Mom, who's talkative when life is going good or fine, and quiet when it isn't. That's not an interpretation. That's a fact.

The other thing I know from group is that it's not my job to change someone else's mood. I try it anyway. When one stretch of quiet gets so long that I check to make sure Mom isn't falling asleep at the wheel, I turn to her and say, "That was the best Christmas."

"It was great. Of course, now we're broke." Mom pushes her hair back. "Gas, food, Adventure freakin' Mountain. And this truck is a gas-guzzler. At these prices!"

Somehow I've made her mood worse. "At least the cabin

was free," I offer. And didn't we have a Christmas budget for everything else?

"The cabin was free, but we had to *clean* it. I worked twice as hard—on a holiday—on that place than I would on a regular paying job, because I don't want Lucy to think I take her gift for granted. Or her tips."

We'd both worked hard. But I thought we were having fun.

"I just never get a break," Mom continues. "Not even on my own vacation. I've been working since I was sixteen, and I haven't had a real break since. I'm tired."

"I know," I say quietly.

"Sometimes I want someone to take care of *me*."

I turn to face the road. I don't know what to say to that.

Who plans every day with her? Who makes sure she always has breakfast and snacks and coffee and water? Who reminds her about her charger? Who helps keep our house clean and fixes her a dinner plate and keeps it warm on the nights when she's late?

I guess it's not enough.

A car suddenly brakes in front of us, and Mom almost can't stop the heavy truck in time. I suck in a breath and bite my cheek so I won't say, *You're following too close!*

"And now," she goes on, "getting through all this traffic there and back when we could have been relaxing at home. It's like it wasn't worth it."

Not worth it. Not worth it to get away together, have our day on the mountain, eat by the fire, stand under the stars with snow falling into our cupped hands.

127

That's not an interpretation. She literally said it.

Everything I wanted for me, for us, and that we got—even if it was only for a few days.

Not worth it?

What happened to gratitude, and all the things she said Christmas Eve about remembering what it takes to be able to have good moments?

We drive straight through, only stopping once for gas and to use the bathroom. No fun detours or road snacks. I text Lu the Adventure Mountain selfie and tell her we're on our way home. **We had so much fun!!** I write. We did, whether Mom wants to think about it or not.

When we're finally inching across the Bay Bridge, I stare out at the view. The sun has just gone down, and the San Francisco skyline stands tall against a purply-gray backdrop. I want to say that she was right: the bridge is a lot prettier on the way back.

We go right to Steve's to return the truck and pick up our car. He hugs me hello, and when my face is mashed to his shoulder, I feel like I'm holding back tears. It's a relief to just be here. I've missed it, and I've missed him.

"Merry Christmas, kid," he says. "Lu's in her room if you want to say hi."

I do want to. I knock on her door while Steve and Mom and Lu's mom, Ann, talk in the kitchen. "It's me."

A second later, the door swings open. "Merry Christmas!" She flings herself against me and then pulls me into her room.

It has this certain Lu smell that's the soap she uses and the stack of library books she always has by her bed. "I'm putting away my presents and stuff." Her bed is covered in clothes and boxes and candy. She picks up stuff to show me. "I got this case for my phone that has this shoulder strap . . . and a Taylor Swift songbook for guitar . . . peanut-chocolate brittle. . . ." She digs through the pile and pulls out a blue sweater with white stripes on one sleeve. It looks so small to me. I don't think I ever fit into anything that little. "Casey got me this."

I touch it. It's soft and cute and perfect for her. I hold the sweater up to myself and joke, "I could wear it as a crop top."

Lu laughs, but the sight of us next to each other in the mirror over her dresser makes me want to turn away. The Adventure Mountain hat makes me look even taller. I take it off; my hair is a staticky mess. I put it back on.

"I love that hat," she says, almost like she's jealous.

Steve leans his head in the doorway. "How about staying for dinner, Keek? Your mom says yes if it's okay with you. I'm just throwing some stuff on the grill. There are also leftovers from yesterday, but I'm in a grilling mood."

I nod, happy. Being with Steve and everyone usually cheers Mom up, and it definitely cheers me up.

Lu helps me help Steve get the food ready. She preps burger toppings, and I make a big salad with everything I can find in the fridge that could go in a salad. Including a little can of sliced black olives I find in the cupboard.

"Ew, don't put those in," Lu says. She stops slicing a red

onion to look at the salad toppings I have lined up on the counter. "Or bell peppers."

"Why are you so picky?"

"I'm not. I just don't like peppers and olives. Or onions." She turns her face away from the chopping board, blinking away tears. She hasn't even started the tomatoes and avocados yet.

"You should always do onions last," I say. "Now they're going to be sitting there stinging your eyes while you do the rest of the stuff."

"I didn't think about it."

"It's common sense."

"Well, I didn't think of it!"

She puts the sliced onions on a separate plate and takes them out to Steve to put on the grill.

I shouldn't have said, "It's common sense," like that. It's almost the same as calling someone dumb.

Casey comes into the kitchen while I finish the salad. "Hey, how was Tahoe?"

"So great," I say. "I loved it." I did love it. But I know I'm leaving out the part about the car ride home, and it makes me think of the look Owen gave me when I didn't tell the whole story of my Thanksgiving.

She picks up a red pepper ring and eats it. "Did Lu tell you? Our dad called on Christmas Eve, and it was totally trauma-tizing. Drunk, crying, angry, guilt trip, self-pity, all of it at once." She stretches her arms overhead. "You're lucky your mom is doing awesome at recovery. I always wonder what that would be like, if he could do that."

"I'm sorry it was like that." Was Lu going to tell me about her dad? I think about what she shared at group, about her dad falling that time and bleeding and no one helping her. I never heard that story before. She keeps things to herself a lot. But obviously I do, too.

I arrange the pepper rings and olives on a side plate, separate from the salad bowl, so anyone who wants them can add them. I get out every bottle of dressing Steve has in the fridge, and Casey helps me carry it all to the table.

At dinner, when the small talk dies down, Steve looks at Mom and says, "I bet it was good to get away, huh? You've been working so hard."

I wait for her to say what she said in the car, about it not being worth it, about how she had to clean, all of that. But she only talks about the fun things we did minus all of the complaints, and makes it sound like it *was* worth it. Maybe driving in traffic put her in a bad mood that's clearing up now. Or, like me, she's just not telling the whole story.

After dinner, she helps Ann with the dishes, and Lu tries playing a song from the Taylor Swift book on her guitar while I sing along. She's on the bed; I sit cross-legged on the floor.

I like it best when it's us like this, being who we are. Without all that school and popularity stuff to interfere.

"I'm sorry for what I said in the kitchen," I blurt out as soon as we're done muddling through the song. "About the onions."

"It's okay. Steve said you're probably tired from your trip."

"I am. I'm sorry anyway."

She strums a chord.

"Casey told me about your dad," I say. She doesn't say anything, so I keep talking. "Have you told Till and those guys about him?"

"No." She plays another chord. "Not yet."

"My mom's been kind of . . ." I shrug. "Up and down. On this trip. And before that."

Lu slips her guitar out of her lap and sets it on the bed. Is it okay for me to talk about my mom, who at least is there and has herself mostly together, when I know how bad things are with Lu's dad? I pull at carpet threads.

"My mom keeps pointing out that holidays are hard when you have kind of a messed-up family," she says. "Even for her. She says they're a reminder of everything you wish could be different. Like, even though this Christmas was mostly okay—except for that one call from my dad—I thought a lot about the ones that weren't."

I nod. "Or you worry about the ones in the future. I did this journaling prompt kind of about that . . ."

Before I can say more, there's a knock on the door, then Ann pokes her head in. "Time to say goodbye, girls. Kyra, your mom is ready to get you guys home."

"See you at group on Saturday?" I ask Lu.

"We actually have a church thing. Do you want to come to that?"

"That's okay."

But as I put my shoes on, I wonder: What if I did go with

her sometime? Would that help us stay closer? She'd probably never invite her new friends. I know sometimes she's embarrassed about being religious.

But I like my higher power how it is. And I want to go to group.

21

I t's only Gene and me and Owen at group, the last one of the year. Lu and Casey are at their church thing, and we have no newcomers. Mom almost didn't get home in time to drive me because she had trouble getting up this morning and got a late start.

She's gotten late starts every morning since we got back from Tahoe. Late starts and late nights.

My prediction that after the trip we'd be normal again hasn't come true. Yet. Technically, it's still kind of the holidays, and Mom still has lots of jobs cleaning up after people's holiday parties, so I'm trying to be patient.

Gene and I sit opposite each other with the space heater and box of tissues between us. He reads the welcome from the binder and passes it to me, and I read the introduction and pass the binder to Owen, who reads the group guidelines we already know. I don't feel like any of us are actually listening.

There's only the shortest pause before Gene jumps in. "Hi, I'm Gene."

"Hi, Gene." Owen says it singsongy, like it's silly to do this every time.

Gene says, "So, I hate New Year's." He leans forward with his hands clasped. His bushy eyebrows are drawn together, nearly touching. "I always hated it. I hated it because every year I promised myself—made a resolution—that it would be the year I'd quit drinking."

Now we listen.

"I knew it was taking my life away from me," he continues. "Little by little at first, and then not so little. My wife left. My kids weren't talking to me. And every December I'd make big promises to myself like I was somehow going to wake up on January first and magically not want to pick up the bottle. But addicts are great liars. Mostly to ourselves. So of course in December, I'd drink my ass off. I'd drink myself sick and not change a thing about my life."

He stops there, and I open my mouth to say thanks for sharing, he was heard, but he keeps going, now squeezing one hand with the other, making his knuckles pop.

"I'd manage to stop for a little bit sometimes. But by the end of the month or the end of the week or sometimes by the end of January first, I'd be drinking again." He slides his hands under his thighs. "So I kind of hate this time of year now. It reminds me of wasted time and broken promises and how

135

much I let myself down over and over. I abandoned myself, just like my dad abandoned me, and—"

His voice breaks.

Suddenly, I want to cry, too. Owen folds way forward in his seat so his head is almost touching his knees.

Gene clears his throat and finishes his sentence: "And I abandoned my kids."

I think about *my* dad, who I guess abandoned me, but I don't think about it like that, because he was never there in the first place. I don't feel anything about him. Then how come it's so hard not to cry at what Gene is saying?

He goes on. "And I hate hearing people talk about their New Year's resolutions. Starting in January they're gonna do this, starting in January they're gonna do that. That's what we call *magical thinking.*" He flutters his fingers to emphasize the words. "There's nothing special about January first. It's just another day you have to take life on its own terms. And it's another day I get the chance to work on forgiving myself for all the years I kept hurting people, including me." Finally, he looks up. "That's it. Kind of a rant. Thanks for listening."

"Thanks for sharing," I manage to say. Owen still has his head down. "You were heard."

Maybe Mom hates this time of year, too, and I never noticed. Maybe that's what's going on. Like Lu's mom said—holidays are just hard.

"Oh!" Gene says. "The day I finally did quit? Just a boring Wednesday in March 2004." He holds out a hand. "Sorry, I shouldn't have kept going after I said I was done. That's it."

Owen lifts his head, eyes rimmed in pink. "I have a question. It might be crosstalk."

"Go ahead," Gene says.

"How could you do that to your kids?"

The way he says that straight out, like the time he said he hated his mom, makes my stomach jump. But when I look at Gene, his face is open.

"Like," Owen continues, "how could drinking be more important to you than them? How could you choose *that*, not them?"

"Well . . ." Gene thinks for a few seconds. "The second step of Alcoholics Anonymous says we start to believe a higher power can restore us to sanity. That's because we're not sane. Nothing we do in the service of addiction makes sense. Or I should say, it makes sense only to the addict. Our whole logic is built on rationalizing another drink."

Owen groans and leans back in his chair, staring at the ceiling. "It's so freaking selfish."

"You're right," Gene says. "And you can lose your sanity, too, trying to change the addict."

"Yeah, I feel that." He straightens up and looks at me. "Sorry. That's all. You want to go?"

I take a deep breath and say, "Hi, I'm Kyra," before I think about what I'm going to say.

"Hi, Kyra."

Now I'm the one staring at the tissue box. "Um . . . I had a good Christmas with my mom. We went to Lake Tahoe and stayed in a cabin that one of her clients let us stay in for free.

It was the first time I'd been to the snow. The air was, like . . . different."

There was the cold and the altitude and all the trees, everything sharp and clear and fragrant. I know from science class that humans breathe in what trees breathe out. Up there it really felt like that. Like the air was alive.

"It was perfect while we were there. I felt close to my mom. But then on the drive home, her mood changed. And she talked about the trip like it wasn't worth the trouble and I felt . . . I felt like it was my fault."

I didn't know how much I felt that until I say it aloud. I bend down to grab a tissue from the box.

"It was me who begged her to say yes when her client offered us the cabin. I wanted to go so bad. I think she did it for me and then afterward, she was unhappy. Thinking about everything we don't have." Maybe if I hadn't pushed, we could have had a nice Christmas at home. "She's been sad and quiet ever since, and she's never like that." I blow my nose. "Except, actually, she was a little like that at Thanksgiving, too. I don't know what to do. I'm trying to help and be good so she . . ."

So she what?

I hear in my own words all the things that newcomers to group say. Talking like I can fix it, when I'm supposed to know better. Talking like if I do enough, I can change whatever she's feeling.

I'm talking like someone whose parent is an active alcoholic.

"Active alcoholic" is what they call someone still drinking.

Or drinking again. I'm talking like someone brand-new who's afraid of causing somebody else to drink. And I want Gene and Owen to think I'm smarter than that by now, and anyway it wouldn't apply to me because my mom is sober. She's just having a hard time right now holding it all together, that's all.

"Thanks for listening," I say, cutting myself off before I say more.

Gene waits. Then says, "Sure you're done?"

I nod and press my lips together.

"Thank you, Kyra. You were heard." He squeezes his hands together again. "Do you mind if I speak to that?"

"I don't mind."

"From what I see and hear, you're doing the very best you can. If your mom is unhappy or struggling, you're not the one making her feel that way. Even if you're not perfect. I know you know that. But it's good to be reminded. That's why we're here. To be reminded of the things we know."

"Are you worried she's going to drink?" Owen says. Again, he just *says* things.

I jerk my head toward him. "No!"

He holds up his hands. "Just asking."

"No," I say again. "She's just tired. It's the holidays."

"Okay."

Gene flips through the binder and reads the closing, and then instead of reading one of the prayers or declarations, he pulls out a laminated blue card. The affirmations.

I let out a breath as he hands it to me. Whenever the blue card comes out, we each get to pick one and read it aloud.

There are a lot I like; it's always hard to choose. I skim through the list.

"'It's okay to have fun and celebrate,'" I read. It feels right for this time of year and for wanting to hold on to standing in the snow with my mom. Those hand-sized flakes.

"Pick two," Gene says. "We've got time."

"Um . . ." I scan the card again, and a certain one jumps out at me because of the journal prompt I did in Tahoe. "'It's okay to not know everything. I know enough, just for today.'"

I hand it to Owen. He stares at it, jiggling his leg, then reads, "'It's okay to feel angry.'" He passes it to Gene.

"I'm gonna go with . . . 'It's okay to give myself a break.' And"—he glances at me, then back down at the card—"'It's okay to dream and have hope.'"

PART III: JANUARY

Live and Let Live

22

Three weeks later, I'm still waiting for the return to normal.

Mom isn't back to the person she was before the holidays, and Lu and I never sit at our old table together anymore at lunch. We're either both with the eighth graders or just she is while I go to the library or eat outside. I still feel like I don't know Till at all. I try to start conversations with her at lunch when I eat with them, but she's so quiet, and meanwhile Jaymison won't ever shut up! They've been wearing their pink ankle bandannas every day since school started again, and I refuse to ask them what it means because I don't want them to think I care.

At home, I make a fruit fly trap with vinegar and soap in an old jar, and every day there are a few more fly bodies floating on the surface. They just needed a reason to come out from wherever they were hiding.

Group got canceled twice because Gene got the flu and it took him a long time to recover. If Mom were her old self, I could have asked her to sponsor us while he was sick.

But she's not.

Work should have slowed down now for her, but she's still gone a lot, late a lot, in her room a lot. I'm starting to think it's not work that's been the problem. The things about her that were up and down through Thanksgiving and Christmas and winter break are all down now. Down and down and down through January, which is almost over.

I'm worried all the time but try not to be. I try to think, *Just for today*, but every day there's something to worry about. I listen to her phone calls when I know I shouldn't, to see if she's talking to Antonia. I used to only check her dot on the GPS when she was late and I needed to figure out when to start making dinner. Now I follow it all the time, to see if she's going to meetings or stopping too long anywhere else between jobs. It's easy to tell what's a meeting if she's stopped for an hour *on* the hour. That hasn't happened, though. Her stops are at random times, in random places. I snoop in her room, looking for her recovery journal, and can never find it.

Mostly I try not to think about what Owen said at group and one certain word that no one who loves and needs and lives with someone like her, someone in recovery, wants to say.

Relapse.

That's when an alcoholic who hasn't had a drink for a good

143

stretch of time starts again. And I hadn't thought of it—or hadn't let myself think of it—until Owen asked it at group. Now I can't get it out of my head.

That worry is a fruit fly that keeps reappearing after I thought I killed it.

There's a test in Social Studies today. Multiple choice plus two essay questions about everything we've learned this month in our California history unit. Which I feel like I kind of know from living here my whole life so I didn't prepare very well. Since school started back up, I've gotten more incompletes on my assignments than I did through the whole fall.

And I'm running late.

I take a shower without putting my head under, and the steam leaves my hair in a frizzy triangle. I wish, for the millionth time, that it were still long. I used to always have it long enough to braid or have in a ponytail, anything to keep it out of my face. Then right before seventh grade, Mom said, "Don't you want a change?"

Questions that start with "don't you want" are hard for me, especially from her. They don't leave very much room to say, *No, I* don't *want*. The question should be "*do* you want," because then there couldn't be a wrong answer.

So Mom said, "Don't you want a change?" and I said, "Okay," and it hasn't been the same since, and I keep getting impatient while waiting for it to grow through awkward stages and I cut more off myself.

I take my Adventure Mountain ski cap from my dresser,

pull it on, and shove my bangs under. Christmas seems like it happened in another lifetime, to other people.

In the hall outside Mom's room, I take a deep breath and push the door open but don't go in. "Mom?"

She's awake. She lifts her head and squints at me. "What time is it?"

"Eight-forty-one." Homeroom bell is at eight-fifty.

"Are you kidding me?"

"No."

Mom swears and throws back the covers. I wonder how long it's been since she's washed her sleeping T-shirt or sheets, because everything in here smells old and sour.

Sour like the bottom of a dirty wineglass? Or sour like unwashed clothes in a stale room? I can't tell.

"Do you have clients today?" I ask.

"No." She rakes her hand through her hair. "I mean . . . this is Thursday, right?"

A pang shoots through my stomach. "It's Wednesday."

She swears again and digs into the jumble of covers, sliding her hand under the pillows. "Help me find my phone."

Her phone is her life. Everything for her business is on there. She can't lose it. I get down on my knees to look under the bed. No phone. Nothing under there at all, not even a dust bunny. I toe through a pile of laundry on the floor.

"Babe, go check the car while I get dressed?"

I watch her try to fix her tangle of hair. "Can you drive me to school, though? I'm ready now."

"Good for you. I'm not."

145

Another pang. *Good for you.*

Mom claws through her dresser drawers, pulling out jeans, a bra, a different shirt. "Why didn't you wake me up sooner?" she's saying. "Check the car for my phone. Then we can go."

I grab the car keys off the hook in the kitchen, but when I get outside I can see the phone sitting on the passenger seat and the door is unlocked. I open it to grab the phone and am hit with the smell of smoke. I think. Then it's gone. Except maybe a hint of it? She must have been back to that one client whose house is saturated with the smell.

I can't think about it because I just want to yell at Mom about leaving the car unlocked and her phone on the seat. *Someone could have taken it, then you wouldn't have access to any of your work stuff!*

I could never be that careless.

On top of everything, the phone is totally dead. Inside, I plug it into the charger we keep on the kitchen counter. I open the fridge to see what I could do for breakfast, but in my mind all I see is how empty it was under her bed. Why, if her whole room is a mess, would she have cleaned under there? I wonder if I'd checked yesterday, would there have been bottles? One bottle?

I slam the fridge shut. The *Easy Does It* magnet slides halfway down the door. I don't *know* if she's drinking again.

The feeling I have reminds me of how, when I was a kid, I'd question myself about if I really saw all that beer in the fridge or only imagined it. But even then, her being drunk was obvious. The way she'd crawl into my bed, smelling of it and

146

so sorry. And she drank in front of me back then, red wine or a water glass with clear liquor mixed with juice like when I was in the bath, or while we watched TV, her laughter or tears or outrage at a show getting louder and louder the longer we sat there.

If she's doing it now, it's different.

She hasn't smelled like alcohol that I've noticed, or acted drunk. I can't find any proof. I don't *know*. I only feel it. And we say in group that feelings aren't facts.

"Well?" Mom calls from her room. "Was it there?"

"Yeah."

"Can you please bring it to me?" It's the kind of "please" that makes the request actually sound rude, not polite.

"It's dead. I'm charging it."

She swears *again*. I watch the phone light up with calendar reminders, bank notices, and texts. One from yesterday says:

I thought we were scheduled today but it looks like you didn't come. Maybe I got mixed up?

Another says:

Hi Meg, no big deal but I think you left the bathtub faucet running, so just make sure to double-check next time thank you!!

I stop reading and run through what I can remember about California history for the test. The Ohlone people lived here before the Spanish missions came. Gold rush. Railroads. Immigration through Angel Island, where we're going on a field trip next week. I don't know if I have it all in the right order. Except the Ohlone. I know they were first.

147

Mom comes in and grabs the phone, scrolling and swearing, scrolling and swearing. "I really thought . . ."

She really thought today was Thursday.

I fill a glass of water under the tap and hand it to her. "Do you want me to help you with clients today?" I ask.

While chugging water, she shakes her head. "No, babe," she says with a gasp after she drains the glass. "I'll get you to school."

"It's too late."

"I'll write you a note."

"I hate walking in late. Everyone stares." I point to the phone. "You need more charge on that before you can go anyway."

"I'll charge it in the car." She unplugs the phone and slides it into the back pocket of her jeans, then looks at the empty coffeepot. "You didn't make coffee?"

"I overslept, too." If she can, why can't I? "And you lost the car charger last week, remember?"

I watch her try to remember that. Her eyes are somewhere between blank and anxious as she turns in a circle in the kitchen, like someone lost. I look away before she can catch me watching.

"I'm going to be so behind." She pulls at a piece of skin at her throat, a thing she's started doing when she's worried. I don't like the sight of her skin stretching out, like her neck is beige rubber.

"If I help, you can get all caught up. Easy." Mr. Ocampo will let me do a make-up test if I have a note saying I was sick.

Mom puts her glass under the tap for more water. "What if . . . what if you help me this morning, and then I take you to school at lunch and you can go to your afternoon classes."

I feel a tiny bit of control back in my hand, like I'm catching the frayed end of a rope. Or a tether, like the ones we used on Adventure Mountain to keep our tubes together. I take hold of it in my mind and pull and pull as if I can gather it into my hand and coil it around my wrist, and anchor us.

"Call me in sick for the day and I'll make breakfast," I say, "then we'll go get everything done."

"I can't take you this afternoon. This one city client is there when I clean and she wouldn't like it."

"Let me help with everything else, then."

She finishes her water. "Just this once, Keek. Okay?" I nod and she reaches out to touch my face. "I'm sorry. I'm . . . I'm going through something." Before she looks away I see one of the little glimpses I've been getting of the real her. They go by so fast. "I'll handle it," she says. "I promise."

I turn to the fridge and try to avoid eye contact with all the slogan magnets before I open the door. "What do you want for breakfast? I can make you a smoothie. Or fried rice with eggs."

"You pick." She lowers herself onto a kitchen chair and opens a bottle of vitamins and a bottle of Tylenol. "Thank you, babe."

When we were on the first inner-tube run, when I was still getting the feel of it—like how to shift my weight enough

149

to steer but not too much—my tube slid off the center of the path. For a few seconds that felt longer, I careened left and then right and off a snowbank before the hill flattened out. And after steep hills, there's a mini hill going up to help you slow down. The course is designed so nothing bad can happen. You can careen and slide all over. The sides of the run keep you from going too far off course or smashing into anyone else.

With Mom the way she's been since then, I feel like she's careening down in a tube and *I* am the sides of the run and the snowbank, but she might still go off course.

23

We're fed and Mom has coffee and we're on our way, and I'm happy to be riding in the opposite direction from school.

Aside from everything with Lu and the pink bandannas, there's also still Juan and Gabe calling me Whitney and making other comments. Yesterday, I got a bathroom pass from Mr. Banks during Language Arts because I'm having my period and I could tell I needed to change my pad, like, *now*. I took my whole backpack with me because the pads were in there and I didn't want anyone to see me taking one out to put in my pocket. It felt like everyone knew, and I imagined them watching me as I walked out and hoped I wasn't leaking.

When I was done in the bathroom, I came out into the hall right when Gabe was going into the boy's room. For once,

Juan wasn't right next to him, and I thought he might not say anything. Then he looked at me and said, "You smell."

I froze. I wanted to say something back to him, like that I'd showered that morning and my clothes were clean and I washed my hands in the bathroom and I smelled fine. But he said it like he knew something about me I didn't. Then he laughed and walked away. It all happened in a few seconds, but it felt way longer than that.

When I got home, I wanted to ask Mom—*Do I smell? Can people tell when you have your period? Do I smell different? What's wrong with me that Gabe and them are always looking for something to say to me? What's wrong with me that Till doesn't want to get to know me and Jaymison always wrinkles her nose at my lunches?*

But of course Mom wasn't home.

I lay down with a heating pad for my cramps and wished someone would make me soup instead of me always making it. I wished I had a dog, a little terrier from the shelter who I'd name Gonzo, after the Muppet, and he would be there every day when I got home from school and we'd take a walk and then he would jump up onto the bed next to me while I did my homework.

I fell asleep thinking about Gonzo and imagined the heating pad was his little warm body. By the time Mom got home, I was back to worrying about her again, and I didn't tell her what Gabe said or ask if it was true.

When I'm cleaning with Mom, like we're doing today, at least I don't have to deal with the school part of life. And it lets me make messy things neat. I mean, literally, that's what cleaning is. But it feels that way in my thoughts, too. My mind gets dusted and polished when I'm cleaning, or put in recipe order when I'm cooking.

Also, when I'm cleaning with Mom, I know she's okay.

"This guy is extra picky," she says when we get to the house in Daly City. She checks her phone for the door code and lets us in. "If I put a dish back in the wrong cupboard, I get a text. If I fold the towels wrong, I get a text."

"You should fire him."

"I wish."

She does fire clients sometimes, but only if they're *really* bad and only if she has enough other clients where she doesn't have to worry about losing the money. Based on the texts coming up on her phone this morning from clients, though, she's probably the one who should worry about getting fired.

We take our shoes off and leave them by the front door. It's a two-bedroom, two-bath house that reminds me of a nicer, newer version of ours except we only have one bathroom.

"He uses the second bedroom for an office, at the end of the hall," Mom says. "You can start there. Make sure you do the windowsills. He checks. I'm going to get the bedding into the washer."

I take a cloth and the furniture polish down the hardwood hallway.

I do the windowsills first, so I don't forget. Then the bookshelf. He's got a lot of books. Thick ones about ancient

153

presidents, a set of classics with black covers and white titles like we have at the school library, and a whole shelf of books with spines that all look exactly the same. I pull one out—*Securities Regulations: Cases and Materials.* On top of being picky about his house, I bet he's boring.

When I turn to the desk, I see it.

A bottle of whiskey.

There's a glass, too. When I sniff it, there's that familiar smell I don't like, that reminds me of being little and not knowing what was wrong with Mom.

I look around for a liquor cabinet so I can put it away, and don't see one. The day we found the beer in the fridge seems so long ago. I feel like a different person now, and so does Mom. That day, we dealt with it together, and then she wrote about it in her journal and she read it to me. Now I don't even want to ask her where I should put this stuff.

I pick up the bottle and the glass and walk quickly to the kitchen. I put the glass in the dishwasher and start opening cabinets in hopes of figuring out where it goes.

"Up here."

Mom's voice makes me jump. She's come in and is standing by the sink, pointing to a cabinet above it. She reaches out and I hand her the bottle and watch her put it away next to other bottles.

"Thanks," I say. And I wait a second for her to say something about it. To acknowledge it, like she did with the beer.

She says, "Did you get those windowsills? When you're done in there, how about you take a look around the house for anymore dirty dishes, then go ahead and run the dish-washer."

"Okay."

She turns to get some cleaning stuff from under the sink, and I go to finish the office.

My thoughts are a jumble, a sudden heap of dirty dishes.

I crawl on the floor to run a damp cloth over the base-boards. They aren't even dirty, but with picky clients you can't skip anything.

The thought that there's probably alcohol all around Mom when she's working, every day, overwhelms me in a different way now than it did when we found that one beer.

A couple of years ago we went to a cookout at Steve's house, and there was so much alcohol because that's how he likes to host, and Lu was all anxious about it because it was her first time at one of Steve's parties. She'd only ever seen people who drink lose control, like her dad. And my mom talked to Lu about it, and Lu felt better. Back then, I wasn't worried about all the alcohol because I knew my mom wouldn't drink, and my mom knew she wouldn't drink, and Steve knew she wouldn't drink.

Now I don't think I know that.

What's changed since then?

Mom's job is the same. Our house is the same. Our higher power is the same.

Thanksgiving she was tense. Then Tahoe was so good, until after. It doesn't make sense.

Is it me? I've changed a lot in two years. I'm bigger, taller, smarter. Maybe I'm also weirder. Maybe I'm too much. Lu keeps saying I talk too loud at school. Jaymison says, "Can you *stop?*" when I jiggle my leg. Mom pushed me off her.

Maybe it was easier for her to love me when I was younger and smaller, a little girl.

I know what she'd say to that. "No, babe. Honey, no. I love you the same," she'd say.

Addicts are good liars, Gene says.

I lean back and sit on my knees, holding the dustcloth in one hand. I close my eyes.

I picture the ocean. It's there now. We saw it on the drive here, and we'll see it on the way home. It was there yesterday. It'll be there tomorrow.

In another part of the house, the vacuum bellows. I fold myself over, put my head down on my legs, try to make myself small.

Should I tell?

Tell what?

That I'm scared my mom is relapsing.

Tell who?

I don't know. The group? Gene? Lu? Am I allowed to call Antonia?

Maybe if I wait a little bit longer, I won't have to. If something's really truly wrong, Steve will notice. Antonia will say something. But if they don't . . . I could tell just one person. One safe person who knows exactly what it feels like to worry and hope and be afraid.

Lu. She knows, because she's been through it with her dad.

I try to stand up, but the pinpricks from my legs falling asleep make me stumble, so I crawl on my hands and knees to finish dusting the hallway baseboards.

24

How come you weren't at school today?

I'm surprised when I get the text from Lu while I'm making dinner. We don't even meet at the rock every day now. Sometimes she's there and sometimes she isn't, and if she isn't, I don't wait. When I eat at her table, they're always trying to make videos and Jaymison usually has some comment, like didn't I wear those pants yesterday or how can I eat so much tuna or I should get my hair straightened.

Group getting canceled hasn't helped.

I start to answer with the truth, that I helped Mom with work and then she dropped me off at home before going to her client in the city. Then I imagine Lu telling her mom or telling Steve or maybe even Till, and then my mom getting in trouble somehow.

Worst cramps ever, I answer.

She replies with a frowny face. She doesn't even have her period yet that I know of, and I *think* she would have told me.

Will you be at school tomorrow? she asks.

Probably. Why?

You'll find out if you come :)

I stare at the phone. *Tell one safe person.*

Can I come over after school tomorrow?

The pause is long enough to make me wish I hadn't asked. I open the oven and poke one of the baking potatoes with a fork. Not done yet. Dinner is going to be simple: baked potatoes, broccoli, and cheese sauce from a jar. It was on special last time we went to the store. And I'm making a bunch of extra potatoes because they're good for lunches or I can make twice-baked potatoes for another dinner this week.

Mom promised she'd be home to eat with me tonight.

Finally, Lu answers. Let me ask.

That's as bad as a *We'll see* from an adult.

I set the table and watch Mom's dot on my phone.

In the morning, Mom sleeps through her alarm again, even though she was home early enough for us to have dinner and go grocery shopping after and still go to bed by ten-thirty. Again, I get her up. And I make coffee. And I make breakfast. And I pack her lunch and snacks and water. She takes me to school and we pull up exactly as the first bell rings. Lu is waiting at the rock.

"Right on time," Mom says, but it's with a lot less enthusiasm than she used to have.

With one leg out of the car, I turn around and blurt, "You should call Antonia."

I didn't plan to say it, and I immediately wish I hadn't, because her whole upper body recoils and then her eyes go instantly from tired to hard. "Kyra? Live and let live, okay?"

It feels almost exactly the same as when she pushed me off her and all I can do is react like I did then and say, "Sorry," and feel big and awkward and get out of the car.

As I'm walking up to the rock, I start crying. I try not to, but I can't not. I listen for Mom to say, *Wait!* or, *Keek!* or, *Babe!* because she *has* to know how wrong what she said is. "Live and Let Live" doesn't mean "Don't Care About Me" or "Never Try to Help" or "Butt Out." She *knows* that. But her car is already leaving.

I'm brushing tears away and trying to fix my wobbly mouth as I cross the lawn. As if things aren't bad enough, Juan is crossing from the other side at the same time. I brace myself, but he's walking fast with an expression on his face that's not that different from mine and doesn't even notice me.

"What's wrong?" Lu asks when I get to her.

I sink onto the rock, then the second bell rings and I immediately stand up. The only thing worse than being late and having everyone watch you walk in is having everyone watch you walk in while you're crying.

And anyway, now I don't even want to say what's wrong. Maybe talking about it is a bad idea. My mom is the one that Lu and Casey and Owen and anyone else with an alcoholic parent wishes were theirs. Over five years of sobriety. And

160

she talks recovery talk and has been to a million meetings and understands why I go to mine. She works and pays bills.

She has to be okay. She's the only family I have, and she can't relapse or be mean or not be there for me. She can't.

I hold my hand over my lower stomach and say to Lu, "Hormones," with a shaky voice and pull her inside the building.

"Well, try to feel better. And eat lunch with us. I have an announcement."

It's taco salad day in the cafeteria, and Lu and the other Pink Bandannas are in line. I know it's one of Lu's favorite lunches, even though I can make a way better taco salad than what they have here. Unfortunately, I'll have to eat it. I was so busy making sure Mom had everything she needed that I forgot to grab my leftover baked potato.

They're all clustered toward the middle of the line, and I stand sort of nearby, waiting. If this were a few months ago, Lu would have waved at me and given me cuts, and if someone complained she'd say, *Oh, I'm not giving her cuts, I was just saving a space*. She doesn't even notice me there now, so I go to the end of the line.

Turn around, I think toward Lu's back. *Turn around*.

I wish she could feel how much I need her. I need her to do more than ask, "What's wrong?" and then accept my dumb excuse.

I reach toward my shoulder before I remember my braids aren't there anymore and haven't been for a long time. I used to twist the tips between my fingers and put them in my

161

mouth when I was anxious. Now I do it to my hoodie string instead.

Jaymison leans toward Lu and whispers something, like my telepathy went to her instead of Lu. Lu looks behind her; I try to smile.

"Come sit with us when you get your food!" Lu says.

I wave her toward me. After a hesitation, she runs over. "What?"

"Can I . . . can we . . ." The hoodie string, which I'd forgotten about, falls out of my mouth. "Do you know yet if I can come over after school?"

She shifts her eyes to the side and then back to me. "Till and Jaymie are coming over."

I don't expect her to add, *But you can come over, too.* I don't even want her to say that. I want her to say, *But if you really need to talk, I'll tell them not to come.*

The line is moving forward. Abbie cranes sideways from her spot to call, "Lu! It's almost your turn!"

"Lu . . ." I say in my smallest voice.

She looks at me and calls back to Abbie, "I'll wait with Kyra."

My mouth starts to wobble again. I press my lips together to stop it. She rubs her hand on my upper arm and knows not to ask me any questions right now. I wave my hands in front of my eyes and take breaths.

We move along in the line, and I feel her checking me every thirty seconds. Then she says, "Did you get the text that Gene is better?"

I nod.

We get our taco salads and the little bags of chips that come with them. At the table, I crush my chips and dump the fragments over the ground beef and lettuce and salsa, wishing the whole thing were on a baked potato.

"Are you okay?" Abbie asks me while she crushes hers. "You look kind of upset."

"My period," I mutter.

"Ugh," Till says. A lot of her sentences are made of one or two words. *Ugh. Oh no. What? For real.*

Then Lu finally makes her announcement. Her thirteenth birthday party is in a few weeks and it's a combination of her birthday and her mom and Steve's anniversary, and Steve's going to do a cookout, and she wants us all to come.

Jaymison, of course, thinks this is a bad idea and says, "Wouldn't you rather go, like, ice-skating in Union Square or something?"

"Oooh," Till says. "You should rent out the Exploratorium!" She's talkative today.

I can't even imagine how much the Exploratorium would cost for a whole party. Anyway, they've never been to one of Steve's cookouts.

"I think it sounds perfect," I say. "His cookouts are the best," I tell Abbie. "It's more like a block party. He makes a million pounds of food and also gets every kind of chips and dip. Giant buckets of ice and soda and water and . . ." Beer. "Everything."

Lu looks at me and smiles. "Yeah. It's the best."

163

"But what will we actually *do*?" Jaymison asks. "Besides eat?"

I roll my eyes. If she's so boring that she doesn't know what to do at a party without a set activity, how is anyone supposed to explain it? But Lu looks down at her lunch, like she doesn't know how to answer.

Maybe it was her pat on the arm or Abbie asking how I am or me just being tired and fed up, but I say to Jaymison, "Are you coming or not? It's an invitation to a party. She wasn't asking for suggestions."

Till laughs; Jaymison almost drops her fork. "Okay, calm down!"

Abbie says, "I'll be there."

"Me too," Till says.

"Me three," I add.

"I have to check the date," Jaymison says. "But . . . me four, probably."

In sixth period, a note folded into a tight triangle drops onto my desk. When Mr. Ocampo looks down at the textbook open on his desk, I unfold the note and smooth it down. It's Lu's messy printing in blue gel pen.

K,

I'm glad you're coming to the party. I hope you and your mom can come. You don't have to bring anything if you don't want to, I just want you there. I'm sorry about how everything is. In the lunch line I wanted to say that you're my friend but you're not my only friend, you know? I hope you understand. You should come over soon, though, just us. It's like a different vibe when it's me and them than when it's me and you. Write back.

Lu

". . . so what does that tell us about how the Gold Rush affected the native populations here?" Mr. Ocampo is asking. His eyes scan the room and land on me. "Kyra? I know you missed yesterday, but any thoughts?"

"Um . . . the Gold Rush people took over everything. And whoever was here already got pushed out? Like always."

"Right." He takes his focus off me. "What else? Anyone?"

I start to write a reply to the note.

I know I'm not your only friend. But you're my only friend. And I was there first.

Back in fifth grade, Lu was the new girl and I was her first and best friend. And when I found out her dad was an alcoholic like my mom, and that her new stepdad was one of my mom's oldest friends, I thought it was fate.

We did a song at the talent show. We went to each other's houses all the time. Last summer, we all went camping on the Russian River. Everyone got along so good.

We started going to group at the same time.

I wish nothing had changed. I wish I hadn't grown six inches between fifth grade and seventh. I wish I didn't already wear a grown-up-sized bra. I wish I could be eleven again and stay there. I wish she would have asked more about why I was crying this morning.

I don't really know if I can come to your birthday party.

That's a lie. I know I can and I know I will. But I keep writing.

My mom might need me to help her with work. I've been doing that lately. It's been hard and I don't know but I think maybe she's

I suspend my pen above the sheet of binder paper. If I write it down or say it, I can't take it back. And there's still a chance this is all a strange hard time that will soon end. That this, too, shall pass. Mom said it herself—she's going through something. She'll handle it.

I crumple up the note until it disappears into my fist.

25

I stand outside Mom's bedroom door.

"It's seven-fifteen."

She asked me last night to do this. "I set my alarm," she said, "but could you also kind of gradually remind me of the time while you get ready for school?"

I don't know how *this* is "Live and Let Live." Still, I'm glad she asked because it seemed almost like a kind of apology at the time.

Now there's no response. I start a pot of coffee for her, warm up a mug with hot tap water, take my shower, and come back to the door.

"It's seven-forty. There's coffee."

It's too cold in the hallway to be standing here wrapped in a towel with drippy hair. I go to my room to dry off, get dressed.

"It's eight-oh-five," I say to the door. I tap lightly. "Mom? Do you want me to bring you coffee?"

I eat a banana and a big spoonful of peanut butter because now I don't have time to make anything more for breakfast *or* lunch, which means I'll be stuck with school lunch again. Back at the door, I say, "It's eight-twenty." Louder. "Mom. It's eight-twenty!"

Finally, the door opens and she comes out with her blanket around her shoulders and dragging behind her. Dark circles under her eyes. No matter how much she sleeps lately, she never looks rested.

"Keek," she says, her voice hoarse with sleep. "I'm sorry."

"Did you hear me? Did you hear your alarm?"

"I kept snoozing it."

"Mom!" I mean for it to come out exasperated, but what happens is a weird thing between a yell and a sob. It scares me, and I don't want to start off another day crying. I put my hand over my mouth.

"Baby . . ."

"Mom, just tell me that you're okay," I say, as steady as I can. "Or if you're not."

"I . . ." She tightens her blanket around her. "I *will be* okay. I think you should probably plan to get yourself to school from now on. Do what you need to do to go on time. Don't wait around for me. And don't worry about me. I know you are and I feel guilty and I . . . I just don't want you to, all right?"

No. Not all right. I will my voice to be angry, not sad. "You *told* me to help you wake up and I did and I made coffee and you still didn't get *up*."

"I know. I know. I *promise* you that you don't have to do it anymore. You don't have to get me up or make coffee or pack my food for the day," she says. "You don't have to help me work, and you don't have to wait up."

"But . . ." The panic is a hot spot on top of my head, even though my hair is still wet. The heat oozes down my face and the back of my neck, and I can't hide anymore that I'm going to cry. It's like she's telling me to give up on having what we always had before. Almost always. "It's too late for me to take the bus today."

"I'll write you a note."

"Mom, no." I want to grab her, hold on to her. I'm afraid she'll throw me off. Pull away. I shake my hands to keep them busy.

"Honey, Kyra, take a breath."

"And what if you don't get up? What if you keep not getting up and you miss clients again? What if—"

"That's my responsibility. Okay?"

"Stop wanting me to say 'okay'! It's not! It affects me, too!"

She holds up a hand and closes her eyes. The blanket slides off one shoulder. "Kyra." Her face crumples, and now we're both crying. "I know."

"Mom . . ." I plead through tears. I don't know what I'm pleading for. I don't want to have to know. I want *her* to know.

She opens her eyes. Hers are gray-blue and rimmed with red and spilling over with tears. I have my dad's hazel eyes, she says. I wonder if it would be better if he were here, if things had worked out so that he'd always been here. Or if I had a sister or brother. All I know is I don't want to be alone, and I don't want to ask her if she's drinking because her lying to me right now would feel lonelier than her not saying anything.

"I promise," she says, "I promise I'll do better. I swear it." She picks up the mug I warmed up for her, dumps out the tap water, and pours herself coffee. "Let me write you that note."

All day at school, I feel on the edge of that same panic I felt in the kitchen.

The heat creeps over my head off and on, and I swing between having no thoughts or feelings and being certain I'm going to explode at the next person who talks to me.

When Lu texts me to ask how come I never wrote back to her, I say, *Forgot, sorry!*

At lunch, Till asks Lu what she wants for her birthday. "Do you have a wish list? You can send the link."

A present.

I hadn't thought about that. There's still time, but time isn't going to solve the problem of me not having money. Lu's note said I didn't have to bring anything, but I guess she probably meant foodwise. It's her birthday; I'm supposed to get a present. And she's showing us some things on her phone that she wants. This one pen case. A book. And makeup, since her mom said she can start wearing it after her birthday if she wants.

"What about guitar stuff?" I ask.

Jaymison tilts her head at Lu. "You play guitar?"

"That's cool," Abbie says.

They don't even know she plays guitar?! What do they think that thing is in her room when they go over there? That *guitar case*?

I can't take this. Before I can start screaming at them, I pick up my tray and go to the waste station to separate out my trash, recycling, and compost. I feel sorry for whatever plants have to use this sad half a fish stick for fertilizer. My container of tartar sauce slides off the tray to the floor and lands with a splat.

"Way to go, Whitney."

I whip around to see Gabe, of course. And his annoying little shadow, Juan.

"Why do you call me that?" I ask.

Juan darts his eyes to Gabe, who only smirks. Then Juan says, "Mount Whitney."

"What?"

"The highest mountain in the United States?" Gabe says.

I get it. I'm the tallest girl in school. I'm adult-sized. I'm a lot.

"*That's* why? That is so *stupid*."

Mr. Simmons, the lunch monitor no one likes, strolls over. "Everything all right here?"

Gabe points to the ground. "Whitney dropped her mayo."

"It's tartar sauce!" I scream it into his dumb face and storm out of the cafeteria.

26

I walk home instead of taking the bus. It's a long walk, but I can't deal with the stuffy bus air and being jostled by people I don't like.

To help it go by faster and to keep worries out of my head, I think as many of the affirmations from group as I can remember.

It's okay to not know everything. I know enough, just for today.

It's okay to feel angry.

It's okay to cry.

It's okay to dream and have hope. That's the one Gene likes.

But it's hard to dream and have hope when your best friend has new best friends who don't even *know* her, and your mom might be relapsing but you're afraid to ask, and the one person you mostly want to talk to is the same one with all those new best friends.

What could I have hope about? What could I dream? I'll think of what dreams I have until I get to the stop sign at the end of the block.

Having a car someday so I can drive myself to school and back.

Getting a job in a restaurant that has one of those giant mixers you can make a hundred pounds of pizza dough in. Or saving up and buying my own stand mixer for home.

Going to Tahoe again and maybe taking a friend with us? Maybe Lu would want to come. She said she still likes it when it's just us, and I know she'd love Adventure Mountain. She could play her guitar by the fireplace while Mom does dishes from whatever I cooked. Except the Mom that could do that, that would do that, is the one that's missing.

But I'm not supposed to worry about that.

I think up more dreams and hopes:

Mom and Grandma working out their problems and Grandma not being so judgmental so that I could have a grandmother I get to go visit or who could come see us on holidays. Mom doing a DNA test and discovering she has a brother who can't wait to meet her, and then he's my uncle and we could visit *him* on holidays, or maybe he already lives right here. Maybe he's a popular chef in San Francisco and he saves me a special table one night a week and makes me whatever I want, for free. Me getting a DNA test and finding out *I* have a brother. Or a sister. Or a bunch of aunts. Maybe they're rich. Maybe they could loan or give Mom money to expand her business and hire help. . . .

I realize I passed the stop sign two blocks ago, and my dreams are turning into little-kid fantasies of things that deep down I know won't happen. That's not what the affirmation means.

The affirmation means I can hope that things will get better, even in simple ways. I can dream of a life for myself where not all my thoughts are about Mom.

Worrying seems easier than that kind of hope.

When I finally get home, I'm hungry and tired and sweaty even though it's still January-cold out today. Mom's car is gone, and her dot is in San Bruno. I text her that I'm home, and drop my bag before going to the fridge for a snack. The *Practice an Attitude of Gratitude* magnet has slipped down, and part of the vinyl is peeling off the magnetic part.

I grab an orange out of the produce drawer, where I keep them because I like cold oranges. But when I dig my fingernails in to peel it, the nail of my index finger bends back. I shriek and drop the orange. It's the worst feeling—not exactly pain, but it gives me bad shivers and makes me want to cry anyway.

When I bend down to pick up the orange, I see crumbs and dust and a coffee stain on the floor. I swept it last night after dinner, but I haven't been doing a good enough job cleaning since the holidays. I stand up and look around and all I can see is what's wrong. Like where the paint is bubbling on the wall near the stove and how one cupboard door never stays closed because the hinge is coming off and we can't find the right kind of screw for it.

My fingernail feels funny and there's grime on the floor and everything is broken or peeling or dirty and I feel suddenly hot again like I did this morning, and tingly on the top of my head. Like if I don't get out of here, I might sweep my arm over the counter so that all the dirty dishes there crash to the floor. I might scream or rip my fingernail off or something worse.

I walk back outside and go fast.

"It's okay," I say, even though I don't know if it is. Every affirmation starts with those two words. I chant them while I walk. "It's okay. It's okay." I say it with every step until I cross the highway and walk down onto the beach.

The water is flat and gray. There's no sharp horizon today; the ocean just dissolves into the sky.

I sit there for the longest time, letting the air cool me, letting my hands open and close on the sand. When I don't feel like screaming anymore, I say to the ocean, like a prayer, "I want it to be okay. I just want it to be okay."

If Mom *is* drinking again. If. If the worst thing is true, and it's happening and I knew *for sure* for sure, what would I do? I haven't let myself think this far ahead, but I have to.

I would tell Steve. Lu, also, but Steve is a grown-up who knows her and cares about us. I promise myself that if it's really really really happening, that's what I'll do.

The waves keep going in and out.

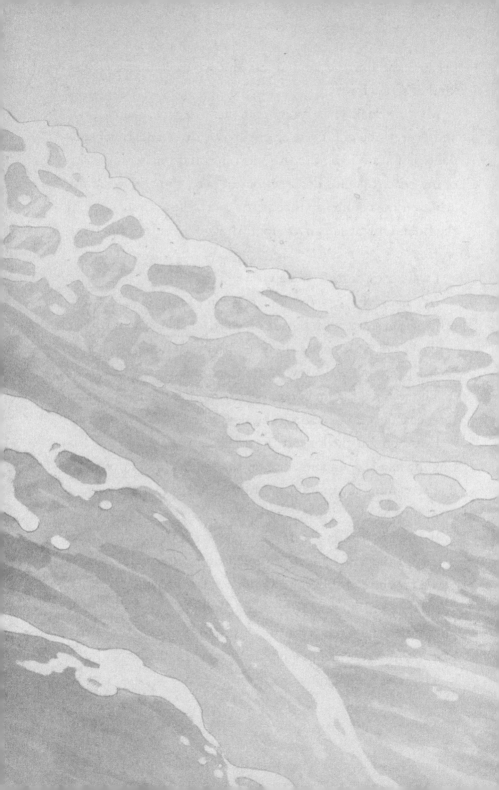

PART IV: FEBRUARY

One Day at a Time

27

It occurs to me, when Lu and Casey pick me up on Saturday, that Lu never wears the pink bandanna to group.

Is she not wearing it because she doesn't want to hurt my feelings even more, or because maybe it's a secret from Casey, or maybe a rule of Pink Bandanna Club is don't wear it when you're not at school?

I don't care. I'm just happy to finally have group again.

We stop to pick up Owen. He lives up one of the steep hills in the back of the valley where the big houses are, but he's not waiting in front of a house, he's waiting on a corner with his hands jammed in his pockets and his hoodie up.

He has to squish into one of the small seats behind us in Steve's truck.

"Hey," he says, once he's buckled in. His voice is right behind my head, close enough to feel his breath. That grosses me out a little; I lean forward.

"Which house is yours?" I ask, turning toward him slightly.

"Um, it's up on Everglades." He hesitates for a couple of seconds before adding, "My parents don't know I go to this. I just tell them I'm hanging out at my friend Jack's."

"Oh."

"Yeah," Owen says. "My dad's not exactly to AA step one yet. He might never be."

Step one is admitting you have a problem—that you're powerless over alcohol or the alcoholic. For some people it's the hardest step. Maybe that's the one both me and Mom need to go back to.

Gene bought a new, bigger space heater for the basement and set up our chairs more toward the corner since this heater's cord isn't very long and can't reach the outlet otherwise.

"I don't know about you guys, but I'm tired of freezing my butt off, and that little one wasn't cutting it," he says. "I almost bought a bunch of gloves at the dollar store to pass out."

I hold my hands out to the space heater, like it's the crackling fire we had at Tahoe. "It's not that bad."

"You're young and resilient."

It's the usual people—Gene plus the four of us that came together in Steve's truck. I take the meeting binder out of the box, the laminated cards, the brochures we don't need.

"How come we never get new people?" Owen asks, walking over to the box with his hands in his pockets.

"Sometimes we do," Gene says. "You were new not that long ago. How'd you find us?"

"I Googled. There was this one day I thought I might actually kill my dad and I just looked up every possible phrase that might help me, and I found this group. How come you don't advertise?"

Gene rubs his hands together near the heater. "Well, twelve-step groups like this are traditionally based on the idea that people who want help bad enough will find us. We don't market ourselves."

"What if they don't, though?" Lu asks. "Find us?"

"Twelfth step," Casey says, and grabs the meeting binder. "We better get started."

The twelfth step says something about carrying the message to others who need it.

"I think we should have a big billboard on the highway," Owen says. "I don't think people know how much better it feels to just talk about the one thing you're not supposed to talk about."

"Yeah, maybe you're right about the advertising," Gene says. "Like you said, the sharing is powerful. One of the rules of alcoholic families and all kinds of other dysfunction is 'don't talk, don't trust, don't feel,' right? Talking to each other in a safe place sure helps us do the other two."

"Speaking of sharing," Casey says, "since it's been so long since we met, maybe we could skip over the opening and stuff? I know we're not supposed to, but it's just us, and we need to catch up."

Gene scratches his face. "Well, one of the reasons this is a safe place is because we have these rules. Even if they seem silly, they never change. It might be the one thing in our lives that doesn't."

"Yeah," I say. "I like the rules." Knowing exactly what to expect is what I need right now.

Casey sighs, and we do the opening readings just like we're supposed to. Then Casey shares first.

"My dad just hit thirty days of sobriety," she says. "After he was drunk at Christmas, he quit again. And, like, I'm happy about it, I guess? But I still feel like . . . I don't really know him or like him, and he hasn't been a dad for years, and now that he's gotten one *month* of sobriety, I'm supposed to be all into a relationship. That's what I think he thinks. Meanwhile, I'm used to not having a dad. I don't call my stepdad 'Dad,' and I don't feel like I want or need a dad at this point. I barely even care about it anymore. Now I'm expected to celebrate every day he adds onto his sobriety and . . ." She rakes her hand through her dark hair. "Frankly, I don't give a damn."

Owen snickers.

I wonder what Lu is thinking. She hasn't talked to me about her dad since Christmas. I didn't know he had *any* sobriety.

"That's all," Casey says. "Thanks for listening."

"Thank you, Casey. You were heard."

Then Lu goes. "Sometimes after Casey shares I don't even know what to say because she's better than me at describing it, but also I might not agree with her. I think thirty days is good." She shrugs. "I'd rather he have thirty days than none."

181

I wish you'd told me, I think. *Even though we didn't have group, you could have told me*. We don't have to be *so* alone in this.

"Hi, I'm Kyra," I say. "My mom . . . I don't know what's going on, but she's having a hard time. I've been trying to 'Live and Let Live.' It feels lonely. I know we're not supposed to try to fix people or monitor everything they're doing, but it's only me and my mom. When I'm 'letting live,' I hardly see her, and I worry. But I'm supposed to 'live' like I'm not worrying?" I say this last part to Lu. Maybe she'll ask me about it later. "Anyway," I continue, "I'm trying, but it's hard right now. I know we're supposed to focus on ourselves . . ."

I can't hold it in anymore. It's too much for me to be thinking about all by myself.

"But I don't think my mom has been talking to her sponsor or going to her meetings. She's missing work." I can't look at them. My eyes are on my hands. "And I don't have enough friends. Or family. It's a lot to carry. More than other people have, it feels like. And I'm just . . ." My chin quivers and I feel my mouth tug into wavy, dangerous shapes. "I know we talk about how we can be okay whether the alcoholic is drinking or not, but I don't want that. I want her to never drink again. And I'm sad right now." I reach for the tissue box on the floor. "That's all."

"Thank you, Kyra." Gene's voice breaks; he clears his throat. "You were heard."

After we say the words of serenity and the meeting is officially over, Casey comes over to me. "Can I give you a hug?" she asks.

182

I nod. She wraps both arms around me, and I cry some more.

"It's okay," Lu's small voice says, her hand on my arm.

Then Owen says, "Group hug? Okay?"

"Yeah," I say. Then his arms, skinnier and longer than Casey's, are around me, too.

I feel a big, warm hand on my head. That's Gene.

"It'll get better," he says in his gruff voice.

"When?"

"I wish I could tell you," he says, "but that's not something any of us can know."

In the truck on the way home, I'm in the middle front, and Owen is next to me since he needs to be dropped off first, and Lu is in the jump seat behind.

She says, "I know what happens in the room stays in the room, but how come you didn't tell me about your mom? Is she going to be okay?"

I explode with, "How come *you* didn't tell me about your dad? Thirty days is a big deal."

"Guys . . ." Casey says.

Owen leans over and says to her, "Let 'em talk."

I turn as much as I can from my middle seat. "Do your new friends know about him yet? Did you tell them about group? Did you tell them I'm in it?"

"No!" she yells back at me. "I told Till a little bit. I told her I go to a group that helps."

"And me? What did you say about me?"

There's a very long pause, and I know she told. Even though every single week we read from a card talking about how important confidentiality is—what we talk about, and *who* is there.

"I think I mentioned it. Like when she asked how we became friends. I don't talk about your mom or any details or anything."

Casey groans. "Lu. You shouldn't do that."

"Sorry! Kyra's so open about things I didn't think she'd care!"

"I'm open with people I *know*. I don't like Till knowing this big thing about me when I know nothing about her! She barely talks. She speaks in two-word sentences."

Owen laughs a little, covering his mouth. "Dang, I forgot about middle school drama."

Lu's hands are on my shoulders. "Don't be mad. I don't talk about you like that. Like it's bad. I tell them you're like family."

"Aw," Owen says.

Casey shoots him a look, and asks me, "So what do you think is going on with your mom?"

I'm still thinking about what Lu just said, and what I might feel about it. Is it better or worse to be like family instead of friends?

"I don't know," I say. "But it's not good."

"Do you want to talk to Steve about it? Do you want us to?"

"No! No." Mom feels like he's been rescuing her since she was fifteen. And if he hasn't noticed anything himself, I'm not

184

going to say it, either, unless I know *for sure* for sure.

"Okay," Casey says. "But you know you could."

"I know."

Mom is up watching TV when I get home, sipping from a mug with a tea bag hanging in it. Since she doesn't ask, *How was group?* I say, "Group was really good." I pause. "Did you finish work in time to go to yours?"

Her eyes stay on the TV. "Unfortunately, no."

"Don't you miss it?" I don't exactly know how long it's been, but whatever it is, it's too long.

She turns to me, and I think she's going to snap, *Live and let live*, again, but instead she says, "Not that much. Maybe I've been kind of burned out on that whole thing."

That whole thing? The whole meetings-and-journals-and-talking-about-it thing? Or the whole not-drinking thing?

"Hey," she adds, "I got a couple of voice mails from your teachers saying you've got some makeup work to do."

Yeah, because I've been distracted and also missing classes to help you!

"Maybe *I'm* kind of burned out," I say, and get up to go to my room.

28

On Monday, I skip school to help Mom again.

It's not supposed to happen. I'm supposed to be worrying about only myself, not her, and *she's* supposed to be the one dealing with her stuff, not me. I'm supposed to not help her with work anymore or miss any more school, and she *knows* I'm falling behind.

But there's a crisis.

She forgot she agreed to do two vacation rentals by the airport before one p.m., and it's a big client who has a lot of rentals in the area and gives her a lot of work and who also has high standards. She can't let this client down, and that's a lot to get done in that time, even for both of us.

She calls school to tell them I'm sick.

"I know," she says into the phone. "It's that time of year!"

She listens. "No, no fever. Just kind of blah. Mm-hmm. Great. Okay. Thank you! I'll tell her."

She sounds so normal and cheerful.

"Tell me what?" I ask when she's done.

"Mr. Aranda hopes you feel better soon."

On the drive to South San Francisco, I keep thinking about her phone call to school. It's hard not to remember, again, what Gene said—that addicts are great liars. And there are so many things every day she could be lying to me about. If she lies as well to me as she just did to school, I'd never know.

The rentals are bland beige cubes in an apartment community. Beige carpets, tan curtains, oatmeal upholstery. When Mom comes out of the bathroom with her long gloves on and a scrubber brush, I say, "How many different words are there for 'blah'?"

"What, honey?"

"Everything in here is beige or white."

She snaps her gloves off. "Did you get behind the coffee-maker?"

"Yes."

"The load of towels should be ready for the dryer."

I go to the hall closet, where there's a stackable washer and dryer, and move the towels. They're all beige and white, too. Sand. Taupe. While those are drying, I dust and Mom mops the kitchen and bathroom.

If this were a few months ago, she would have played the game with me of finding all the words for "blah." When am I supposed to give up waiting for her to become herself again? Gene says we don't know when things will get better, but he seemed confident they will. And I guess Mom isn't as bad today as she has been. She doesn't look as tired, doesn't look as lost. I almost feel guilty for letting the word "relapse" into my brain.

We finish the first unit, and walk down a corridor to do the next one. When Mom uses the code to open the door, she swears, says, "Sorry!" and closes it again. "Come on," she says to me, and we start toward the parking lot. "There are still guests in there. They were supposed to be gone hours ago."

I sit in the car while she calls the property manager's office. It's cold and gray today, and we're on the bay side of the peninsula so we don't get to see the ocean.

"The property manager is going to deal with it," Mom says as she gets into the car. "She'll let me know when they're gone." She rests her hands on the wheel and her head on her hands. "I'm sorry. You shouldn't have missed school for this. I'm really doing an amazing job being a parent."

"It's okay."

"No," she says, shaking her head, "it isn't."

I agree with her, but also it *is* okay and it's just today and we don't need to blow it all up. "I know," I say. "But it also is. Life can be not okay and also okay at the same time."

She lifts her head and looks at me with an uncertain smile. "You've noticed that, too?"

In this moment—*this* moment—I think I could ask her if she's drinking and she would tell me. I form the question and take a breath.

She says, "Hey, do you want to go to the airport? Like we were going to do at Thanksgiving? It's so close."

I let the breath out. "Yeah."

It only takes us a few minutes to drive to the terminal; longer to park and walk in.

"You won't be able to see much on this side of the security gates," Mom says, "but maybe you can kind of get the idea."

I know I'm too old to be nervous about getting on an escalator, but I get stuck watching the steps move past and can't pick one to get on. Mom wiggles her hand at me; I take it and step up with her. At the top, she lets go of my hand and walks me to a big directory so I can see where we are and where everything else is.

"When Lu took her trip at Thanksgiving, there was this other girl from school on the same flight." I trace the terminal map with my finger, wondering where she was when that happened. "They're, like, best friends now."

Mom puts her hand on my back. "I've never liked the word 'best' or 'favorite' to describe relationships," she says. "No one person can be everything. We all need enough people who are each good at being a friend in their own way. No one has to be the best."

It's the most we've talked in a long time about anything important, or the most we've talked about anything important in *my* life, not hers.

"Well, I don't have enough people." I walk around to the other side of the directory, where it has lists of restaurants and shops.

Mom follows and reads the directory with me. "A lot has changed since I was here last."

"I need to get Lu a birthday present."

"Right," Mom says softly. "Is that this weekend?"

"Yeah."

"Do you know what you want to get her?"

"No. I don't know. She has a whole list, but—"

The ringing of Mom's phone cuts me off. She answers it, says, "Mm-hmm. Okay. Will do." After she ends the call she tells me, "The apartment is ready. And based on what I saw when I got a peek earlier, we should be prepared for a mess."

There's stuff everywhere. Pizza boxes on the bed, blankets and pillows on the floor, recycling container overflowing with wine and beer bottles, and lots of dirty dishes and almost-empty takeout containers. Mom won't even let me look in the bathroom.

"They're going to pay a bonus," she says, "because we need to do this super fast and get it right."

Before I put on gloves to start with the dishes, I check my phone in case Lu's wondering where I am. There are no notifications.

29

A few days before the party, I still haven't gotten Lu a present.

I didn't want to bring it up with Mom again. I've barely seen her since Monday, anyway. I thought we had a pretty good day, but now it seems like she's avoiding me. She's pretended we never had the conversation about meetings and my homework. If she wants to pretend, I can pretend, too.

I eat with the Pink Bandanna Club and act as excited about Lu's party as they are. Jaymison still sometimes seems like she's playing a game only she knows about, where the goal is to not think about me existing. I do like Abbie, though. She seems more independent and rolls her eyes a lot at Jaymison.

I have about twenty-three dollars in my sock drawer. I don't want to use it on a present, in case we need groceries or I need a bus card or have some other emergency. Even if I did want to spend it, there's nowhere around here to shop for anything good. I'd need to take a bus somewhere farther away.

While daydreaming in Mr. Ocampo's class about one day having my own catering business—I could start it with some of Mom's cleaning contacts, and then she could get clients from *my* catering contacts—I imagine what I'd do if I were hosting the cookout instead of Steve. For Jaymison, I'd make three-bean salad and bean dip and white bean chili. Everything would have beans. I'd also do a cookie bar. There'd be a basic cookie dough and then people could add their own mix-ins and toppings, and then I'd bake them all together. There are a lot of things you could do like that. Pizza bar. Baked potato bar. Taco bar. Sundae bar.

Toward the end of class, Mr. Ocampo passes back our papers on the Ohlone. He looks at me over the top of his glasses when he hands me mine and bends down to whisper, "What happened? You can do much better."

"Sorry."

His note on the bottom of the first page just says, *Sloppy!*

I turn it face down. All my grades are bad right now, and I don't want to think about it. So I go back to thinking about my imaginary cookout menu. And I realize I could make cookies for Lu. That could be my present. I think I have all the ingredients for her favorite—salted caramel chocolate chip. Or at least they used to be her favorite. Anyway, "favorite" doesn't matter, like Mom said. As long as they're good. I can do that and put them in a nice cookie tin.

When I get home from school, there's a note from Mom:

Babe—I'm doing a move-out job this afternoon that will probably go into the evening. Don't worry about me and don't wait up. I'll see you when I get home.

xo Mom

A move-out job is what it sounds like. Someone has moved out of a house or apartment, and Mom cleans it all out until it looks like new again, or good enough for someone else to move in. It's hard because it means washing walls and inside cupboards and sometimes the way people leave their fridge or oven is disgusting. But it's also kind of fun because there're no furniture or knickknacks in the way. And it pays more than a regular cleaning.

I can catch up on my homework. I lay it out on the kitchen table and check online for which assignments I should focus on. Then I move it to my desk because my room is cleaner. Then I think I'll do it on the couch with the TV on because otherwise it feels too lonely. Then I get distracted by a baking show and decide I should make Lu's cookies now because the kitchen is all mine for hours, and I can put them in the freezer when they're cool. The morning of the party, I'll take them out and they'll be just like fresh.

The easy way to make these cookies is with store-bought salted caramel, but we don't have any, and making it yourself is cheap. Caramel is just sugar, butter, and cream. And for salted caramel, salt. All things we have on hand.

I clean up first. That's how real chefs do it: they start with a clean kitchen and keep a tidy work area. Also, they lay out all the ingredients instead of taking them out as they go. You don't want to find out halfway through a recipe you don't have everything you need.

I wish life could be like that. With a tidy system and a way to make sure you have what you need for any given situation and a clean area before and after.

As I put everything out for the cookies—flour, sugar, eggs, baking powder, baking soda, butter—I try to imagine how it will feel to be at the party with Lu's new friends there, too. In a way, Steve's house is *my* territory, and them coming is an invasion. Of course, they've already been there. With their own vibe. Are they going to wear their pink bandannas? Will Mom notice I'm not wearing one and ask me about it? Maybe I could find a bandanna like that at Walgreen's. And just wear it and see if they say anything.

The butter and eggs for the cookies come to room temperature while I make the salted caramel. Some will go into the cookies; some gets drizzled on top. This is the second time I've made this recipe. I find the video that I used before, and prop my phone up on the kitchen counter to review the steps.

While I'm watching, a thought comes into my head, uninvited and out of nowhere.

Mom's note could be a lie.

Addicts are great liars.

Maybe she doesn't really have a clean-out. Maybe she's just

saying that so she has an excuse to not come home or not go to a meeting or whatever else she is trying to avoid. Like home. And me.

I know from group that we can't spend our lives watching to make sure our parents don't drink, or wondering if they are, because we have no control over that anyway and we're only making ourselves unhappy when we try to control the things we can't. It's so hard not to, though, when it affects you.

I'm not paying attention to the recipe. I jump back twenty seconds to see what I missed. With this recipe, you don't need a candy thermometer, you just watch the color. Also you have to stir constantly while the sugar melts and goes from clear to amber.

Once I remind myself how caramel works and start making mine, thoughts about Mom slip in again. I think about my plan, how if I know *for sure* for sure, I'll tell Steve. Maybe I shouldn't wait until I have proof. I know feelings aren't facts, but they also aren't nothing, and when a gut feeling doesn't go away, you listen to it.

When the melted sugar seems to be about the right color, I add the butter. Then I remember the video said to be extra careful with this step because it could bubble up. The second I remember is a second too late. The butter bubbles over and splatters onto the stove and droplets of hot caramel hit the hand I'm stirring with.

I yank my hand back reflexively. The pan tips over and boiling-hot caramel spills near my left foot and splashes up onto the skin showing between the hem of my jeans and the tops of my sneakers.

After I yell out, my mind goes completely blank and my vision blurs from the pain. When I come back to reality, I'm on the kitchen floor and my left shoe is off and I'm rubbing at my ankle furiously to get the caramel off, which is still hot.

I've had burns before, and I know I'm supposed to try to cool it immediately. But those were always little ones, like accidentally touching a hot pan for a second, or brushing the top of my hand near the broiler. Those I could hold under running water; this one I need to submerge. I crawl to the sink and pull the dishpan out from underneath, stand up, and fill it with cold tap water.

I'm going too fast when I try to move the full dishpan to the floor. It spills.

I fill it again, take off my shoe and sock, and put my foot in, sinking down to the floor. I also dip in the hand that got splattered. After a second, I realize the gas burner is still on; I reach over and turn it off.

The skin is turning red everywhere that caramel touched me but especially around the front of my ankle. When I put my fingers on the burn, I can feel it's still hot, even in the cold water, and the skin is already starting to bubble. That's when I cry.

The burn hurts so much. That's not it, though. I mean, it's part of it.

The rest is everything else. How Mom should be here. How I'm scared about *why* she isn't here. How I shouldn't be alone so much. How Lu should be a better friend. How I want a dad. How I want more than an ocean and a once-a-week group to rely on when everything is such a mess.

I could list more things and cry harder, but I have to think.

I don't know if I should call 911. When I was nine, I twisted my ankle while I was home alone jumping from the couch to the armchair and back again, which I wasn't supposed to do. It swelled so fast that I thought I broke it, and I couldn't reach Mom, so I called 911, and firemen came. Later, I found out we got a big bill because they treated me with a splint, and also Mom got a visit from Child Protective Services to make sure I wasn't getting neglected.

We can't afford that kind of a big bill right now. We can *never* afford a big bill. And I don't want Mom getting in trouble when we already have enough to worry over.

But my skin is still burning in a way that feels deep and painful.

I take my foot out of the water long enough to get my phone off the counter, then I put my foot back in the water and hold the phone in both hands.

I know I have to call her. But the thing in my gut that's been telling me something's wrong is telling me now that she won't be there. That she hasn't been there for me to rely on. We haven't been a team. We're not Kiki Krash and Meg the Marauder. I'm just Kyra, over here on the floor by myself, and she's only Meg, and she's given up.

I tap her star in my favorites and close my eyes.

It goes straight to voice mail and says her inbox is full.

197

I throw the phone across the kitchen and start crying again, and cry some more while I crawl back over to it.

Lu's house. They still have the landline Steve's parents had in the house back when they lived there. Someone has to be home, and I don't want to sit here calling four different cell numbers.

Casey answers. As soon as I hear her voice, I start crying harder.

"Who is this?" she asks.

"Kyra."

"What's wrong? What happened?"

I manage to say, "I need help," through my sobs. "Is Steve there? Or your mom?"

"They took Lu to Serramonte to get something for her birthday. What happened?" she asks again. "Do you need me to come over? My mom's car is here."

I'm thinking *Yes, come over*, and also *No, get a real grown-up*, and also, *Just be here now already*. But I can't get any of the words out.

"I'm coming over," Casey says. "I'll be there in five minutes."

I sink to the floor and sit with my foot and hand in the water, shivering and crying, going back over and over in my head to the moment before I put the butter in when I was supposed to be careful. The recipe says *be careful*. It plays in my head like a video loop, over and over, like if I think about it enough I can somehow go back in time and not make a mistake and not have to call Mom and not get her voice mail and not call Lu's house and make her sister come over to help me because I screwed up something I should know how to do. It's like what Mom said about her history with Steve: her being desperate, him saving her. Now I'm adding to that history.

Casey gets here fast and knocks hard on the door.

When I let her in, she looks all around the living room like she's searching for something. "Where is she?"

". . . she?" I ask through a sob of relief that I'm not alone anymore.

"Your mom."

"She's not here."

"So it's not about your mom?" Casey asks, confused. "I thought . . ."

"I burned myself." I point down to my ankle.

She swears and kneels down. "What did you do?" She touches the burn and I jerk my foot back. "It's blistering," she says.

I know.

I go back to the kitchen to the pan of cool water. Casey follows and sees the spilled caramel and my cookie ingredients. I stare at the white skin separating and pulling away from the red part. It makes me want to throw up, so I make myself look at Casey's boots and how they're leaving black scuffs on our kitchen floor along with the rest of the mess I made.

"Did you call your mom?"

"It went to voice mail."

She crouches next to me and puts her hand on my back. "I thought maybe she was here and passed out or something."

"She has a big clean-out job today. It pays extra. She prob-ably let her phone die. I didn't remind her about her charger this morning."

"That's not your job."

"It is, though." The heat in the burned part of my skin is finally fading. "I think I'll be okay." There's first-aid cream in the bathroom drawer. I can use that and maybe a bandage.

"No, Keek. This is bad. The burn could get infected or something." She sits down on her butt and we're both leaning against the kitchen cupboards. Now I stare at her hand on her leg to avoid looking at my puckering skin—the pewter rings she always wears, the thread bracelets, only her pinkie nail painted black. "Are you scared you'll get in trouble?" she asks.

"It says in the recipe to be careful, and I wasn't."

"You made a mistake. You're allowed to make mistakes."

I glance up at the fridge. We have a magnet for that.

"What if I'd started a fire and the house had burned down?" I say. "Where would we live? We'd be homeless."

"Well, you didn't. And if you did, you could live with us." She stands up. "Where's your phone? Let's try your mom one more time."

I get it out of my back pocket. Now that my foot is hurting less, I start to feel the burns on my hand more. I examine it and see tiny versions of the blister on my ankle bubbling up. "I was making cookies for Lu's birthday because I can't buy her something right now. Now I won't have anything, and the Pink Bandanna Club will have one more reason to think I'm . . . whatever they think about me."

Casey laughs. "Is *that* what they're calling themselves?"

"No. I just call them that in my head."

"Don't worry about what they think."

I hand her my phone. I can't hear Mom's cheery voice-mail message again. "Her number is in my favorites."

Casey makes the call. It goes to voice mail again. "I'm sending a text, just in case."

When she hands me back my phone, I check for Mom's dot just in case she has her phone on do not disturb. It searches and searches and then says, "Location not found."

Casey looks down at me and the caramel sauce—now cold and sticky—splattered all over the floor, and says, "I'm going to clean this up, and if your mom doesn't call back by the time I'm done, you're coming with me."

30

Right as Casey parks in front of their house, Steve's truck pulls up, too. It's getting dark out, but I can see Lu sitting between him and her mom.

"Stay here," Casey tells me. "I'll go explain what's going on. My mom might want to just take you straight to the doctor."

I stay. I've got a wet towel wrapped around my hand where I got splattered, and another one around my ankle. It's kind of rough, though, and whenever I move even a little bit, it hurts. My mom hasn't called or texted; her dot has not shown up.

Steve gets out of the truck while Casey talks to her mom and comes over to the car, Lu following behind. What I don't want is to cry any more in front of them. I can't stop it, though, when Steve opens the door and leans into the car and says, "Hey, Keek. You doing okay?"

"Yeah," I say through my tears, even though I'm not doing okay and even though I'm clutching at his jacket and pressing my forehead into his chest.

He cups his hands around my ears and smooths my hair down.

"What happened?" Lu asks from behind him.

I don't want to say I was making cookies for her. And that I can't reach my mom. I don't want to say anything. I want to go back in time to before it happened. By now I'd be cooling the cookies on the counter and getting the kitchen back to perfect, and planning what to make for dinner.

"Can I see your foot?" Steve asks me.

I nod and move so I'm kind of sitting sideways in the passenger seat with my good foot on the ground and the other one crossed over my knee. I carefully take the towel off the burn. "It hurts a lot less now except when the towel brushes it. I put it in cold water right after."

"Good." He takes my wrist and looks at all the tiny blisters on my hand. "How about these?"

"Mostly they sting."

Even though I keep my eyes on my ankle, I can tell Lu is staring. Or it feels like she's staring. I'm embarrassed and feel like a problem—the one who always needs more than anyone else does, and I can't help it, and I don't know why. More patience and more kindness and more attention and more help.

When Steve goes back the truck, I say to Lu's feet, "What did you get at Serramonte?"

She pauses as if it's a silly thing to be asking right now, but then she answers. "Some stuff at Cost Plus. To redo my room."

"Oh."

She's been talking for a long time about getting the old flowered wallpaper down. We were going to do it together, and paint the walls. Now she's probably doing it with Till.

Then Lu's mom is standing there, too, with her arm around Lu. She asks me how I am and I say fine and this time I don't cry.

"Well, I think you probably *are* fine," she says, "but I'm going to run you over to the urgent care clinic just to make sure we've got everything we need to keep it from getting infected. I don't feel okay about making a decision not to take you just because we can't get ahold of your mom, okay?"

Then I do want to cry again. I nod.

"Can I come, too?" Lu asks.

Her mom thinks for a long few seconds, then says it's okay with her if it's okay with me. I nod.

Pacifica doesn't have an urgent care clinic, so we have to drive over the hill into San Bruno. Sharp Park Road winds like a snake; I tend to get queasy. Barfing in Lu's mom's car would make everything that's already bad so much worse. I keep my eyes on the road ahead with Lu in the backseat.

She asks me again what happened.

"I was making salted caramel." *For your birthday*. "It splattered, and then I spilled it."

"Do you always do those kinds of cooking projects when

you're home alone?" Lu's mom asks.

What does she mean? I cook breakfast and dinner for us almost every day. Is that a "project"? "Sometimes."

"And that's okay with your mom?"

"I'm thirteen," I mutter to the window. My breath makes a foggy patch on the glass. Steve's the one who taught me safety tips for chopping and using the stovetop and keeping my hands and surfaces clean. Lu's mom should know by now that I know what I'm doing.

"Oh, I know you are, honey," she says. "But caramel is so tricky. You have to be—"

"Everyone makes mistakes, Mom," Lu says, interrupting. She puts her hand on my shoulder for the rest of the ride.

The clinic takes forever, and there's a whole thing about "pending parental consent" that my mom will have to sign later.

The good thing is that the doctor says I did everything right, and because of that it should be a lot better in a few days even though it's a medium second-degree burn. I'm supposed to keep it loosely wrapped, and she gives me some cream to put on it to help with the healing.

"Elevate your leg a little tonight while you're sleeping. Just put a couple of nice fluffy pillows under your ankle, and that should help with any inflammation." She pats my knee and says, "You know you can buy caramel in jars."

It makes me so mad that she says that. Of course I know you can buy caramel in jars! Doesn't she think I would do things the easier way if I had that option? My life is not that simple! It's like what Grandma said to Mom a long time ago when she first started going to meetings and calling her sponsor every day. "Why don't you just not drink?"

I'm too tired and hungry and know I can't scream, *You don't get it!* at a doctor, so I say, "I know," and clamp my lips together.

By the time we leave, all of us are starving. Lu's mom takes us to Five Guys on the way home and we eat it in the car. Between bites, I check my phone.

The thing is, she would never let her phone die on the job. If she forgot her charger, she'd come back for it. All her work information—the job addresses, the key codes, each client's specific instructions—it's all on her phone.

Which means she turned her phone off, or put it on do not disturb *and* turned off her location. The only reason she'd do that is if she didn't want to be reached.

And I know my gut is right. If things were normal or just a little off, she would have called by now. She would say, *Baby, are you okay?!* Her dot would be speeding home. And she'd be waiting for me at Lu's house to take me back to our house and she'd let me sleep in her bed with her and she'd make sure my foot was propped up all night.

But things aren't normal. I know that. I've known it. Now I know that things are way more not-normal than I thought. I finish my food and try not to think of all the worst-case scenarios of where she might be and what she might be doing.

31

Steve is waiting in the living room, and I can see from his face that he knows more than he knew when we left. He and Lu's mom exchange a glance that must be some kind of secret language, because Lu's mom steers her toward her room and says, "Let's get ready for bed," and then they're gone.

"How's the foot?" he asks me.

"The stuff the doctor put on it stings some, but it'll be all right."

"Good." He gestures to the couch. "Let's sit and talk for a minute."

My stomach hurts as he sits in the armchair and I sit on the edge of the couch closest to him. I'm still stuck in a loop of: If I hadn't messed up the caramel, this wouldn't be happening. I'd be home, brushing my teeth and putting on pj's. Mom would come home and it wouldn't matter where she'd been or if she'd lied.

"You know I've known your mom forever," he says. "Since we were kids."

"I know."

"I remember her folks—your grandparents."

I know that, too. He's told me before what he can remember about them. My grandpa drank like my mom, and he died from it. My grandma got mad when *her* mom gave *my* mom the house. My mom was single and pregnant and a little older than a lot of people are when they're single and pregnant, but lived like she was still in her twenties, and the house changed everything for her, for us. But instead of seeing it as the best thing that could happen for Mom, Grandma saw it as the worst thing to happen to *her*. Neither her nor my mom's dad were good at being parents.

"One thing I can tell you about your mom," Steve says now, scratching at one of his sideburns, "is that she loves you more than anything in the world."

I nod. I know she loves me. And I know she's better at being a parent than hers were. Before he can say whatever he's trying to, I tell him, "She hasn't been going to meetings, I don't think. Or talking to Antonia. I think . . ." I still don't want to say it aloud. "I don't think she's doing too well. I think . . ." I look at him.

"Go ahead," he says gently.

"I think she's drinking again."

He lets out a breath and leans back in the chair. "I think you're right."

We sit there for a minute. Steve stares at the floor, and I stare at Steve, waiting.

"I did get ahold of her," he finally continues.

"You did? You got her to call back?" Why would she call Steve back but not call or text *me*?

"Well, no. I got in my truck and went looking in a few of her old spots."

Her drinking spots, he means. Even though she used to go to bars with the "party posse," she told me once that she stopped doing that because getting drunk at bars would mean she's like her dad, and she didn't want to feel like that was true. So I don't know where she goes, but I guess she had lots of little hidden places for drinking. Has.

"I found her and we talked a bit," Steve says. "Not a lot. But we decided you'll stay here the rest of the week. Then she'll be here Saturday for the party and we'll all talk and figure some things out."

Now it's my turn to stare at the floor while Steve watches me. Everything I worried about since Christmas, everything Mom told me not to worry about, everything I tried to talk myself out of thinking . . . It was all true. I was right the whole time.

"Is she okay?" I ask. "Is she going to call me?"

"Not tonight." He sighs. "And listen, Kyra, she *is* okay. At least, she can be. I've seen her much, much worse. So have you. She's been hiding it really well, which she wouldn't be able to do if she'd slid all the way back down."

I nod. "I know she's been hiding it, but also . . . did you notice anything was weird? I did. Did you?"

"No," he said. "I didn't. But we've both been busy."

"Aren't you her best friend, though?"

"I'm her oldest friend. That's a little different. But maybe I should have noticed. I don't know." He gives me a sad smile. "I can't read minds."

"Me neither."

"She'll drop off some clothes and your schoolbag first thing in the morning." He pauses. "Then she's going to call Antonia and clear her clients for a few days and go to a morning meeting."

I nod again and watch a tear splash onto my pants, leaving a little dark spot. "I think Tahoe got her depressed or something. She was busy and tired and stressed out before Christmas, but I kept telling her I wanted to go. I basically begged her to ask you for the truck. She didn't want to."

"What? You guys had a great time in Tahoe. It made her happy. I was happy to lend the truck."

"But afterward," I say, and watch the dark spot on my knee grow, "she was different. Or maybe at Thanksgiving I shouldn't have let her call Grandma. That upset her, too."

He sits forward in his chair. "You can't look for reasons or blame. You know that. Meg chooses what Meg does, no one else."

I look up. "Why, though? Why would she choose . . . to start drinking again? When she knows what it does to her? And me?"

"I don't know, Keek. I don't know it about your mom and I don't know it about Lu and Casey's dad and I don't know it about your grandpa. It pisses me off that they do that. I don't get it. But I do know that for some people it's just this real serious, difficult thing." He reaches out to touch the hand that isn't burned. "And I do know it's not your fault."

People in group, people in recovery, they're always so sure that no one can make an alcoholic drink and no one can make them stop drinking. That's what everyone says. But how can you really know? Maybe it's just something people say to try to feel better.

My foot throbs slightly; I pull away and run my hands on the fabric of the couch. "Can I sleep out here? I'm supposed to prop up my leg."

"I was thinking we could set up a camping mattress in Lu's room? So you can talk? Do you want me to do that?"

I shake my head. "No thanks."

"Do you want—"

"I just want to go to bed."

He says okay and he'll get me something to use for pajamas.

I only sleep a little bit and only off and on. The burn feels hot again and my stomach won't stop hurting and every time I think about my mom, I start to cry. Not because I'm sad. They feel more like the kind of tears I get when I can't figure out my math homework or it's been one of those days when Gabe won't leave me alone. The kind where I want to scream into my pillow.

At 3:12 a.m. I start writing a text to Mom on my phone.

Why didn't you call me when you knew I was

211

hurt??? Why didn't you even text? Did you even
really have a clean-out or were you lying? Have
you been going to your jobs at all? What's going
to happen when we don't have any money?? How
can you

I backspace it all and instead try to find an audiobook to
download from the library. Something to talk over the voices
in my head that are yelling at Mom and also at myself. When
I find a book, my phone gives me a message I'm out of data
because we're on the stupid cheap plan, so I have to get on the
Wi-Fi. But when I try that, the saved password doesn't work.
Steve or Ann must have changed it.

My thoughts get stuck in the loop again. If I hadn't hurt
myself. If I hadn't tried to make the cookies. If I had just
spent some of my money on a present for Lu. If I were cooler
and smaller and cuter instead of Mount Whitney and Lu's
new friends liked me. If I hadn't made my mom take me to
Tahoe. If my grandma wanted to know me. If my dad wanted
to know me. Why don't they want to? What did I do? What's
wrong with me?

The urge to scream is still there, but now I *do* feel sad and
I can't stand it. I hold one of the sofa pillows and curl into it
and hum to myself until I fall asleep.

32

Steve has to leave for work while it's still dark out.

Him leaving wakes me up, but I try to act still asleep while watching with one eye as he puts on his coat and gets his keys off the hook by the door. When he opens it and starts to step out, he stops for a second and bends down. Then he turns back inside and sets something down on the living room floor.

It's my schoolbag. And a canvas grocery store bag stuffed full of clothes. I can see the edge of my Adventure Mountain hat. I don't even like it anymore because it reminds me of how Mom was on the drive home from Tahoe.

Steve glances toward me before he leaves, carefully closing the door behind him.

I check my phone. There's finally a text from Mom.

I dropped your stuff off. I hope you're feeling ok. I misplaced my phone last night. Sorry for everything. See you Saturday ok?

No, I think. *Not okay*. And she didn't "misplace" her phone! She turned off her dot. She hid from me on purpose. Why is she still bothering to lie?

I write back: ok.

I use the bathroom and wonder if I'll get in anyone's way if I take a shower now. I'd better not. I fold up the blankets I used and stack them on one end of the couch. Pretty soon, I hear Lu's mom in the kitchen and smell coffee, so I go in, too.

She hears me and turns. "Hey, sweetie. How are you feeling?"

"Fine." I'm wearing one of her nightgowns that looks a lot like the one she has on, and I feel embarrassed that a whole grown-up's clothes fit me just right.

"We usually let everyone fend for themselves at breakfast, but I have a few minutes to make you something if you'd like?"

"I'm okay."

"Help yourself to anything in the fridge." She picks up her coffee and adds, "*Except* the yogurt and boiled eggs. Those are Casey's and she'll have a fit." She takes her coffee and heads back to her and Steve's room upstairs.

After what happened yesterday, I don't feel like cooking anything on the stove. I find some tortillas and cheese and make a quesadilla to heat up in the microwave. It's not as good as when you do it in a pan, but it's faster and easier.

Lu is the next one up. She blinks when she sees me and says, "I thought you were my mom for a second."

"I'm not."

This feels different from the times I've slept over for fun. It's too early and we both have to think about school. She fixes herself a bowl of cereal and sits across from me. I'm on my last few bites of quesadilla.

"Do you think I could take a shower?" I ask.

"Ummm . . ." She looks at the clock on the microwave. "Like a three-minute one if you go right now. Then Casey will be in there."

I get up, put my plate in the sink, and get a towel and wash-cloth from the hall closet where Steve has always kept them. It all takes me more than three minutes, though, because I have to unwrap the bandage on my foot and be careful when I'm drying off. I can only pat it gently and even then it hurts. There's a big, white, wrinkly patch where most of the caramel got me.

When I come out, holding the towel and nightgown in front of me and shivering, because the doctor said to use cool water only, Casey is leaning on the wall outside the door. "Sorry," I say.

"It's okay." Her morning voice is hoarse as she brushes past me. "You can use my room to dress in if you want."

The bathroom door closes before I can say thank you to her face, but I really need to say it. For yesterday and for offering me her room when it feels so hard to ask for anything more from anyone here. "Casey?"

215

"Yeah?"

"Thanks."

"Yeah," she says again, light and final, like she never even thought about not helping.

When Lu's mom drops us at school, Till and Jaymison are waiting out front with their pink bandannas tied around their ankles. Lu doesn't have hers on, but as soon as we're to the rock, she gets it out of her jacket pocket and crouches down to tie it on.

"What does that thing even mean?" I ask.

Jaymison watches us and says something to Till while looking at me.

"Nothing." She stands up and brushes off her knee. "I mean, it means, like . . . we have each other's back. Like you mess with one of us you mess with all of us. Jaymison thought of it."

"Is someone messing with you guys?"

"No. Maybe it works." Lu hesitates, then asks, "Do you want to wear it?"

I know it's the nicest thing she can do right now, and I want to grab it and say yes, but I know it wouldn't mean the same thing on me. I don't think it's the bandannas that are working. I think it's them already being popular that's working.

Abbie's dad's car pulls up and she gets out right near us. She says hi to me first and also says, "How's your burn?"

How does she know? I look at Lu, who explains, "We texted."

Based on the tone of her voice, I don't think it crossed her mind at all that I might not want anyone to know. That it might be embarrassing to me not only that I spaced out and had a kitchen accident, but especially that I had to sleep over at Lu's because my mom didn't even care enough about me to call me back.

I turn on my heel and veer off onto the lawn to walk around to one of the side entrances so I don't have to keep talking to them when they go in the front.

"Kyra!" Lu calls after me.

I wave my arm like *Leave me alone.*

"Kyra, wait up."

Her voice is getting closer, and she's breathing heavily from running after me. People turn around to look. Just what I wanted: more people staring. I keep walking faster even though I know she's going to catch up. When she reaches me, she grabs my arm right where some of the caramel splattered me. I yank it back and hold it against me.

"What?" I ask.

"I didn't know I wasn't supposed to tell about that. It's not like group. It seemed like something I'd tell *you* if it happened to Till and she was staying at my house."

"It didn't happen to her. It happened to me."

"I know, but . . ."

The first bell rings. Some kids go in, but some are still staring.

"I don't care." My nose is starting to run, and tears won't be far behind.

217

"You do, though! I'm sorry!"

I stop and turn to her. "I don't want to cry at school," I plead. "Let me just . . ." I flap my hands in front of my face, press my fingers under my eyes to block the tears. "Let me go to class."

This she understands. "Okay," she says quietly. "Sorry. I'll walk with you."

We pick up the pace to try to get in before the second bell rings, and she doesn't say anything else. In the hall, we have to pass by Juan and Gabe. They like to loiter in front of their homeroom, across from ours, and make everyone else's life miserable.

Gabe says in a high, trembly voice, "Draaamaaaaaa!"

It must be obvious that I'm still fighting tears.

"Catfight!" Juan adds.

Lu stares straight ahead and grabs my hand to keep me walking, too.

But after we pass, Gabe starts fake crying. Really loud. I tear my hand out of Lu's and spin around. "Shut up!" Not as loud as I wanted it to sound. I want to be louder than him. I say it again. "Shut up!"

"Eek! Bigfoot is after me!" Juan says in a high voice. He and Gabe laugh, and so do a few other people, before they disappear into their classroom.

Bigfoot? Is that what they're calling me now? The hall empties out and I'm just standing here.

"Come on," Lu whispers. "You said you didn't want to get upset."

A teacher down the hall—Ms. Ellis—leans out of her classroom. "Everything okay out here?"

"Yeah," Lu answers.

She takes my hand again, more gently this time, and leads me into our homeroom.

I didn't make a lunch at Lu's house, so I have to get it from the cafeteria.

Lu stays close. I don't know if she's doing it because she really cares or because she's guilty. Maybe it doesn't matter; I'm just glad to not be alone.

It's Thursday, which means French bread pizza. It comes with a side of cucumbers and raisins for the vegetable and fruit. Who came up with the combination of cucumbers and raisins? They're a reminder I'd rather bring my own lunch, which is a reminder that I'd rather be staying at my own house.

Jaymison, Till, and Abbie don't ask me anything else about what happened. I assume Lu told them in their special group chat not to, and instead they're talking about random stuff. Videos and songs and memes and school and what they want to do for spring break, which feels so far away. I eat and listen, except I'm not really listening. I'm thinking about what Juan said. When all that's left on my tray are raisins, there's a pause in their talking.

I ask, "Do people call me Bigfoot?"

Jaymison laughs a little, then says, "Sorry."

"They were calling me Whitney and I told them it was dumb and now it's Bigfoot?"

219

"I don't think so?" says Till.

Lu is sorting her raisins into groups of three.

Abbie looks me in the eye. "I've heard some people say it. Not a lot."

"Have you heard it, Lu?"

She looks up at me and nods very slightly.

"When people call you names," Jaymison says, "you have to clap back. Tell Juan he has chicken legs. Tell Gabe he has beady eyes. He does."

"I don't want to call people names. People can't help how they look."

She sighs impatiently. "Then I guess you just have to take it."

"Who ever called you names?" I ask.

"I was in seventh grade once, too, you know," she replies. "This group of eighth-grade boys always harassed me in the halls. They called me horse face, pancake butt, chompers. Because of my big teeth?"

I never noticed her teeth.

"I always had good comebacks and they eventually left me alone. They were scared of what I'd say."

"Congratulations," I say, "now you're a bully, too."

She shrugs.

"Ignore them," Abbie says to me. "That's what I do."

Till nods. "Me too. If they can tell it bothers you, they'll do it more."

"Kyra can't hide her feelings," Lu says to them, explaining the obvious.

Jaymison leans forward. "That definitely makes it harder.

But if you don't want to be mean, probably ignoring them and trying to stay above it is your best option. Personally, I'd rather be mean."

She laughs and flicks a raisin at me. It hits me on the cheek. I flinch at first, but then I flick one back. She ducks and squeals. I think I might be starting to understand her, just a little.

33

I take a long nap on Casey's bed after school while she's babysitting for a family on their block.

When I wake up, there are two texts from my mom.

I hope your day was okay, babe. I met with Antonia today for almost two hours. She helped me make a plan.

And then:

How is your foot feeling?

The skin is tightening up and itching a little. I put on a new layer of ointment, but don't answer my mom. She's telling me she's going to "make a plan," but we skipped over the part where she tells me what happened, what's been going on, and where she was when I needed her.

Maybe Jaymison is right and I need to learn how to hide my feelings. Stay above it.

Fine, I answer.

Later, I help Steve make a big pot of chicken noodle soup for dinner. It's sort of homemade and sort of not. It involves a rotisserie chicken from the store and some cartons of broth, but then we chop our own carrots and celery and sauté them in butter and some spices to bring out the flavor. And we parboil the noodles separately so the soup doesn't get gummy.

"Needs thyme," I tell Steve after tasting it carefully. Even the steam makes the tiny blisters on my hand and wrist sting.

I rub a large pinch of thyme between my palms and let it fall into the soup. I saw in a video once that crushing them like that helps bring spices to life after they've been sitting in a jar for who knows how long. Then Casey gets back and Lu's mom comes out of her upstairs office where she's been working, and we have soup and bread.

They all talk about their days. When they ask me how mine was, I say, "Fine." I don't want to talk about what Mom told me. For one, Steve probably already knows. For two, I'd rather listen to them and let my own feelings keep settling somewhere deeper down, where they can't constantly be coming up, and I can stay above them.

When Lu and I are the only ones left in the kitchen and are loading the dishwasher, she says, "I really am sorry I told about your burn. I didn't think it was like talking about group."

I place a bowl on the top rack. "What did you say to them about my mom, though? Like why I'm staying at your house right now?"

She clutches a bowl in both hands. "I said you burned

223

yourself and your mom was working and . . ." She hands me the bowl to load, then turns her back to me, rinsing silverware under the faucet.

"And what?" I ask.

"And she didn't answer her phone and stuff." She leans over the machine, putting the silverware in the basket.

That's a lot. That's a lot to say about someone's mom. Because all anyone has to do is read between the lines, and they'll know something isn't right about that. "And stuff" can mean anything. Everything.

I watch her rearrange dishes to make everything fit and tell her, "They're going to think my mom doesn't care about me."

Finally, she looks at me. "I don't think they'll think that," she says. "Do *you* think that?"

"How would you feel? If it was your dad?" I can feel my voice breaking. "If you really needed him in an emergency and you didn't have Casey or your mom and he just . . . wasn't there?"

She clutches my hand. "I'd hate it."

"And you wouldn't want anyone to tell." I pull my hand back. I know she's sorry and I can forgive her, but I don't want us to stand here crying in the kitchen. "I was making your favorite salted caramel cookies when I burned myself. For your birthday. It was going to be your present."

"You were?"

"Yeah. I didn't know if my mom was going to be able to take me shopping like I wanted. So I thought I'd do something homemade."

224

"I love those cookies. That's really nice."

"It was, until I messed it all up." I wipe my eyes with my hands, then wipe my hands on the apron I took from their kitchen drawer. "Anyway. That's why I won't have a present on Saturday."

"I don't care about that."

Right then, Casey walks in, holding her phone. "You invited Dad to your birthday?" she asks Lu, and doesn't sound happy about it.

"Yeah . . ." Lu looks at me. "He's doing good with his sobriety."

"For *now*," Casey says.

What if Mom starts being like their dad now, always off and on sobriety? That's a thought I have to stay way, way above.

"It's *my* birthday," Lu says.

Casey scoffs. "And Mom and Steve's anniversary."

"Mom said I could."

Casey throws her hands up. "Amazing." She looks at me. "I feel like we need group *now*. I don't know if I can wait until Saturday."

"Me too," I say.

"Wait, I'm a genius." Casey starts texting. While still looking down at her phone, she says to us, "Finish cleaning in here and meet me in my room in half an hour."

34

Owen says he wants to come, and Casey leaves to pick him up.

"What's good?" he asks when they come back. I know "what's good" is just an expression that doesn't even need an answer, but I blurt out, "Nothing."

"Still sucks, huh?"

"She got a second-degree burn," Lu says as we walked down the hall to Casey's room.

"Lu!"

She claps her hand over her mouth, but then takes it off and says, "He's gonna see your bandage!"

That's true. Group always involves a lot of time staring at each other's feet. But, "Can you please just let me tell my own stories?" I say.

Owen and Casey exchange a glance like they think Lu and I are amusing. Or maybe they only think it about me. I curl my hands into fists and shove them in the pockets of my windbreaker, which I'm wearing indoors because Mom only brought me T-shirts and the house is chilly. It's not even a jacket I wear anymore. I don't know what made her think I want to wear this old yellow one with the hot chocolate stain on the cuff of one sleeve.

We sit in a circle on Casey's floor. She reads from her phone the same opening statements that we always do. Then she finds a set of meditations and we pass around her phone, taking turns reading.

I'm trying not to listen too carefully. We've been learning about black holes in our astronomy unit in science. Ms. Scheiner said they're these things in outer space that have a gravitational field so strong nothing can escape once it gets too close, not even light. Everything gets sucked in. Where does it go? No one knows. Well, billions of years later it *might* get spit out on the other side, Ms. Scheiner said with a little too much enthusiasm.

There's something like that inside me since the moment I spilled the caramel and knew I couldn't rely on Mom before I even tried. Something opened, something powerful and scary, and I don't want to get too close to it. It feels like if I have one bad feeling, like disappointment or hurt, I'll get sucked into all of them—anger and sadness and fear of the unknown and other feelings I don't even know about yet—and I won't be able to handle it.

227

Maybe someday that feeling of avoiding the black hole will make me want to drink. Or make me mad all the time like Grandma. Or be mean first before anyone can be mean to me, like Jaymison.

When the phone passes to Owen and he reads something about shame, I want to put my hands over my ears. Not hear and not think. I don't want to hear Bigfoot or Whitney or feel the hot caramel on me or see the words *I misplaced my phone* in my head or think about Mom's easy lying.

I'm next to Owen, but when he passes me the phone, I pass it back to Casey.

She says, "I'll share. That part we just read about shame is intense. Like, I know it's not my fault my dad drank or left us or did any of the other stuff he did, so why do I still feel like it is? Why won't this feeling ever go away? Is that the shame they're talking about? Like if I were a different person, he wouldn't have left or . . . I don't know. Also, like, the fact that he could only finally get some sobriety *after* he left makes me sometimes think we were holding him back or something."

In the gap when she pauses, I stand at the edge of that black hole. The swirling thoughts are: What if it *is* true, though? What if there's something wrong with every one of us in this room that makes our parents need to drink, and we only tell ourselves it's not our fault because otherwise we would hurt all the time knowing we were the problem all along? At least when Casey and Lu's dad left, they still had their mom. If it's better for my mom to leave, if she can only stay sober without me, I won't have anyone. I don't want to sleep on Steve's couch the rest of my life.

Maybe it's my fault Gabe and Juan call me names.

My fault that Jaymison doesn't want me in the Pink Bandanna Club.

My fault Lu would rather be with new friends than with me.

My fault I burned myself and my fault my dad doesn't want to know me and my grandma is going to resent my mom forever. After all, if Mom hadn't been pregnant with me, she probably wouldn't have been given the house that Grandma thought she was going to get. So in one way, everything was my fault from the beginning.

Suddenly, I realize how quiet it is. Everyone is looking at me. I guess sharing is about to be over and they want to make sure I have a chance. It could be my imagination, but Lu and Casey might be staring extra hard. I stare back at Lu. Hard.

If she likes talking about me so much, maybe she should just share for me.

I shake my head.

Then Casey breaks the no-crosstalk rule, where we don't comment directly to each other during group time or refer to another person's share.

"I'm glad you called us last night," she says. "I'm glad I'm the one who answered and got to come help. It was scary, and I know you wanted your mom. But I'm glad I was there for you, and I'm glad you let me be. And whatever you're feeling right now, this week, next week . . . you're allowed to feel it."

I make myself so detached from the gravity field of the black hole that all I can say back is a flat "Thanks."

But for some reason, Owen is crying.

And Lu is sniffling.

Then Casey puts her head in her hands and lets out a sob.

There's a box of tissues on Casey's bedside table. I stand up, feeling the skin on my ankle stretch tight, and get the box and put it where everyone can reach.

35

When Owen's gone and we're getting ready for bed, Lu tries to talk to me, saying, "At least tomorrow's Friday, right?"

"I guess."

"Well, it is."

"I know. That's not what I meant."

One day of school, and then her party on Saturday. She's excited about it since she's turning thirteen, and I'm probably ruining her excitement by having a crisis, but I can't fake looking forward to something I'm dreading. All of her other friends will probably give her great presents. I'll have nothing to give. And my mom will be there so we can talk about "the plan." Goodie.

I avoid the hallway and bathroom while she brushes her

teeth and does all her stuff to get ready for bed. I'm not mad at her anymore, just exhausted from so many feelings and don't want to have any more of them tonight.

I go sit on the couch that is my bed, even though I can't go to sleep yet because I need to work on make-up assignments.

Steve comes into the living room, and I pretend to be absorbed in my math even though I have almost no idea what I'm looking at on this worksheet. Grids and numbers and blanks to fill in.

"Need anything else in here?"

"No. Thanks." I write down an answer in one of the blanks, then immediately start erasing it. I swipe the eraser dust off my paper. It shows on the cream-colored carpet. "Sorry. I can vacuum tomorrow."

"Don't worry about it, Keek."

"You don't have to be so *nice* to me," I say with a sigh.

He runs his hands on the fabric of the chair. "I don't?"

I shake my head. The numbers on my math sheet blur. So much for not having any more feelings.

"Well, that's good," he says. "Tomorrow I'll need help getting ready for the party. I'll put you to work. I'm not going to be nice about it, either, so I hope you like doing dishes."

"I do," I whisper, and watch a tear hit my paper. The blot spreads.

When he's gone, I lie down and pull a blanket over my head, and let the black hole suck me in.

My second night on the couch is almost as bad as the first.

The burn itches worse, and the ointment only helps for ten

minutes after I put it on. Crying off and on all night doesn't help. Neither does the text from Mom that comes around one a.m. that just says:

I love you, Kyra.

I don't know how that could make me feel worse, but it does.

When I see myself in the bathroom mirror in the morning, I want to start crying all over again. My face is blotchy and pale at the same time, and somehow I also have shadows under my eyes. I just look so sad and tired. I look like Mom. And that makes me sadder.

I stand under the shower a long time, even though it's not hot, and even when I hear a knock on the door and know I need to get out. While I'm standing there, I get a strange urge to slap myself. I've never wanted to do anything like that before. It scares me. I hurry to turn off the water and dry myself before I can do it, and I shove the thought out of my mind.

"Sorry," I say to Lu as I pass her in the hall.

I dress quickly in her room. I wish I had all my clothes to choose from. Then I could at least try to feel good about how I look when how I feel about everything else is so scary. But all I've got is the bag Mom brought, obviously put together in a rush without any attention to which of my clothes I actually *like* to wear. Lu's closet is open, and I eye it jealously. Nothing in there would fit me.

Casey's in the kitchen when I go in there to find breakfast. She sees me and says, "Are you okay? You look like sh—you look tired."

"I *am* tired."

She opens the fridge and takes out a yogurt and two boiled eggs. She hesitates a second with the door still open and then says, "I've got an extra lemon yogurt if you want one. Or eggs. Or both."

"Really?"

She hands me a yogurt and two boiled eggs.

We sit at the table and peel our eggs. I do not think this is a good flavor combination, by the way. Or a good texture combination. It's nice not to have to decide what to eat, though, and nicer that she shared.

When we're done, she asks if my mom lets me wear makeup.

"I've never asked."

"Let me do yours. Come on." She stands up and sweeps all our bits of shell onto one plate and then into the garbage. When I hesitate, she adds, "Don't worry, I won't do yours like I do mine. Just some concealer and a little cheek color. It'll look natural. You won't look so tired."

It can't hurt. I follow her to her room; we pass Lu's closed door.

She has me sit on the edge of her bed while she unzips a canvas case of makeup and sorts through it. "Look up toward me a little." I do. She adjusts my chin so I'm looking a little higher. I close my eyes against the glare of the overhead light.

Fingertips dab at my face—under my eyes and on my forehead and chin, then they feather over me like they're carefully rubbing lotion in. A few more dabs on my cheeks, then she says, "Okay. You're done." I open my eyes. She looks through her bag again and hands me a small tube. "Use this, too, if you want. It's lip balm with just a little bit of rosy tint to it."

"Okay. Thank you."

"Don't you want to look in the mirror?"

I get up and go to the mirror that hangs over one of her closet doors. It doesn't look as natural as she said it would, but it's not weird or anything. "Thanks," I say again.

"Do you like it, though?"

I don't know how to feel about myself. "Yeah."

She stands behind me and stares at the mirror-me, and I steal glances at the mirror-her. Casey is the coolest older sister anyone could have, and it's another thing that makes me jealous of Lu. I don't think Lu appreciates it. Even in her pajamas, Casey looks cool. Her dark hair is pulled back with some kind of hair wrap thing and she's got on black bike shorts and a big black sweatshirt. She could go to school like that and no one would know she'd slept in it.

"Do you ever wear red?" she asks suddenly.

"Not really."

"It would look good with your blond hair and your skin tone."

"What's my skin tone?"

"Sort of pale pink. Not peachy."

Casey reaches into her closet and digs through a heap of clothes that have been stuffed onto a shelf. She pulls out a fuzzy red cardigan sweater. "Will this fit? You can wear it instead of that yellow windbreaker."

"Probably not."

She holds it up next to me. "I think it will. Just try."

I pull it on over the Muppets T-shirt my mom had put into the bag, forgetting that I hadn't worn that since starting seventh grade because I worried people would think it was weird to still like Muppets. I was planning to snap all the windbreaker snaps so Animal and Beaker don't show.

"See?" Casey says. "It's a little short, but it fits. Do you like it?"

It really does fit. And I really do like it. I nod and start to button the buttons all the way up.

"Leave a couple open. The T-shirt looks cool with it."

"Are you sure?" She doesn't know Gabe and Juan.

"Positive. I'd wear this outfit." She takes a handful of my hair and pulls it back, makes a face, and lets it drop again. "Better down."

Lu appears at the open door and says, "We gotta go!" When she sees Casey, she says, "You're not even dressed?!"

Casey swears and moves like lightning to riffle through her closet. "I'll be out in two minutes." Lu stomps away, and I'm still standing there. "Go!" Casey says to me, making a shooing motion with her hands.

In the living room, Lu asks how my foot is, how I slept, if I have all my stuff before she really looks at me. When she finally does, she says, "Are you wearing makeup?"

"Is it obvious? Does it look bad?"

She shakes her head. "No. It looks good."

"Casey did it."

"Is that her sweater?"

"I didn't even ask. She just gave it to me."

Casey's voice from down the hall says, "I didn't *give* it to you. You can *wear it today*."

As we're all walking out to the car, Lu says to Casey, "Will you do makeup for me tomorrow? For the party?"

Casey sighs like it's a big pain. "We'll see."

But we both know she will.

36

In science, we make Black Hole Books, which is the kind of half-fun, half-learning project we only get to do on Fridays. It reminds me of sixth grade.

"I didn't make this up to get out of lesson planning," Ms. Scheiner says as she passes out stacks of sheets. "This comes straight from NASA's website." When she puts mine on my desk, she asks, "How's that makeup work coming?"

"Um, fine."

The sheets involve coloring and a word search on one and some puzzles and fill-in-the-blanks. Ms. Scheiner passes out plastic containers with crayons and glue sticks and some other supplies. When I open mine, the smell of crayons is cozy and safe, like someone just put a fuzzy blanket over my shoulders and a cup of hot chocolate in my hand.

I lose myself in coloring. When I'm finished with the NASA sheets, I turn the paper over and draw my own galaxy. It's mostly just patches and blocks and blobs of color I make in big strokes and many layers. Ahead of me still are lunch, language arts, and social studies. I already had math and PE, but I didn't dress out for PE because of my burn. Mrs. Pak had me organize the equipment closet.

Thinking about the whole rest of the day makes me even more tired than I already am, so I don't think, I just color. I wonder if I could stay in here all day with paper and crayons. That should be an elective. Paper and Crayons.

Lu's desk is one behind and one over. When I feel someone watching me, I glance up and over my shoulder. I can see she's on the word search page and probably wondering what's wrong with me since I just noticed the way I'm coloring is making a lot of noise.

"*What?*" I ask her. I'm not nearly as mad at her as it sounds like I am when I say it.

She shifts in her seat a little. Other kids are talking and don't pay attention to us. On Fridays, Ms. Scheiner doesn't care if we talk, as long as we're also doing our work and not getting loud.

"I'm just worried you're getting crayon on Casey's sweater," Lu says.

"I'm not." Then I check to make sure, and rub off the little bit of waxy dust that actually did get on there.

After that, it's not as fun anymore.

I had another text from my mom this morning asking me

if I'd gotten her text, the one saying she loves me. I told her I did. I know she wanted me to say I love her, too, but I couldn't. My hands just froze on my phone and I couldn't say it.

"Are you wearing makeup?" Jaymison asks me at lunch.

"No." I don't know why I lie.

Lu looks at me—along with Till and Abbie—but doesn't say anything.

"It's just concealer," I say, as if I don't know that counts as makeup.

"It looks good." Once Jaymison approves, Till and Abbie say it, too.

"I like your Muppet shirt," Till adds.

She seems like she means it, though a part of me wonders if they're being nice because they know I'm staying at Lu's house for some reason having to do with my mom not taking care of me and there being no dad. Or other mom. Or uncle or grandma. No one I belong to.

Before I can thank Till, Lu says, "Me and Kyra did a Muppets song in our fifth-grade talent show. I played guitar and she sang."

Abbie says, "I could never get up in front of people like that."

"But you run track in front of everyone," I say.

"That's different."

"Yeah," Lu says.

"Why?" I don't know why it would be any different. Either way, people are watching and judging.

"It's like . . . it's just running," Abbie says. "It's natural."

"Not for me."

No one says anything to that. I'm tired of talking, anyway. The school lunch is a burrito. I can't even tell what's in it. I start pulling it apart and picking through it. It maybe has beans, or it could be some thick goo around chunks of meat that's probably chicken. This is the last school lunch I'll eat. Even if I have to live at Lu's forever, I'm going to get Steve to take me to the store so I can get things I like to have for lunch.

"Gross," Jaymison says, making a face at my burrito dissection. She has a Subway sandwich that her mom dropped off for her.

"Yeah." Lu wrinkles her nose. "Eat it or throw it out."

Her tone annoys me. She's telling me what to do like she's a parent or teacher or something. Maybe she's embarrassed and wants to stop me from being weird. Maybe I'm tired of it, too! I'm sick of acting like Lu's needy shadow, or feeling like it.

I hold up a piece of chicken-like substance that I've speared with the end of my plastic fork.

"I can't eat it if I don't know what it is." I get up from the table and, with the fork held in front of me, power walk to the counter where the lunch is served. People are watching. "Does anyone know what this *is*?" I ask the room. I'm being so loud. Louder than when Lu says I'm being too loud.

A couple of people laugh.

"Tastes like chicken!" someone shouts.

"No, it doesn't," someone else says.

241

That makes me stop. They're all watching. "Who here thinks it should say on the menu what it is, instead of just 'burrito,' which could be literally anything?"

A few hands shoot up. Other people laugh. Others get bored with whatever it is I'm doing and turn back around. Someone shouts, "Okay, Bigfoot!"

What *am* I doing?

I keep talking. "Clap if you think it's chicken."

There are some claps.

"Now clap if you think it's *crap*."

Wild applause. A few people whoop. Someone throws a crumpled napkin at me.

The lunch monitor starts walking over. It's Mr. Simmons again. I go right to him and hold my fork to his mouth like it's a microphone. He jerks his head away, disgusted.

"Survey says this is crap. Do you have any comment?"

Everything goes quiet. I feel the whole cafeteria holding its breath. I'm almost as tall as Mr. Simmons, so he can't exactly stare down at me, but he's trying.

"Sit down, Ms. Hale. This is your first warning."

I speak into my fork. "So that's a 'no comment'?" I stick the fork in his face again. His forehead is reddening at the edges of his hairline.

"What's the matter with you?" he asks, his voice full of disdain. "Second warning. If you don't sit back down, you're headed to the office."

Sitting in the school office for the rest of a Friday afternoon sounds easy; maybe they'll give me crayons.

I turn away from him and speak into my fork like a news-caster. "As you can see, Mr. Simmons does not wish to comment on the chicken-or-crap issue. Back to you, Bob."

There are a few giggles.

"Get your things," Mr. Simmons says. "Now."

On the way to get my backpack, I make a big show of com-posting my fork and the bits of burrito filling still sticking to it. Till and Lu have their hands over their mouths and just stare with wide eyes. Abbie is shaking her head and smiling. Jaymison looks gleeful, and the last thing I hear before I get marched to the office is her saying, "That was amazing."

37

I haven't been sent to the school office in years. It used to happen a lot in first and second grade. That was when my mom's drinking was pretty bad. Teachers complained that I wouldn't sit still, was always distracted, couldn't or wouldn't follow directions. I don't really remember what I was thinking or why I did what I did, but I doubt I could help it.

"Do you have drawing stuff?" I ask Mr. Aranda. He's the nice one of the two secretaries that are always in the office, the one who told me he hoped I felt better soon when Mom lied to him. I like his clothes. They're always colorful and interesting. Today, he has a bright blue shirt with a print of tiny yellow ducklings all over it.

He looks at me over the top of the purple frames of his glasses. "Welllll," he says, stretching it out. "I can give you some used printouts from the recycling bin and a highlighter or Sharpie or something."

I don't think he's expecting me to say yes to that, but I do. He gives me a clipboard with some papers clipped to it, and a red pencil and a black marker and says, "You can draw on the back but don't look at the front. There might be top secret school information on there. Mrs. Earnshaw will be back from lunch pretty soon, anyway."

I draw an apple with the red pencil and use the marker to make seeds.

"So what did you do?" Mr. Aranda asks.

"Nothing. I just wanted to know what was in the cafeteria burrito."

"Oh, is that all?" He says it teasingly, like we both know that is *not* all.

The apple is hanging from a tree now, also red. I'm adding some red grass around the bottom when Mrs. Earnshaw walks in. She's older than my mom but not by a lot, and almost always wears her black hair in a bun. She has on what she wears every day: a blazer over a T-shirt and jeans. She has at least nine different blazers. I've counted. Today it's navy-blue with pinstripes.

"Everything okay, Kyra?" she asks me.

Mr. Aranda says, "Mr. Simmons sent her over."

Mrs. Earnshaw raises her eyebrows. "Oh? What happened?"

"Nothing," I say.

"In that case, let's get you back to class."

I flop my hands onto the clipboard and look up at her. "Do

I have to? Don't you want to call my mom?"

"Do you want me to?"

I don't answer because I don't know the answer.

"Would she be able to pick you up if I did let you go?"

"I don't know." Probably not.

"Maybe if you tell me what happened, we can come up with a solution, yeah?"

I go into her office, still clutching the clipboard, and tell her a version of the story, and when she asks me why I think Mr. Simmons sent me to her, I say, "Because he doesn't have a sense of humor."

She moves her tape dispenser from one side of the desk to the other. "Sometimes when we joke around, we hurt people. You know that."

"He wasn't *hurt*."

"Well, it sounds like he did give you a couple of warnings. Sometimes being disrespected can actually make people feel hurt."

I don't like to think about Mr. Simmons having human feelings like mine. "Can I just go home? I can walk. I don't need my mom to pick me up."

I picture going to my own house. Making my own lunch. Picking my own clothes. Sleeping in my own bed. Everything normal.

"No, I can't do that. And you can't hang around the office all afternoon." She gives me a kind smile. "As much as I'd love to have you help Mr. Aranda stuff some envelopes, I'm sorry." She types into her computer. "What class are you supposed to be in right now?"

"Language Arts. I already have an A in that class." It's actually a B+ right now, my current best grade besides PE, but I'm sure I can make it an A again soon.

She's giving her computer a concerned look. "What's with all the missed days lately?"

"I . . ." I swallow. I hate how Mom's choices and lies mean I have to lie, too. I mean, I guess I don't *have* to, but it feels that way. "I keep getting sick."

"You sound okay," she says over the top of her screen.

"Not like colds and stuff. Like . . . headaches."

"I'm sorry. I get those, too." She checks the time on her phone. "Why don't you help Mr. Aranda for the rest of this period, then go to your last class, then the day will be over and it will be the weekend. Does that sound doable?"

I nod.

"So really, though," she says, "what was the issue with Mr. Simmons?"

"The menu should say what's in the burrito. I got tired of trying to guess."

She folds her hands and rests her chin on them. "Everyone with food allergies registered at the beginning of the year and we have all their stuff on file. Same with vegans and vegetarians. They have all the menu details they need." She jots something on her notepad. "But your point is taken. I would want to know, too. Mystery meat is no fun." She opens a desk drawer. "Did you get enough to eat? Do you want a protein bar or something?"

"No thanks."

"Granola bar?"

I hesitate, then she waves it around and it's the one kind I like with peanuts and dark chocolate, so I reach out and take it. "Thanks."

Jaymison waits with Lu and me at pickup.

She goes on and on about how funny I was at lunch. "Mr. Simmons was *so mad*. I can't believe you kept poking that fork in his face. He looked like he wanted to knock it out of your hand. Imagine if he did! You could have gotten him fired. You'd be a hero. Did the office call your mom?"

"No." I make it sound simpler than it was. "It wasn't that big a deal."

"Lucky."

Lu takes a step away from us, leaning into the street to look for Steve's truck. He gets off work a little earlier on Fridays.

"Mrs. Earnshaw basically said I was right," I say.

"Seriously? I love her."

"So tomorrow," Lu says, turning back to us but really only talking to Jaymison, "come as early as you want. Like we talked about."

"Yeah, I'm helping cook, so I'll be there early, too," I say, as if I won't be waking up there tomorrow morning because I have nowhere else to go. "Steve asked me to because he knows I'm a good cook."

Jaymison laughs. "Don't give yourself a third-degree burn."

I laugh back, like that's only funny and not a little bit mean. Lu acts like she doesn't hear any of it. "There he is," she says.

We climb into the truck—Lu first, then me—and as we

248

close the door, Jaymison cups her hands around her mouth and shouts, "Clap if it's crap!"

I turn to the window and put my hands together in a silent clap. It cracks her up.

"What was that?" Steve asks.

"Nothing," Lu says. "Trust me."

38

As soon as we get to Lu's house, I take off Casey's red cardigan and put it on her bed. Then I wash my face, because the stuff she put on it this morning makes my skin feel like it can't breathe. When that's done, my phone pings with a text from Mom.

How was your day? Thinking about you. Can't wait to see you tomorrow.

The black hole of feelings tugs at me. But I won't look in. I double-tap her text with a like so she knows I saw it, then I turn off the phone and shove it to the bottom of my backpack. I sit on the edge of the couch and know that if I lie down and close my eyes, I'd probably fall right to sleep.

Lu comes in. She's changed into shorts and the pink sweat-shirt she likes to wear around the house. "Did you really not get in trouble?" she asks.

"Yeah. I helped Mr. Aranda with a mailing."

"Maybe they know about your mom and stuff and were being nice."

I look down. The bandage on my ankle is so beige and ugly. "No. They don't." She seems upset that I didn't get into trouble.

"Well, I don't know why you had to do that. Everyone was staring."

"Because I was funny."

"Okay." She folds her arms and leans on the wall.

"I have to go help Steve." I get up and walk past her.

"He's not *your* dad," she mutters.

I stop and turn around. The girl with the interview fork in the cafeteria would say, *Thanks for the news flash!* But that's not me. "I know that."

Steve has me help make these meatballs called kofta that are going to go on the grill. It's lamb—which I don't like to think about—and pine nuts and almonds and a lot of spices I don't usually use.

I hold the cardamom jar to my nose. "I like this one."

We're in the kitchen, each standing at different parts of the counter. Lu and her mom went to the store for a few more things for the party.

"Me too," he says. "How are you doing?"

"Fine."

When I'm done mixing, I start rolling the koftas into the oblong shapes that Steve demonstrates, and place them on a platter covered in wax paper. I know I'm not "fine," and he knows I'm not "fine."

But he's not my dad. As Lu helpfully pointed out.

"First, we're going to put these on skewers." He opens a drawer and gets out a pack of wooden skewers. He shows me how to slide them on the long way.

I do one, and he says, "Perfect."

We work quietly. I want to ask him if he ever got in trouble at school when he was my age, and what for, and if he was popular or unpopular or in between. Instead, I ask, "What was my mom like when she was my age?"

He glances at me. "Well, you know it was right around your age she started drinking."

"I know." I skewer another kofta. "Did you?"

"Truthfully, no. I think I was sixteen or seventeen the first time I had a drink."

"But you never had the kind of problem my mom did."

"No. I was just stupid. For your mom, it was something else."

I guess if it goes that far back for her and it was always a problem, then it can't be my fault because I didn't exist. The *idea* of me didn't even exist.

"But," Steve continues, "your mom has also always been a great person. Everyone in school liked her. She was cool with everyone, you know?"

My platter is all done, the skewers perfectly aligned. I wash my hands. I doubt I'll ever be cool with everyone like that.

Steve starts clearing away the kofta stuff so we can work on the next thing—monster cookies. "How do you feel about using the stand mixer?"

Normally, I'd jump up and down and clap my hands. That's how I feel about stand mixers. I'm just too tired to be excited. "Sure."

"'Sure,' she says."

He opens the little wooden box on the counter where all his recipe cards are. Some were his mom's, and some were *her* mom's, and some are ones he's been writing out and collecting since he first started getting into cooking. He flips through the cards and pulls out the one for the cookies.

We go over the recipe. Sugar, butter, eggs, like most cookies. "This one doesn't have flour," Steve said. "It uses oats, so if anyone's gluten-free, they can still partake."

It's a cookie with lots of stuff— chocolate chips and M&M's and chunky peanut butter.

"What if someone has a peanut allergy, though?" I ask.

Steve rubs his beard. "I didn't think about that."

We stare at the jar of peanut butter. I do love peanut butter. "Let's make them, but we'll keep them separate and write a note saying they have nuts."

They're easy to make. I should have done something simple like this for Lu instead of trying to do the salted caramel. But then I wouldn't be standing here with Steve right now, and being here with him makes me feel better, even if he's not my dad.

"If," I say, measuring out oats, "someday, for some reason, me and Lu aren't friends, would me and you still be friends?"

He finishes cracking the third egg and looks at me. "Are you kidding?"

I shake my head.

"How long have I known you?" he asks, still holding an eggshell.

"Since I was born."

"Right. So don't even ask me that."

I pack brown sugar into a measuring cup, making it line up exactly to the top. "It's different, though. You and Lu's mom are married. You and my mom are just friends."

"Keek. Never put the word 'just' before 'friends,' like it's not that important. It's a different kind of love, sure, but it's not something less."

It reminds me of what Mom said about the words "best" and "favorite," and how I don't need to think of people like that.

I put the butter and sugar and eggs into the mixer, and watch the paddle whirl as it creams everything together. At home I have to do everything with a spoon and take breaks when my arm gets sore.

"Speaking of your mom," Steve says, "are you ready to see her tomorrow?"

"No."

He hands me the measured peanut butter and vanilla to dump in. "I bet you're mad. I would be. You want to know your mom is there for you when you need her, and she hasn't been."

Next are the oats.

"I mostly can take care of myself," I say.

"I know you can. But you shouldn't have to, right? Not all the time."

I add the chocolate chips and M&M's.

"Anyway," Steve adds, "it's okay to be mad about it."

I nod and watch the dough whirl.

"Tomorrow," he says, "I'm not doing the alcohol thing."

"What do you mean?" I ask, my mind on cookies.

"With your mom and Lu's dad and all you guys' friends from school—"

"Lu's friends."

"Okay, them. I told the folks we invited for our anniversary that they can bring their own if they want, but I'm not serving."

"If Mom really wants to drink," I say, "she'll find a way. She always tells me that. *You* always tell me that."

"That's true. I thought I'd try it without anyway."

When Lu gets home from shopping, she asks if I want to come in her room and help her figure out what to wear for the party tomorrow. Asking *me* for help with outfits is something she hasn't ever done. She opens her closet and I sit on the bed with my back against the wall. She asks me to check tomorrow's weather on my phone; she's been checking obsessively all week.

"Still fifty-three and partial clouds, like every single other day." That's what Pacifica weather is almost all the time in February. While I'm checking that, I see a text from Mom.

Hope you have a nice evening. Love you.

"I think I wear my overalls too much," she says. "Does it seem like I wear them all the time?"

"They're your favorite." She's wearing them now. They're cute. They're denim and soft and rolled at the cuffs.

"I wonder who invented the idea that you're not supposed to wear the same thing two days in a row," she says. "Or more."

"Wear them," I say.

"What are you going to wear?"

"I have to see what else is in the bag my mom brought. I'm stuck with whatever's in there."

"Today at lunch," she says into her closet, "you *were* funny. It reminded me of how you were in fifth grade, like when we did the talent show."

"I thought you thought I was annoying today."

She pulls something out and turns to me—it's a light blue sweater with a goose on it. "I was surprised is all. And I didn't want you to get in trouble. We're not the kind to get in trouble."

"Maybe I am. That goose is . . . cool?"

Her arms drop. "Kyra, don't turn into someone who's always getting in trouble. Remember last year? Casey?"

I do remember. Last year, Casey got into a *lot* of trouble at school. Mostly for cutting class but for other stuff, too. Then she got into a fight with another girl. Like they were punching and kicking. She got suspended, and Lu's mom and Steve had to go to all these meetings, and Casey's grades were bad, too. She had to go to summer school.

"It turned out okay," I say.

"It was so hard, though, when it was happening." Lu hangs the goose sweater back up and takes out a plum-colored hoodie

256

with an abstract graphic print on the front in white. "I could do this with jeans."

"If the sun comes out, you might get hot."

"I'll do a T-shirt under. Maybe my green-and-white striped one."

I nod.

Lu sits on the bed next to me. "I'm sorry you got burned making cookies for my birthday. You don't have to worry about getting me a present. I don't care," she says. "I know how it is. Before Mom married Steve, she'd give me a budget of five dollars to buy a present when it was someone's birthday. Everyone got invited to everyone's party in, like, second and third grade. That gets expensive! When I was in third grade, it was kind of a fun challenge to find something cheap. But I wouldn't want to have to do that now. Like imagine being invited to a party for Jaymison and trying to find something for five dollars?"

"She'd still like you."

"Maybe."

I pick at one of the tiny blisters on the back of my hand. "Remember the cookout two years ago? When my mom talked to you about alcoholism and your dad and everything?" It had been another big party at Steve's house, at the end of fifth grade. We were brand-new friends. "Now she's drinking and your dad isn't. It's just weird."

"I know. It always feels up and down. Like you can never be sure about anyone."

I look at her. "Exactly."

This is what she meant when she said our vibe was different. Even if she messed up by telling my stories, she's always going to understand this.

She stands and hangs her clothes for tomorrow on the back of the chair by her desk. "Let's go tell Steve what we want on our pizza."

Friday at Lu's house is Pizza Movie Night.

It's the one thing Steve likes to order out instead of cooking himself. They get pizzas and take turns picking a movie, and even Casey stays home unless she has a babysitting job.

The TV is in the family room, a few steps down from the kitchen at the back of the house. There's a big, comfy sectional sofa with blankets in case we need them, but Steve lit a fire in the fireplace, so we don't.

We eat pizza straight from the boxes while we watch the movie. Steve sits next to Lu's mom and Lu sits next to Steve and I sit next to Lu. Casey sits on the floor with her back leaning against the sofa. She half watches the movie and half does stuff on her phone.

I think about Mom's last text. She hoped I'd have a nice evening.

I am.

I'd still rather be home if it were the home I used to feel safe in. But this is good for now.

39

Saturday morning, I wake up while it's still dark and quiet, other than the furnace blowing. I lie there on the couch in Lu's mom's nightgown, with my itchy ankle. This is the day I'll see Mom. I want time to go slow, but I also want to get it over with.

This too will pass. This day will pass. An hour at a time.

I fall back to sleep, then Casey and Lu wake me up and say we're going to Starbucks for hot chocolate and cake pops. I pull on jeans and a T-shirt and my yellow windbreaker.

"Count this as my present," Casey tells Lu after we drive there and get our treats. "So if I disappear later, you can't say I didn't celebrate."

"*Are* you going to disappear?" Lu asks.

"Possibly."

We cross the highway on foot so we can sit at the beach on the same driftwood I like to sit on with Mom. It's cold with high, gray clouds, but there are lots of surfers out. We watch them paddle out into the flat ocean and wait for waves. It's been a long time since I really looked at the ocean.

Last time I did, I told my higher power I wanted everything to be okay, and it wasn't. It's not.

Except, like last time at the beach, it also is.

My hot chocolate is sweet and creamy. The ocean air is clean today. My burn is healing the way it's supposed to. For the first time in a while, I feel like Lu and I aren't drifting further apart. I'm not even mad anymore that Jaymison is going to be at the party.

Right now, it's enough. Right now, I'm okay.

I look out at the horizon, as far as I can see. The green of the ocean makes a sharp line against the sky. I close my eyes, breathe, open them again.

"Are you having a moment of Zen or are you just dissociating?" Casey asks with a laugh.

I shrug and sip my hot chocolate.

"Will you take a picture of us?" Lu asks Casey.

She pulls her phone out of her pocket. "Get up and turn around so I can get the view in the background."

We pose with our arms around each other, backs to the coast. I still feel like a giant next to Lu. Like Bigfoot. So what? I'm tall. I'm grown-up-sized. The only jacket I have for Lu's thirteenth birthday photo is this stained windbreaker. So what?

"Are you gonna smile, Kyra?" Casey asks, angling her phone at us.

"Yes," I say, then I do.

Good morning, babe. I'm going to come early so we can talk. Can't wait to see you.

The text from Mom is waiting for me when I turn my phone on. Three days ago, the most important thing in the world was for her to answer me, for her to come home. Now I'm not ready, emotionally, and also suddenly in a panic about what I need to do before the party: shower and change, put the bedding I've been using into the washer in the garage . . . do I need to pack? Am I going home with her?

How early? I have to help Steve.

It's the most I've said to her in days. And I don't *have* to help Steve.

I'm coming at ten. Steve knows!

It's nine-fifteen now. Ugh.

I take the bedding to the laundry room like I do at client houses, and I put the nightgown Lu's mom lent me in there, too. I'm the very last one to use the shower, and the lukewarm water feels cold on my head but soothing on my burn. The white layer of skin that pulled away from the rest of the layers looks like it could be peeled right off. I resist because the doctor told me not to do that. It's there to protect the exposed layers underneath.

With my hair wrapped in a towel, I put on the cleaner of the two pairs of jeans I have here, and the Muppet T-shirt, and my purple short-sleeve sweatshirt over that. I squeeze and pat my hair dry and add my towel to the laundry.

Lu and Steve are outside, setting up folding chairs on the front lawn. Lu's mom is in the kitchen. My stomach gurgles with hot chocolate and whipped cream. I make a piece of toast while Lu's mom decorates the birthday cake.

"This is the one thing I get to do," she says to me while I spread peanut butter on my toast. "I've been making Lu's birthday cakes forever. They may not be the prettiest, but I'm not going to stop now even if Steve can do it better."

"It looks good."

It's a big chocolate sheet cake with vanilla frosting. She's writing *Happy Birthday—Lu's Lucky 13th* in five different colors from icing tubes.

She glances up at me, then back to the cake. "Are you nervous about seeing your mom? I'm nervous about seeing Lu's dad. I have to get used to trusting him to keep a commitment."

"Thanks for taking me to the doctor and everything" is all I can think to say.

She sets down a tube of purple icing. "Oh, honey, you're welcome. You can always call on us."

It's nine-fifty-one. I finish my toast, drink a glass of water, and then go knock on Casey's bedroom door.

"What."

"It's Kyra."

In a few seconds, the door opens. She's changed into a plaid miniskirt and black tights and a gray sweatshirt with Baby Yoda on it.

262

"Will you do my makeup again?" I ask.

She opens the door wider and gestures for me to sit on the bed like I did yesterday. Without talking, she dabs on the concealer and some cheek color. This time she also has me close my eyes and sweeps on some eye shadow. She brushes my eyebrows and finally talks.

"I love Steve, but I hate his weekend cookouts. It feels like a massive invasion. People wander the house looking for bathrooms, they think my bed is the spot to put their coats, and some people don't *leave* when the party is officially over."

I hear the doorbell ring. Hear the door being opened, Steve's voice mixed with my mom's.

Casey hands me a lipstick. "This is kind of a matte rose if you want to try it."

"That's okay." I hand it back. I don't like the feel of stuff on my lips.

Steve calls my name. I don't move.

"You're going to get through this," Casey says.

I nod.

There's a tap on the door. "Case?" Steve calls. "Have you seen Kyra?"

I stand up and go to the door.

40

"You look so nice," Mom says with a tentative smile.

We're in Lu's room. She's sitting on Lu's desk chair; I'm on the edge of the bed.

She looks good, too. Not so wrung out, not so gray. The citrusy smell of her shampoo is almost overwhelming, and I realize I haven't smelled that in a long time. She's got on clean jeans and a dark-green sweater.

"Casey did my makeup," I say.

"How's your ankle?"

"Better."

She hesitates before asking, "Can I see it?"

I pull up my jeans to show her the white, puckery skin. She swears under her breath, and I cover it back up.

Her hands are clasped between her knees—nails clean and

trimmed. She keeps rubbing one thumb with the other.

I wish her relapse left a visible mark like my burn did, something I could see and touch as evidence that it happened. Something with a healing process I could see with my own eyes.

"I'm so sorry I wasn't there."

"You had a clean-out job," I say, as if I believe that.

"No. I didn't."

Hearing her say it still hurts. She rises to come sit by me. I stop her with "Don't."

She backs away and resettles onto the chair. "I'm sorry I lied to you. I'm sorry I didn't answer my phone or call back that night."

"You turned off your location, too."

"I didn't want to be found."

"Was it because I made us go to Tahoe?" I ask.

"What?" She tilts her head to the side, eyebrows drawn.

"The day we came back from Tahoe, you were depressed and quiet. You said the trip wasn't worth it. I thought that trip was perfect, and I guess I was wrong. Was it that?" I ask. "Was it me?"

She reaches one hand toward me, then pulls it back and runs it through her hair.

"Kyra. I don't even know how much I should tell you. Antonia said 'be honest but brief,' and I'm trying." She looks down and takes a deep breath. "Okay. Last year—*way* before Tahoe—I had some slips."

Slips. Slips are when an alcoholic drinks but doesn't go

265

into full relapse. That's what it says in the books. They might drink or use but then immediately regret it and go back to stable recovery.

"I didn't know."

"Yeah. You weren't supposed to. I told Antonia. Every time. Except the last time, which was the week of Thanksgiving. Remember when I wouldn't let you get the vacuum out of the car? And when I wouldn't let you put the groceries in the trunk?"

I pause. "Sort of."

"I was hiding bottles. Just tiny ones. I told myself only the little ones. And I was paranoid you were going to see them even though I had them under the trunk carpet, in the spare tire well."

It's a lot to hear. There were bottles right under my nose, in a way, and I didn't know. Secrets hiding like fruit flies, until they got drawn out by my kitchen crisis.

"I felt worried and guilty. Not confessing hung over me like a shadow. I wrote about it a little in my journal but then I got paranoid you'd find that."

"And you pushed me off you to keep me from seeing it."

She looks down and covers her mouth for a few seconds, then holds her chin still while she says, "I felt awful after that. Oozing self-hatred. And Tahoe was a break from what was going on, and it was wonderful." She lifts her head. Tears in her eyes. "It was perfect, Kyra, like you said."

I knew it. I knew it was perfect.

"On that drive home," she continues, "I started freaking

out that I wouldn't be able to hold on to that, and I knew I *had* to tell Antonia, and I didn't want to. I resent it sometimes. That I can't drink like a nonalcoholic. Like Steve or my clients or whoever." She leans forward. "I know you can't really understand. Is this . . . Is it too much? I don't know how much to say. You're not eight anymore, I know. I want you to know everything you want to know."

I fix my eyes on her nose. I can't look into her eyes right now, because they do feel like *her* eyes, like she's back and being the Mom I've missed. Except that person hurt me and lied to me, too. She's been slipping and slipping, before I knew anything was wrong. When I thought everything was good.

"How come you didn't call back when you got Casey's text about what happened to me?" I ask. "You knew it was an emergency."

She closes her eyes, opens them again. "I was in bad shape. It was going to be my last night drinking. Never mind I'd already had a 'last night' a bunch of times before that . . . If I called you back—or Steve, or anyone—you'd know. That I'd been drinking, that I'd been lying. I was walking this tightrope of convincing myself I could control it and get back on track before you ever knew I'd relapsed."

I guess I thought that, too.

"Babe, if I didn't think you were in good hands with Casey, I would've . . ."

Her words trail off, and she stares at the floor again. If she was in "bad shape" like she said, she might not have been able to think and decide how to help me.

"Well," she says, "you would've called 911. Right?"

Right. If I hadn't been worried about getting a bill or getting Mom in trouble or thinking that the burn wasn't really that bad. Right.

"What about the time you smelled like smoke?" I ask. "You said it was a client's house."

"It was the smoking patio at a bar."

"I thought you didn't go to bars."

"I went to bars."

"I smelled it in the car once, too."

She pulls at the ends of her hair. "I'd manage my drinking while I was out. Or think I was managing it. When I got the car safely home, I'd sit out there and drink some more. I told myself that if I wasn't doing it in the house, it wasn't that bad. And I know this sounds dumb but one night I got cigarettes, thinking maybe if I smoked I wouldn't drink. I hate smoking, though, so that didn't work."

I pull at a thread coming out of Lu's comforter. It's weirdly wiry and plastic-feeling. I wrap it around the tip of my finger until it turns purple, then I unwrap it. Our silence is so long that I can do this three whole times before she says, "Do you have any other questions?"

I think I know enough.

"Am I going home with you after the party?" I ask.

She opens her mouth, then closes it again and thinks. Then asks, "Do you want to? I want you to. But if you want to stay here another night, I'm sure you could."

I smooth the comforter thread down. "I want to go with you."

"Just find me when you're ready."

After another silence, I stand up and rush past her before she can try to hug me.

Lu is dumping bags of chips into big plastic bowls when I go out into the yard. Nearby, Steve puts ice in coolers for the sodas and bubbly waters while he talks to a neighbor who's walking a dog.

"We're done with your room," I tell Lu.

She squints at the sky. "Do you think the sun is going to come out?"

"Yeah. It has to. It's your birthday."

Then she squints at me. "What did your mom say?"

All I've wanted for weeks was to be able to tell her everything that's happening, but it doesn't feel right now. "I'll tell you later. Here, I'll throw those out." I reach for the empty chip bags; she passes them to me.

I go around to the side of the house where the big cans for garbage, recycling, and compost are. Pretty soon, Jaymison and Till and Abbie will get here. I don't want to be the weird, sad one with a giant blister whose Mom is an alcoholic. I want to be the girl from the cafeteria in Casey's red cardigan who everyone was cheering.

To be fun. To be happy. To be okay and at a party.

I am.

I am okay and at a party.

Maybe I don't feel happy right now. Maybe I don't feel fun.

But I am the girl from the cafeteria everyone cheered. She's me.

I'm also the sad one with the blister and the alcoholic mom.

Sometimes I'm weird.

Sometimes I'm a careful cook, and sometimes I spill and need help.

I can see all of me even if no one else can.

Casey comes around the side of the house with balled-up foil to put in the recycling. "Is there a reason you're hanging out by the garbage cans?"

"It just smells so good."

She laughs. "You're funny." She lets the recycling bin lid fall and tugs down at her Baby Yoda shirt. "Come on. Let's join the other humans."

41

The party is strange and sometimes fun.

Steve and Ann's adult friends are there mixed in with Lu's from school—the Pink Bandanna Club and also some other kids I know or at least recognize.

But that strangeness is what makes it fun. I don't have to get stuck feeling like the odd one out when there's such a jumble of people. Aside from Lu's family, I also know some of their neighbors because I've helped Lu babysit their kids before. And I can keep myself busy by helping Steve with party food stuff if I start to feel like the kids from school are ignoring me.

But they aren't. We're standing around the food table in the front yard, and a couple of them ask me what happened after Mr. Simmons sent me to the office yesterday, and can't believe it when I tell them I didn't even get in trouble.

"I guess I could still get in trouble," I say. "Maybe Monday I'll find out I'm suspended."

"You won't be," Jaymison says. "It's your first time getting sent to the office, right?"

"This year. I used to get sent more when teachers thought I needed to calm down."

"Wait," Jaymison says, studying me. "Did you used to have braids? Are you that sixth grader who melted down during the earthquake drill?"

My cheeks get warm. "Yeah."

It's not that I'm scared of earthquakes. Not more scared of them than I am of anything else. The thing was it was so hot that day, and I'd worn a big sweatshirt with only a thin under-shirt underneath so I couldn't take it off. I got hotter and hotter, and then kids weren't doing what they were supposed to do for the drill, and eventually I screamed at everyone to shut up and follow instructions. Which got me sent to the office.

"That was you!" Jaymison says. She looks at Abbie, her mouth so wide open I could throw one of the grapes from my plate into it. Chompers. Her teeth *are* pretty big. "That was her!"

"You didn't know that?" Abbie says to Jaymison. "I remem-ber. I was glad you yelled at everyone," she tells me. "It was total chaos. Maybe you got sent to the office, but it worked. Everyone did what they were supposed to after that. I've known that was you all along."

"I didn't," Till says, staring like she's only seeing me for

272

the first time. "I thought that girl with the braids changed schools."

The only thing I can think to say is, "I miss my braids."

Jaymison steps toward me and touches my hair. I resist yanking my head back. "Your hair is definitely an issue." She holds up sections and lets them drop. "Wait. Let me just . . ." She reaches into one of her pockets and pulls out her pink bandanna. She rolls it into a kind of headband, and ties it around my hair so it's off my face. "That's cute, right?" she asks the other girls.

"Yeah," Lu says, smiling.

A little later, the kid part of the party goes to the backyard where Lu's presents are piled on the picnic table. In the corner of the yard in side-by-side camp chairs are my mom and Lu's dad. Mom sips a bubbly water; Lu's dad has his hands folded in his lap.

I've only ever seen him twice before. One time at our fifth-grade talent show when he was still drinking and I didn't actually meet him, and then once last summer when I did. He was sober that day and took me and Lu to the tide pools at Moss Beach and didn't say much. It was awkward.

I remember him saying, "Are you sure you're going into seventh grade? You're so tall."

He's not one of those people who knows how to talk to kids.

Seeing them sitting there together is so weird that I kind of want to laugh, but I doubt I could explain it to anyone else. Casey would understand, only she disappeared after her dad got there, like she'd warned she would.

Lu's first gift is an instant camera. That's a really good present. Even though our phones have cameras, it's fun to print them out. I move in closer and find out that Till and Abbie and Jaymison went in on it together.

"You can make stickers, too," Till points out.

The camera is purple, and there are also two packs of film. If they'd asked me, I could have taken some money out of my drawer so that it could be from me, too. Then I never would have been making those cookies, but then I wouldn't have burned myself and maybe Mom wouldn't have confessed and maybe she'd have kept hiding.

Lu opens more presents and I wonder if I'm in the Pink Bandanna Club now and it means they have my back and I have theirs. Or is it only a headband now that I'll have to give back after the party? If I am in the club, do I even want to be?

I glance at Mom and see that she's watching me. She smiles and wiggles her fingers in a wave. Pretty soon we'll have birthday cake, and then it will be time for people to go home. Including us.

When we pull up to our house, neither of us makes a move to get out of the car.

I look at our front door. It feels like more than three days since I last walked through it. Mom reaches over to smooth the back of my hair. I want to cringe away but don't. I don't turn to look at her, which I know is what she wants.

"I'm glad you're back," she says.

I'm supposed to say I'm glad, too. I keep staring at the front door.

"I cleaned this morning before the party," she continues. "Our house, I mean. I know I've been neglecting it. And we can make a grocery list and go to Safeway tomorrow and get everything we need for the week."

Now I do look at her. Even if she had slips or a relapse, even if she's been lying about some things, she still knows me. She knows that having a clean house and a full refrigerator and pantry makes me feel calm and good and safe.

"We're going to be all right, Kyra. I understand if you don't trust me. Or if you're mad. Or sad."

I'm too tired to really cry, but a tear gets out. I brush it off and nod.

"Do you need me to take you to group tonight?" she asks.

I almost forgot it's Saturday. I'm so tired, and I want to unpack in my room and be with my stuff.

"We had group on Thursday." I don't explain more than that. I know Gene will be in the church basement, with the binder and the box, and if anyone comes he'll be ready.

"Should we go in?" she asks.

"Yeah."

42

In the morning, she's in the kitchen drinking coffee and writing in her journal. It's the first time she's been up before me in more than a month. The floor and counters and sink are as perfect as we left them last night after having a bagged salad for dinner that we added tuna and slivered almonds to.

Part of me is so happy to see her there at the table, with her flyaway hairs—like mine—haloed by the light from the window. But I felt happy like this in Tahoe, too, when she'd already been slipping and I didn't even know it.

So when she asks if I want her to make scrambled cheesy eggs, I say, "No, I'll do my own."

I don't ask if she wants any, and she doesn't say she does, so I make them only for me. This means cracking two eggs into a bowl and whipping in a little water, salt, and pepper. A lot of people add milk to their eggs, but actually a little bit of water is better if you like them fluffy. I warm up butter in a pan. The last time I did that was right before I burned myself. I feel okay about it, though, because I've made eggs a billion times.

While the pan heats, I shred a small amount of sharp cheddar cheese and mix it into the eggs. When the butter is foamy, I pour it all in the pan and let it start to set. I put sourdough bread into the toaster oven. Then I go back to the pan and stir the eggs. When everything's done, I sit at the table across from Mom and butter my toast.

"I like watching you cook," she says. "You're so good in the kitchen."

"I burned myself making a stupid mistake."

"Everyone makes mistakes, Keek."

I don't think *everyone* makes *that* mistake.

"I was really mad at myself," I say. I want to tell her about how I felt in the shower on Friday morning. That urge to hurt myself. Has she ever felt that way? I'm not ready yet.

"I know I said this already," she says, her tone changing, "but I'm so sorry I wasn't here. It must have been scary." She leans forward and touches my free hand.

I pull my hand back. "I don't really want to talk about it."

"Okay. You don't have to." She looks down at her journal. "Can I read you something I wrote yesterday?"

My heart pounds. I don't want her to. I have to say it. "I think . . . I think the point of the journal is for private thoughts. Not to share. Not with me."

There is a long stretch of quiet where I can tell she's hurt

277

or wants to argue. But then she closes her journal and gets up to put toast in for herself. "After breakfast, I was thinking we could take care of going to the store." She stares at the toaster. "And then I'm going to go to a meeting. Antonia suggested I try to go every day for a couple of weeks. I know it's a lot." She turns to me. "Then maybe just hang out here? We could watch some old cooking shows and make popcorn if you want. Then I need to make my work schedule for the week and confirm some clients."

It does sound like my favorite kind of Sunday if things were normal.

"That sounds good," I say. "I have some homework." More than *some*.

"I can help if you need help." She smiles. "Unless it's math."

It *is* math. She takes her toast out and smothers it in a thick layer of Nutella, which I do not like to eat or watch other people eat. I rinse my plate and tell her I'll be in my room making a grocery list.

In the afternoon, we find an old episode of *Test Kitchen* about grilling. We only have an ancient charcoal grill that we hardly ever use, but we like to daydream about getting a big, fancy gas grill for the little patch of yard we have in the back.

I let Mom snuggle me on the couch while we watch, and that's what it feels like—me letting her. Not me doing it because I want to. The guy in the video is making salmon steaks. Mom says, "I love salmon," and I say, "yeah," even though what I'm really thinking about is what she told me yesterday.

All the lies since before Tahoe.

She knew she was lying and her sponsor knew she was lying and I didn't know. Something in my gut told me things weren't right, and she kept trying to reassure me they were, or they would be. How she snapped at me and said, "Live and let live." And I worried about her and worried about telling anyone what I thought might be going on and worried about getting her in trouble and worried about her clients and worried and worried.

Now she wants to snuggle and for me to believe her when she says we'll be okay.

"Oooh, that looks good," she says. A woman is pulling apart a grilled artichoke. Mom nudges me. "Doesn't it?"

"Uh-huh."

When the video is finally over, she's leaning on me, asleep. It's early evening and time to make something for dinner. I turn off the TV and pull myself out from under her.

43

Monday morning, I twist the sides of my hair and pin them back, and wear Jaymison's pink bandanna around my neck. I thought about putting it on my ankle, but I don't want to be part of something when I'm not even sure it wants me to be a part of it.

Lu and Till are at the rock when I get to school; they wave me over. As I'm walking to them, I see Gabe from the corner of my eye, jogging across the lawn. He trips on something and falls down, and when he stands up he's brushing a clump of dirt off the knee of his jeans.

Someone yells out, "Clap if it's crap!"

I look around and see Juan and one of his other friends cracking up and pointing at Gabe. They're not even looking in my direction.

"You invented a meme." That's Abbie, who's at my elbow now.

All I can think to say is "Oops," which I guess is funny because she laughs.

The three of them look me up and down. I have on my best jeans and a plain gray sweatshirt over a white T-shirt. And the bandanna. "You look cute," Till says.

Abbie nods.

It's disorienting. I don't know if they feel sorry for me or think I'm the person yelling in the cafeteria and that's what I'll do now, or if it's the power of Jaymison's bandanna, or them seeing me at the party and knowing that what Lu said about me being like family is true.

It's just jeans and a sweatshirt.

I look to Lu for confirmation. She says, "You do."

I still feel uncertain and off balance. Not the same person I was less than a week ago.

When Jaymison gets out of her dad's car and has a new or backup pink bandanna around her ankle, the feeling grows. "You're supposed to put it around your ankle," she tells me when she makes it to the rock.

I reach for my neck without thinking, and then stop. One of the group affirmations I always forget is "It's okay to think about things differently." Basically, to be ourselves. Even if we don't know all the time who that is. I could tell her that it's not on my ankle because my burn still hurts a little, but that's not true.

"I think I like it this way," I say.

"But—"

"It's fine," Abbie says, cutting Jaymison off. She bends down and takes hers off her ankle, and wraps it around one wrist. "Help me tie it."

She holds her arm out to Jaymison, who looks at Lu and Till. "Guys, let's just . . ." She trails off and Lu steps forward to tie a little knot with the ends of Abbie's bandanna.

"Let me get a picture." Lu swings her backpack around to her front and pulls out her new camera, the one they all got her for her birthday. She has us cluster around and points it at us for a group selfie. There's no way on that camera to see if we're all in the frame, so when it comes out, it mostly the tops of our heads. "It's okay, I know who you are," Lu says. "I'll stick it up in my locker."

Jaymison sighs and gets her phone out. "Let me do a real one to post."

We re-cluster, with me on one end.

"Kyra, crouch down," she says. I bend my knees to make myself as short as them.

When we get one good enough for Jaymison, she edits and filters it and then texts it to all of us. The bell rings; we go in to class.

The only meeting Mom could go to today that didn't interfere with work is in the evening, so I'm home alone for the first time since I had the accident.

I decide to try an easy baked mac and cheese recipe, where you don't even have to boil the macaroni, you just stir in the cheese and milk and stuff and it all cooks in the oven. I'm skeptical, but all the reviews say it works.

While the mac and cheese bakes, I study the picture Jaymison took this morning. We're squeezed in tight. Whatever she did to it makes our skin look bright and Jaymison's blue eyes shine neon turquoise. My face got washed out by the filter and you can barely make out my nose.

I take some selfies with my phone and play with the editing until I get a version of me that feels like how I see myself: interesting, capable, sort of serious. But I know I'm also funny, average, and needy. Scared sometimes, mad sometimes. Sad. Worried. A good cook and a good daughter and a pretty good friend, I think. Not *that* bad at math. I can kind of sing.

I want to get that all into a picture and post it and have people understand me.

Mom doesn't want me to have social accounts until I'm fifteen, even though most people I know get them at thirteen. I check Jaymison's from the browser and see she posted our photo from this morning.

She cropped me out.

That's what I text to Lu.

She cropped me out.

What?

Jaymison cropped me out of the picture when she posted it.

I watch Lu's typing dots come and go, and I add:

It's okay.

It is. I wasn't telling her that to get her to feel sorry for me or try to make me feel better, more like to remind her what I said about Jaymison from the beginning. That she's mean sometimes. Not all the time, but sometimes.

Live and let live, right? I say, and add zany-face emoji. **What are you doing?**

Practicing guitar. I'm going to start lessons again I think.

I send a smiley and also smile for real. Her guitar and doing the talent show is how we got to be friends, and she dropped it for a while when seventh grade started.

I'm making dinner. My mom is at a meeting.

Is she ok?

I'm not sure, I say. **Better but I don't know.**

ODAAT, she says, and adds a heart.

One Day at a Time.

I heart her back and put my phone face down on the table.

My kitchen timer goes off. I take the foil off the mac and cheese and stir, then let it cook some more uncovered. I set the table with place mats, shallow bowls, cloth napkins. Two glasses of water—ice in Mom's, no ice for me.

She walks in the door just as my second timer goes off. "Nailed it," I whisper, and then laugh at myself.

"Hey, Keek," Mom calls.

I take the pan out of the oven. The cheese on top is bubbly and just slightly brown. Now it needs to sit for at least five minutes, so I set another timer and go to the living room. Mom is hanging her jacket on one of the hooks by the door. I give her a hug. Her skin is cold; mine is warm.

"I love you, honey," she murmurs into my hair.

My chest surges with an ache, and I pull back. "How was your meeting?"

"I got something for you."

She digs in her jeans pocket and pulls out a white plastic disc, like a poker chip. She has a lot of these from AA. They mark different periods of time she's been sober, like a thirty-day chip and a one-year chip and a five-year chip. I've never seen a white one.

"They call this a surrender chip," she says. "For when you're starting out or starting over." She takes one of my hands and opens it, placing the chip in my palm. It's almost weightless. "I'm surrendering—again—to the fact I can't drink. Not even a little. I want you to have it as a commitment from me."

I close my hand around the chip, then open it up to look at it again. I feel like I should say something meaningful. I don't know what, though. I'm still unsure about where we're going from here.

So I put it in my pocket and ask, "You want to see something magic?"

"Obviously!"

I lead her to the kitchen, and get our bowls off the table. When I spoon up the mac and cheese, I can see that it's perfect.

"The magic is that I didn't boil the macaroni."

"Seriously?" she asks.

"Yep. I just put it in dry."

We sit down and start eating. On the first bite, Mom puts

her spoon down to look at me and shakes her head. "I am truly amazed. This is incredible."

It's not the last thing we say about how good and perfect it is, how easy, how amazing. How it seems like it shouldn't have worked, but it did.

In bed that night, I look at my phone again and the picture I'm cropped out of. AbsyDabsy777 commented: Is Kyra a ghost? and there's ghost emoji and red question mark and a cry-laughing face. Several people liked the comment. I laugh and turn out my light.

PART V: MARCH & APRIL

Keep It Simple

44

Mom's been driving me to group the last couple of weeks because she's leading a new meeting Saturday nights, focusing on step one, where you have to deal with the fact you have a problem. That's at the library, which is only a few blocks away from the church.

Tonight it's me and Lu and Casey and Owen, and a small kid from Daly City named Henry who came a few times last summer and is back, and of course Gene. Before we officially start, there's time for some small talk. Owen asks me if my burn is all healed now. I show him; it is. Gene asks me what I've been cooking lately. I tell him about my magic no-boil mac from a couple of weeks ago, and also a pasta primavera I made recently with spring vegetables.

Casey asks, "How's your mom?" and I shrug.

Then, right when we're about to call the meeting to order, a first-timer walks in.

It's Juan. From school.

That Juan.

He looks terrified. And even more terrified when he sees me and Lu.

I don't feel so great myself.

But the thing about group is that it's a special place outside of school, outside of home, outside of everything. We're all here for the same reason. Which is that our parents drink or use drugs in a way that affects us, and we need to talk about it.

So even though there's this nervous heat in my face and my voice is a little shaky, I say, "Hi," as Gene pulls another chair into our circle.

Lu says it, too. Then Gene starts the meeting.

We go around and do introductions like we always do, and Gene gives any newcomers a chance to say more if they want.

"My grandma heard about this and brought me," Juan says, quieter than I've ever heard him say anything.

We read some of our materials from the binder that Gene passes around. He goes over the part about anonymity, how everything we say here stays here. I think he's caught on that Lu and I know Juan and is trying to reassure us. And him.

During sharing, I go first to get it over with. "Things are a little better at my house. My mom is really trying. But . . ." I think of her white chip in my pocket. "She keeps wanting to have these deep moments where she apologizes or tells me she loves me or asks me how I am, and I don't want to talk about it like she does. She went from talking about it all the time, to never talking about it—hiding and shutting me out—to wanting to talk again. I'm tired. I just want her to do her part and not need me to talk about it with her."

I've been thinking about this a lot. How I thought I wanted things between me and Mom to be what they were before, but really what I want between us has changed. I get to decide how much trust to give, how much of her emotion to let in, how much of my own to let out and to who.

"I've been trying to do live and let live," I say, "and now I want her to live and let me live, too."

Casey nods. It's kind of like what she's going through with her dad, I guess.

"That's all," I say. "Thanks."

Gene and Owen say at once, "Thanks for sharing; you were heard," and Juan looks around, confused. It takes a few times to get used to how group works. I only hope he's not going to go straight to Gabe tomorrow and repeat everything I just said.

"Hi, I'm Owen."

"Hi, Owen."

"I've been coming a few months now," he says. "And it hit me just now that when I first started coming, I just wanted my dad to stop drinking. Like I thought if he got sober, everything would be better. But I've been listening to you guys all this time. And sometimes your parents are not drinking and sometimes they are and either way you have problems you have to deal with, right?" He looks at Casey, who mutters, "Yep."

He continues: "Now I get it. That that's the point. Yeah, I want my dad to stop drinking. But mostly I want to stop being obsessed about whether he is or isn't or the what, when, how, why of it all. I'm graduating this year. I have my own life to live. I care about him and my little brothers and everything, but the best thing I can do is for my brothers is show them we can be okay whether or not our dad is."

Gene smiles a little under his mustache.

"That's all I got," Owen says, opening his palms with a grin.

That makes us laugh, and Juan looks even more confused. Then it quickly turns into something else. I watch his face collapse. He puts his hands over his eyes and shrinks down in his chair. Lu and I exchange a glance. Owen breaks the tissue and no-crosstalk rules and picks up the box to put on Juan's lap, saying, "It's okay, dude. We pretty much all cry here at some point."

Juan takes a tissue, then another. His crying is almost totally silent, but his whole body shakes. It seems like he can't stop. We just sit with him until he gets up and walks out of the meeting room.

Owen says to Gene, "Can I go after him?"

Gene nods.

Henry, the kid from Daly City, has started crying, too. Lu sniffles. It's catching. Like when we had group in Casey's bedroom. Since we're breaking rules, I blurt out to Gene, "He kind of bullies me at school."

291

Gene scratches his moustache. "I see."

"But . . ." I look at Lu, then back to Gene. "Maybe he won't anymore."

"If he does, I can refer him to a different group. Longer drive, but less chance of running into anyone he knows from town. It's probably uncomfortable for him, too."

"We can try it," I say.

"Are you sure?" Casey asks me.

I'm not sure, but, "We can *try* it," I repeat.

Owen and Juan come back. Juan's face is blotchy and swollen. Gene asks him if he wants to share; he shakes his head. Owen does another share, about a fight he had with dad. Things are getting worse between them in some ways, but Owen says, "I handle it better now. I walk away. Sometimes that pisses him off, too, but thinking about it afterward doesn't keep me up all night anymore. Oh, and I got my driver's license and I'm getting a car next week and I think that's going to help a lot. Not feeling trapped."

Then Casey shares.

"I'm grateful for this group. I'm grateful for the safe place where I can say anything and I know it stays here. Like I see Owen at school, but I know he's not talking about what we say here. It's a big deal to have this kind of place in a world where everyone shares everything all the time online or whatever. It's special. It feels miraculous, almost." She repeats, "I'm so grateful. I don't know what I'd do without that security."

The whole thing seems like a message to Juan, and maybe to me and Lu.

292

After group, I watch Juan from the corner of my eye while Owen and Gene talk to him some more. Gene pats him on the back and then Juan is walking across the room, toward me.

"If you don't say anything, I won't," he mutters. "They said you won't." He gestures with his chin toward Gene and Owen. "So I won't."

Lu comes to stand near enough us to be halfway in the conversation. "Me neither," she says.

"Okay." I take a big breath and say to Juan, "We don't have to be friends outside of group, but . . . let me live."

"Yeah." He lifts his head. I didn't think he could cry anymore, but he is. "Sorry, man," he says, like he's trying to sound cool even though his voice is breaking.

I don't know what to say to him other than to repeat another slogan that we have on a fridge magnet at home. "You're not alone."

It only makes him cry more. Owen and Gene come back over, and I go outside to wait for my mom.

Casey and Lu wait with me, and none of us say one word about what happened at the meeting, even though I know we're all thinking about Juan being there and also what Owen shared. Then Mom zooms her car into the lot and I get in after saying goodbye to Lu and Casey.

We didn't have time for dinner before group, and Mom wants to stop at Taco Bell at the beach before we go home. It's the one she always went to when she was in high school. We get a few tacos and sit on the back deck to eat, where we can see the ocean. The sun has gone down, but the white foam of waves is visible even in the dark. The sound is a distant, comforting roar. When we're done with our tacos, we sit and stare out, hunched against the cold and damp.

"Do you think Grandma will ever understand about what a higher power is?" I ask.

"No." She laughs. "Maybe."

"I might want to try to get to know her. Like, you guys don't have to be talking for me and her to talk."

I feel her look at me. "Seriously? I don't want her to hurt you again, Kyra. After what happened last time, I swore I wouldn't let her."

"I know. I'm only saying I might want to try. To give her another chance."

She's quiet a while, then says, "I hope this doesn't sound weird, and Grandma definitely would not understand, but you're a part of my higher power. The ocean, yes, and also . . . my job as a mother, my responsibility to you, the fact that you're my family and I'm yours. I'm realizing I have to surrender to that every day. It helps keep my compass straight."

That makes a certain kind of sense to me, and it also feels like more than I need to think about.

The word "surrender" reminds me of the white chip. I take it out of my pocket and lay it on the table.

"I think you should keep this," I say.

"But I want you to have it."

"Mom, you're the one who has to do whatever you have to do to stay sober. Not me."

The ocean is still there, wave after wave, crashing into the beach.

She picks up the plastic chip and turns it over in her hand.

"You're right," she says. She sounds sad. "I know you're right."

45

April in Tahoe is a lot different from December.

There are patches of snow on the ground, but it's slushy and heavy, not crisp. The temperature can get up into the low sixties or even warmer during the day, and it doesn't get so freezing cold at night. The stars are still bright, though, and the trees are so *big*, and there are so many. Breathing.

Mom's client Lucy was here last weekend with friends, and they left a mess because they knew we were coming. That was the deal to get the cabin for spring break. When Lucy offered it, Mom told me, "We don't have to if you hate going somewhere we also have to clean. We can stay here at home, if you prefer, but we can't afford any trip we have to pay for other than gas and food."

"You're the one who got depressed last time about having

to clean it," I reminded her. "Depressed" felt like a shortcut word that actually meant a whole lot of different things, but it was easiest.

Anyway, she knew what I meant.

"Our time there was special," she said. "I would love to go again."

"Me too."

This time we took our own car after checking the weather to make sure we weren't going to be stuck in a storm or need chains. That saved a lot on gas compared to using Steve's truck. I was in charge of our shopping list, like before, and got stuff for soup, enchiladas, and breakfasts.

"What about goodies?" Mom asked, as we pushed the cart through the store this morning. She stopped pushing and said, "You know what we could do, Keek?"

"We could get a cake mix?" And a can of frosting.

"I was going to say was we could make those salted caramel cookies."

I hadn't done anything too complicated in the kitchen since the accident. It's not that I was scared, I don't think. But there were plenty of other things to make that couldn't boil over and give you a second-degree burn.

"Those are Lu's favorite, not mine."

"I know. But this time I could be there and help you and nothing bad will happen. It will be like . . ." She got lost in her thoughts for a second, then laughed lightly. "Never mind. I guess I'm still trying to redeem myself and rope you into it. We can get a cake mix."

I scanned the baking aisle shelves. "I do want to try molten lava chocolate cakes. Those are supposed to be easier than they look."

"'Molten' sounds a little . . . *hot*."

"It sounds that way, but really you just undercook the middle in a certain way."

I looked up a recipe on my phone and got the stuff to make them from scratch. We loaded all the groceries into the car and got straight onto the road. An unwanted thought floated through my mind, about the wheel well in the trunk and what could be hidden there, but after it hung there a minute I let it float past.

When we got here, the mess was bigger than we expected. Now we're cleaning up so we can unpack and start our vacation.

"They didn't even rinse their dishes," I say.

"Must be nice, right?"

We fill the dishwasher and hand-wash the rest, then change the beds and put a load of sheets in the laundry. I run the vacuum while Mom cleans the fireplace and takes out the trash. Eventually, everything is in order. Warm from cleaning, we sit on the couch with our feet up.

The clocks got changed for spring forward a couple of weeks ago, and so even though it's almost six, it's still light out. Tomorrow, when we're not so tired, we can walk down to the lake to watch the sunset.

"Tonight we're just doing veggie burgers and chips," I say, hungry and thinking about dinner. "I knew we'd be too tired to make a big meal."

She leans her head back and closes her eyes. "Smart."

"In the morning, I'll do French toast and bacon."

There's a longer pause this time before she says, "Great."

"That trail around the lake that we couldn't do last time because of snow should be clear. If we want to do that after breakfast."

"Sounds good," she murmurs.

She'll be asleep in a minute.

I get up and go to what will be my room, and unpack my bag. I set my clothes in the dresser drawers, and put my Adventure Mountain hat on the bedpost. I like it again, because I've decided I can let it remind me of what I loved about Christmas and not the part after. And anyway, the bad parts, the good parts, the messy parts . . . they're all what make it whole.

When I close my door to change into something comfy and clean, I see there's a scratched old mirror hanging on the back of it.

My hair is almost long enough for my old favorite braids again. I've never been any good at doing my own braids. I try anyway and wind up with something crooked, but good enough to keep my hair out of my face for dinner and sleep.

I take a mirror selfie and send it to the group text I'm on with Jaymison, Abbie, Till, and Lu.

Did my own braids lol

Within seconds, they've all replied with different emojis. Then Jaymison sends:

Lemme do frenchies when you get back.

I give her heart eyes.

The three of them will be going to high school next year while Lu and I are in eighth. I wonder if we'll keep our group chat or if it will die off the way things do when people move or change schools. Owen and Casey are going to graduate. Technically, they can keep coming to group for as long as they're eighteen, but I wonder if they will.

It's kind of funny, though, how right now I'm friends with Jaymison and in a group where Juan gets to hear my most personal thoughts. Mostly he listens and still cries now and then. All I know is he's there because of his older brother. I think that would be harder in some ways than being there for a parent. Easier in others, maybe.

Anyway, he's stuck to his promise to leave me alone at school, and Gabe hasn't bothered me, either. I don't know if Juan told him anything about group. I can't really care about it too much, whether he did or not. I can't control whether or not people talk about me if I'm not there, or what they say.

Now, Till sends a selfie of her and Lu. They're camping at Lake Berryessa with Steve and the rest of Lu's family. Me and Mom were invited, but we decided to stick with our plan instead. Mom figures that the more Lucy gets used to us using her cabin for free, the more chances we'll get to do it.

Maybe next time, I can bring friends.

In the morning, I sleep in until past ten and only wake up because I smell bacon.

I go into the kitchen, and Mom is in yoga pants and a sweat-shirt, hair wet from the shower. She's leaning on the kitchen counter and writing in her journal with one hand, a mug of coffee in the other.

"I slept twelve hours," I say. She's got everything set up on the counter for French toast: the egg mixture on a shallow plate, the thick bread we got yesterday, the griddle on low.

She puts down her pen and comes to kiss my head. "You needed it. The mountain air helps." She fills a glass with water from the tap and hands it to me. "I got breakfast started. I hope you don't mind. The bacon's staying warm in the oven."

"Did you put cinnamon in the batter?"

"Of course."

"And nutmeg?"

"I couldn't find any here in their pantry."

I go to one of the shopping bags sitting on the counter and dig through it until I find the small container of ground nutmeg I got yesterday. I peel the seal off and sprinkle some into our egg mixture.

"You think of everything," Mom says.

I snap the cap back onto the nutmeg. "I think of everything because I have to." I take a fork and stir the batter a little more, and lay two pieces of bread in it. I'm tearing up, thinking about the truth of that.

"Babe," Mom says gently. "Kyra."

I look up.

"You're right," she says. "And I'm sorry you've had to think of everything."

My chin wobbles. I think she really is sorry. I keep pushing on the bread, even though my shoulders are shaking now.

"I see how much you do," Mom continues. "I see how much you are."

I press the heel of one hand into one eye, still poking bread with the other hand. She comes around the counter to me and pulls me gently away from the task while still talking.

"I'm sorry you've had to be more of an adult than I am sometimes." I feel her warm hand on my arm, and I let it stay there. "I'm sorry I've made it hard for you to trust me the way you should be able to. I'm sorry for lying."

This apology isn't like her old ones, where she couldn't say exactly what she was sorry for. This is specific; this is real.

She makes an attempt to pull me closer, but I'm not ready. I turn away and collapse onto my elbows on the counter and put my head down, crying. It's a relief to let go.

"It was so much," I sob. It's loud. I let it be, knowing the trees that surround the cabin will soak up any sounds that get out, hold it in their branches. "I didn't know what was happening."

I want to tell her all the things. How lonely it was. How confusing. What was going on with Juan and Gabe and Lu and everything, and how much I needed her. How I even thought about hurting myself.

Before we go home this time, I will tell her all of it.

"I can't make it up to you," she says. "And because it's just us, there *are* things you have to do that you might not have to if there were more of us to share the load. We just have a little more to carry. And you don't have to say it's okay. It just is."

I lift my head enough to look at her. She's the Mom I know,

the one I missed. And also, maybe, someone new.

"You know we're not all alone in the world, though, right?" she asks.

"I know." I lift my head higher, and reach for a paper towel to blow my nose.

Steve's family is *almost* like our family. Lu and I are more like sisters than friends sometimes, bickering and trying to control each other, but always there. Group is a different kind of support for me, and Mom's meetings are support for her. There are people who are there for us, clients who lend cabins, friends at school.

"That doesn't mean it's not still hard," I say. "To be just us."

"That's true. That's very true."

She takes a deep breath in and lets it out. I know she's dying to hug me and choosing not to force it. She sees me now. That I'm not quite ready.

I do what I know to do next: turn up the heat under the griddle and drop a blob of butter onto it. I flip the pieces of bread over in the batter and push them down to soak it all up. When the butter starts to foam, I lay the first two pieces of bread onto the griddle, and put two more to soak in the batter.

"Is the syrup—"

"Right here." Mom holds up the bottle.

"We should warm up—"

"Plates? They're in the oven with the bacon."

The toast on the griddle starts to smell delicious. "I'm so hungry," I say.

"Me too." Mom opens a drawer to get out forks and knives. "Do you want me to make you a super-sweet coffee with milk?"

"Yes, please." I take the first pieces off the griddle and put on the next two.

"I don't want you getting hooked on caffeine like I am. Not yet. But it's vacation!"

She makes me the coffee and I pile bacon onto our plates and set the oven timer so I don't forget there are two pieces of French toast still cooking. We sit at the table and devour our first helping, and after that, our second.

"Did I do all right with the batter?" Mom asks as we eat our last bites.

"You did it perfect."

That evening, we take our sunset walk by the lakeshore. The sky is orange and yellow at first, then darker purple above that. Mountains and foothills surround the water like they're gathering it in for the night. The lake isn't the ocean, and Ms. Scheiner says that Lake Tahoe is one of the few bodies of water around here that never even flows into it, wasn't a part of it once.

Still, it's a part of something. Something all around me, all the time, that wants to gather me in, too.

It gets so much darker so much faster here, without all the light from the streets and houses like we have in Pacifica, and we have to use the light on Mom's phone on our way back. It only lets us see a few feet ahead at a time—a few feet then a few feet then a few feet, over and over, and pretty soon we we're back to the car, then back to the cabin.

We stand outside for a few minutes when we get out of the car, and stare up at the tips of the evergreens, up at the stars.

The trees breathe out; we breathe in.

AUTHOR'S NOTE

Kyra's Saturday night group is a fictionalized version of Alateen, which is part of Al-Anon, a worldwide fellowship offering support to families of alcoholics and other addicts. The hopeful message of these groups is that those of us affected by the alcohol use or drug use of a loved one or family member are not alone and there are tools available to help, whether or not the alcoholic stops drinking. The organization Adult Children of Alcoholics & Dysfunctional Families is another helpful resource if you're a grown-up who is still affected by addiction, abuse, or neglect by those around you in your childhood. This book is not an endorsement of any group or of the Twelve Steps recovery model. There are many paths through, and we don't have to walk alone.

www.al-anon.org
www.adultchildren.org

ACKNOWLEDGMENTS

This is my tenth novel. I could not have made it to this milestone without the care and attention of the many people I've been lucky enough to work with on my books for the last twenty years. I also couldn't have made it without the booksellers, reviewers, librarians, and readers who have found and shared the stories. Thank you.

Special thanks on number ten to Elysia Case for the cover art; my insightful editor, Jordan Brown; and Michael Bourret, who has been my agent and friend for nearly two decades.

In her book *The ACOA Trauma Syndrome*, Tian Dayton writes, "One does not need to create some powerful therapeutic intervention in the life of a [child of an alcoholic] in order to make a big difference. An open door, a couch to curl up on, an after-school snack, or a place to play can make the essential difference for CoAs: they just need a place to go that isn't in a state of chaos, somewhere where they feel they can relax."

A library, a church, the living room at a friend's house, the classroom of a particularly astute teacher. These were places

nd and that found me when I was a kid living in the
 of alcoholism. Without those places and the people who
watched over me in them, I don't know how I would have
fared. I'm grateful for all of them, and to everyone who modeled possibility to me when I needed it most.

ACKNOWLEDGMENTS

This is my tenth novel. I could not have made it to this milestone without the care and attention of the many people I've been lucky enough to work with on my books for the last twenty years. I also couldn't have made it without the booksellers, reviewers, librarians, and readers who have found and shared the stories. Thank you.

Special thanks on number ten to Elysia Case for the cover art; my insightful editor, Jordan Brown; and Michael Bourret, who has been my agent and friend for nearly two decades.

In her book *The ACOA Trauma Syndrome*, Tian Dayton writes, "One does not need to create some powerful therapeutic intervention in the life of a [child of an alcoholic] in order to make a big difference. An open door, a couch to curl up on, an after-school snack, or a place to play can make the essential difference for CoAs: they just need a place to go that isn't in a state of chaos, somewhere where they feel they can relax."

A library, a church, the living room at a friend's house, the classroom of a particularly astute teacher. These were places that I found and that found me when I was a kid living in the chaos of alcoholism. Without those places and the people who watched over me in them, I don't know how I would have fared. I'm grateful for all of them, and to everyone who modeled possibility to me when I needed it most.